BAND OF ANGELS

Other titles by Witi Ihimaera and published by Robson Books

The Uncle's Story
The Whale Rider

BAND OF ANGELS

WITI IHIMAERA

ROBSON BOOKS

For Te Whanau a Kai iwi
Te Whanau a Kai pana pana maro

First published in Great Britain in 2005 by Robson Books, The Chrysalis Building, Bramley Road, London W10 6SP

An imprint of **Chrysalis** Books Group plc

First published in 2004 as *Whanau II* by Reed Books, a division of Reed Publishing (NZ) Ltd, 39 Rawene Road, Birkenhead, Auckland, New Zealand

The author has made every reasonable effort to contact all copyright holders. Any errors that may have occurred are inadvertent and anyone who for any reason has not been contacted is invited to write to the publishers so that a full acknowledgement may be made in subsequent editions of this work.

British Library Cataloguing in Publication Data
A catalogue record for this title is available from the British Library

ISBN 1 86105 832 2

Typeset by SX Composing DTP, Rayleigh, Essex
Printed by Creative Print & Design (Wales), Ebbw Vale

CONTENTS

AUTHOR'S NOTE
From *Village Sunday* to *Band of Angels*

In 1969 I married Jane Cleghorn and, the following year, we came to the United Kingdom on our honeymoon. I couldn't get a job in London, where we rented a bedsit at 67 Harcourt Terrace, South Kensington, so Jane suggested I stay at home and pursue my dream of becoming a writer. I was twenty-six and, while Jane caught the Tube out to Hounslow to teach, I stayed in the bedsit and over a three-month period wrote *Pounamu Pounamu* (short stories, 1972), *Tangi* (1973) and a novella called *Village Sunday*.

On our return home to New Zealand in 1972, I rewrote the novella into a novel, and it was published as *Whanau* in 1974. I was influenced by the film adaptation of Dylan Thomas's marvellous play, *Under Milkwood*, starring Richard Burton (1973). Like the play, the film focused on various characters of a Welsh village which Thomas named Llareggub (read that backwards and you'll get the meaning). The main character is, in fact, the village itself, and the various members (and ghosts) of the village are reflections of that character. The entire activities of the village take place over a day and night.

For the last thirty years, however, I have been unhappy with my work in *Whanau*, which was never released in the United Kingdom. The intention was always to write a documentary novel about the physical, emotional and psychic impact of European settler history on a small Maori valley. Last year I therefore rewrote and extended it — you can put this down to an author's constant pursuit of excellence — and it now appears in this new novel, *Band of Angels* (2005). Although it is about a Maori village, its resonances are universal.

I am so thrilled and honoured that *Band of Angels* is being published in this special edition and appears, for the very first time, in the great country in which the original was written.

Witi Ihimaera
Auckland, New Zealand, 2005

Band of Angels

CHAPTER ONE

It was four o'clock, Sunday morning. The sun was coming, a pale wash spreading above the foothills, and the clouds were steaming from the valleys. The shadows on the lowland receded as the sun climbed in the sky. They lingered on a small wooden bridge. First morning light touched the wooden spars and criss-cross shadows slashed an old truck as it rumbled across. The headlights were still shining.

Charlie Whatu was driving. His wife, Agnes was sitting beside him and, next to her, Maka, one of the old ladies of Waituhi. They were all tired, and Charlie's eyes were squinted and bloodshot. He was a solid man in his mid-forties, and his hands gripped the steering wheel tightly as the road momentarily blurred with brilliant sun. In the lapel of his black suit he wore a wilting carnation.

'I sure can't wait to hit that bed,' Charlie yawned.

'Make sure you don't hit the bend first,' Agnes said. 'I don't want to be a statistic.' Ever since her cousin, Mohi, had been killed on this stretch of road she was always on the lookout for old man Death. He was sure to be out there, doing some target practice, waiting this time to take a potshot at her.

Charlie slowed down for her sake. 'Okay, dear,' he said, 'it's been a long night.'

Agnes realised her tone had been sharp. 'For you and me, yes,' she answered, patting his arm. 'But not for those fellas on the back.' She nudged Maka to take a look. Maka was famed for her eyes, which were big and googly and able to look in two different directions at once. Sure enough, Maka made one of her eyes swivel in its socket to look backward while still keeping the other eye on the road.

'We're not as young as we used to be,' Maka intoned like a lugubrious old owl. 'I'm so tired my eyes are falling out. Not enough sleep, that's the trouble.'

'You mean too much booze, that's the trouble,' Charlie laughed.

The villagers on the back of the truck were young and boisterous, with the invincibility that the young have about living forever. Without a canopy, they were all at the mercy of the wind and dust if Charlie didn't keep his speed up and outrace both. They were past caring about the way they looked. The women's dresses were crumpled, the men's suits stained. But, after all, who would see them out here? If the lipstick was smeared or if the wind had totally demolished the carefully combed hairstyle, tough, the time for being beautiful was long over. Anyhow, they'd soon be able to sleep it off, close those red-veined eyes and, by the time they woke up, hey, they'd be as good as new. Until then, they tucked the blankets under because the wind was bloody cold, and kept singing to Blacky's guitar.

There were eleven villagers on the back of the truck. Only seven were still singing. The other four had flaked out under the blankets, too drunk to keep on partying. Couldn't keep up at George Karepa's wedding yesterday. Man, oh man, what a party. Great food, plenty of booze and dancing, and the band was fabulous. Trust Charlie Whatu to want to come home so soon. He was a spoilsport, spoiling all the fun. Not to worry: you didn't have to be at a wedding to enjoy yourself.

Blacky's song ended with laughter. Eyes flashed with pleasure and voices punctuated the steady drone of the truck's motor. Sam Walker took the opportunity to light a cigarette. He'd already ruined his throat with drinking and raucous singing. May as well trash himself for good.

'What's another song?' Hine Ropiho yelled. She was twenty-four, wide awake and still ready to party. Not like Jack, her husband, or her best mate, Mattie Jones. Both of them were out to the world, sleeping the beer off.

'Never mind about the song,' Sam interrupted. 'Just pass that bottle over here, Hine. I know you're trying to hog Mister DB to yourself.'

'Mister DB and I are in love with each other,' Hine answered, smacking her bottle with her lips. 'What's wrong with the bottles you got in your corner, Sam? Find your own. Come on, Blacky, play another song.'

'Wait your hurry,' Blacky said. His real name was Joe but people called him Blacky because, for a Maori, man, was he oh so Colgate white? Was he what. Line him up in the dark with the rest of his mates and he was the one you could see.

Hine leant back against the side of the truck. She was blissed out by the booze. That was the great thing about Mister DB. He made a girl happy and got her to stop thinking about what her life was really like. Mister DB was her darling, the one to make her forget the crap and her rotten marriage to Jack. 'Jeez,' she whispered, 'it was a great wedding all right. That girl from Te Arawa is lucky to have a man like George Karepa. Did you see the way he was flashing his money around? Her dress must have cost a thousand bucks.'

'They were still partying when we left,' Sam answered. 'Maybe we should go back.' Muscular, the leader of the group, he was still stoked and running on empty.

'I like that idea,' Hine said. She was remembering her own marriage. Up the duff to Jack, in a registry office. As for her dress, it had been some cheap thing already stretching across her stomach. Ten years later? She scowled at her sleeping husband. Shovel it on, Lord.

'Yeah, let's go back,' Sonny added. 'Get Dad to turn his truck around, Sam. He'll listen to you.'

With a nod, Sam Walker banged loudly on the roof. 'Hey, Charlie,' he yelled. 'Charlie, you deaf bastard —'

'What's up back there! Somebody want to get off and have a piss?'

'Charlie, be my darling,' Hine Ropiho pleaded. 'Take us back to the wedding?'

'Don't listen to her, dear,' Agnes reproved.

'Next time,' Charlie answered, 'I'll leave everybody behind and they can catch a ride with somebody else.' He put his foot down, and Sam, Hine and Sonny Whatu got the picture. The only place Charlie was taking them was home to Waituhi.

Pissed off, Hine consoled herself with Mister DB. She saw a little head pop out of the blankets beside her. 'Can't you sleep?' Her son, Boy Boy.

'You fellas are making too much noise,' Boy Boy complained.

'Sorry, son. Maybe if you pull the blankets over your head, that'll help.' Hine was also tempted to suggest that Boy Boy wrap the blanket around Jack's neck and strangle him with it. 'We'll be home soon and you can have a long sleep in bed.'

But tempers were still frayed and Sonny Whatu was looking for somebody to pick on. 'Come on, Blacky, attack that guitar!' he began. Then he saw that Mattie Jones was waking to the world. 'Hey, Mattie, welcome to the land of the living dead.' He fumbled for her.

'Keep your hands off me.'

Reaching up from the darkness of her dreams, Mattie clawed her way back to the land of light. Her voice was low and hoarse with anger. She pushed Sonny away, lifted her head to the light, and the sun skewered her. 'Oh, fuck.' She looked like she was going to heave her guts.

'Not over me, you don't,' Hine snapped. 'I told you not to mix your drinks.'

'Fuck you too,' Mattie answered. 'What's the time, Sam?' she asked. 'That's not the sun, is it? Oh my God, it is too.' She struggled to sit up.

'Easy, girl,' Sam soothed. 'Easy.' Mattie was always like this when she woke up. Every morning was like a boxing match. The bell rang, the referee nodded, and Mattie came out of her corner fighting, as if this was what life was all about. 'What were you up to last night, eh? What did George's best man do to you after the dance! Did he hit you? Did he give you that black eye?'

'George's best man?' Mattie remembered some arrogant arsehole, sure of himself, wanting to take her outside. 'What black eye? Don't you know the difference between a black eye and mascara? I never went with nobody last night, did I Hine?'

'Don't ask me,' Hine answered. 'Can't you remember, you dumb bitch?'

'No, and I don't want to, either,' Mattie said. 'Anyway, Hine Ropiho, you were supposed to look after me. Big friend you are.'

'Don't blame me, Mattie,' Hine answered. 'What you do is your own business. If you want to make a fool of yourself, that's your worry. I was too busy holding up Jack to worry about you as well.' She looked at her husband with disgust and kicked him. 'Jack? Wake up! I'm not carrying both you and Boy Boy to bed.'

Everyone laughed. Sonny was still looking for some fun. 'You think George Karepa will bring his missus back here with him?' he asked Sam. But it was Mattie he was after.

'Back to Waituhi?' Sam answered. 'Not likely! Him and Hayley are off to Australia. What's he want to come back here for!' George was a top football player in Aussie league. The clubs were chasing him over in Sydney. 'No, he's making big money and good on him too.'

'The lucky bastard,' Sonny said. Then he pounced. 'Another good man gone down the drain, eh, Mattie?

Sam was on to him. 'That's enough, Sonny.'

Sonny didn't listen. He went for the jugular. 'George ditched you, eh, Mattie? Went after somebody younger and prettier. Has he got a big one, Mattie —'

Mattie had the measure of him. She brought up the edge of her left hand and chopped at Sonny's throat. 'Back off, you little shit,' she said. 'I suppose you've got a bigger one, have you?'

Hine came to Sonny's rescue. 'Don't take any notice of him,' she said. 'He's just a stupid kid making stupid jokes.' Sonny was gasping, trying to breathe.

'Tell him to keep his damn jokes to himself,' Mattie answered. 'All you fellas, leave me alone, eh?'

Sam restored order. 'Can't you take a joke, you stupid bitch?' he asked Mattie. 'As for you, Sonny, you deserved that.'

But once started, it was often difficult for Mattie to stop. She was so wired. Trembling. Shaking apart. George Karepa was gone, gone, gone.

Sam saw that Mattie was out of reach. He shrugged his shoulders. 'You all right, Sonny?' he asked.

The truck turned a corner. Straight ahead, below a crown of spiked and rugged hills, was Waituhi.

PART ONE

Look Over Jordan

CHAPTER TWO

The village is eighteen kilometres from Gisborne, on the outskirts of the farming district where mountain ranges break the blue of sky. Huddled close to the foothills amid farms that grow kiwifruit, grapes and other fruit crops, it is far from the main arteries of traffic pumping commerce to Wellington and Auckland. There is no reason why it should be here except this: the Te Whanau a Kai, the descendants of Kai who gave his name to the tribe, live here. This has always been their home and this will always be their land. It is their hearth. Their parents lived here before them, and their parents before them, and so it has always been. They are the *tangata whenua*, the original settlers.

To get to Waituhi, you head inland, west from the city. In the distance you will see Maungatapere, a prominent flat-topped hill. There's only one highway in or out of Gisborne unless you take the circuitous road around the East Coast, which is an alternative route north. For Waituhi, you take the highway south to Wellington. Just past Matawhero, you come to a concrete bridge. In the old days a red, one-way bridge spanned the river, famed because of the races to the bridge by two competing shearing gangs — the Mahana gang from Waituhi and the Poata gang from Hukareka. On the other side of the bridge is a roundabout with three destinations to choose from. One is the highway south to Wellington, and most traffic takes this route. The second takes you to Ngatapa; if you followed this road to the end, you would reach the place where Maori rebels were executed by government troops at the siege of their clifftop mountain fortress in 1869. The third road takes you to Waituhi. Go to the Patutahi turnoff, hang a right past

11

the pub, primary school and war memorial — after the Pakeha Wars, all this land was confiscated from Te Whanau a Kai — and you will come to a small bridge, the one Charlie Whatu's truck rolled across at dawn. Once you are over the bridge, you know you are nearing Waituhi.

The entrance to Waituhi is a powerful-looking hill, Pukepoto, an ancient Maori fort with serrated edges cutting into the sky. Beyond Pukepoto, a sharp corner curves into the foothills and, opening up, is the Waituhi Valley; it is protected by the fort at one end, a sacred mountain at the other, and a river runs through it.

Historically, the valley has always been home to three main family settlements. The first you come to is Pakowhai, with a small wooden church nearby, roof steeply slanted. Taake Kerekere, priest and scribe for the Kerekere family and Te Whanau a Kai, used to sit on the verandah of his house and wave to the children as they went past to go swimming in the river. Mairia Hawea, David's wife, lives there today. She is Taake's oldest living descendant. Before you reach the second family settlement, Rongopai, you pass through a settled area of houses strung along the road. Some are almost hidden in the vine and kiwifruit paddocks; others seem to be planted in furrows along with the maize and the potatoes. The tented hospice — the Ship of God — which the great Spider Woman of Waituhi, Riripeti Artemis Mahana, built during the 1918 flu epidemic, was raised in the hills behind Rongopai. The meeting house itself is on the left of the first bend, its painted eaves sloping to an apex which thrusts like an arrowhead at the sky. The old outside kitchen, Te Pao, which once stood behind Rongopai, is still there but its function has now been taken over by the large new dining-hall, Te Mana o Riria Mauaranui. The dining-hall is a popular gathering place. A children's nursery operates from it, and sometimes you will come across people line-dancing there to country and western music.

From this point, scrub-covered foothills begin to crowd the sky. The road winds around the bottom of the hills to the third family settlement, Takitimu, on a small promontory overlooking the road. In its heyday in the 1940s and 1950s, Takitimu was where the cultural singing and dancing practice sessions used to be held. Opposite are the paddocks where the hockey and football matches took place whenever Waituhi was host to the great Maori sports tournaments. Haare Matenga lived just below Takitimu, and Gilman Tamatea, who lived close by, was one of a line of great prophetic speakers for this third family settlement. There's a lane opposite, and that is where Miro Mananui lived, and where all her old mates gathered to play cards. The houses along the lane look very old, with rusted roofs and paint peeling from the weatherboards. Some are little more than shacks. They are ancient, sagging cottages in eccentric shades of salmon pink, toothpaste green and mauve, belonging to a hardy people who have suffered for decades and are too realistic to hope for better. Curtains flutter in the windows. Some of the windows are boarded up. Flax and flowers grow wild in the gardens. Tin sheets act as windbreaks. Dilapidated caravans are hitched up outside, obsolete tin horses tethered to the houses by electric cords.

Miro Mananui's house is the blue one. From her front step you can see the family graveyard on Tawhiti Kaahu, the hill above Takitimu meeting house. A tiny tombstone and a cross mark the place where she now lies. Beyond the bend is farming country again. Taumata o Tumokonui, the place where Tumokonui lived, is on the left. Also on the left is the Wi Pere Estate, established by Waituhi's most famous son, Wi Pere Halbert, a Maori Member of Parliament in the nineteenth century, for the benefit of all his descendants. Wi Pere's grandson, Turuki Pere, was the family orator. Indeed, Waituhi was not without great spokesmen and women — Hine Te Ariki, Mahea and Blackie Haronga, Perapunahamoa Ihimaera Smiler (with his close links to Tuhoe via the Te Hanene Ringarore Meihana connection), Karauria Ruru and Pimia Ruru among them. One of the greatest speakers in Gisborne, Kani Te Ua, often visited from across the river. So did Uncle Bill Kerekere, tinkling the ivories at weekend dances.

As for the river, it is called the Waipaoa. It threads its sovereign way through the valley. Logs to build the meeting house, Rongopai, were floated down it. People were baptised in it, white-gowned moths fluttering across the water. Old man Bulibasha once swam it during the winter to get a doctor from Waihirere, on the other side, to come and deliver his and Ramona's son, Joshua. It was Joshua who declared to his son, Simeon, that there was no sweeter tasting water in the entire world — and he was absolutely right.

This is Waituhi. During the time I was a boy, the demographic shock of the rural to urban migration had already diminished the population from its 500 to 600 maximum in the 1940s and 1950s. Even so,

13

physically, it hadn't changed much, and it still looks more or less the same today. The people know every knoll, every fold, every physical feature. Each landmark, large or small, has a story attached to it because the people know this land in the biblical sense; they are intimate with it. Although the village is near enough to Gisborne for shopping, work, school, sport or for going to the pub or the pictures, it is far enough away for its geography and history to remain intact, as it has always been. Other Maori places in New Zealand have been obliterated or overlain by other geographies, other histories, but not Waituhi. The generations are marked only by the houses that decay and the old people who pass away.

The village has a proud, distinctive history. Most people who pass through would be unaware of it. Few ever stop. If they did, what would they really see? For most, Waituhi is just another Maori place. A village out in the middle of nowhere, that's us, lost in time and space. A couple of muddy roads, three meeting houses, fields of grapevines, kiwifruit and maize, and old wooden houses. Not worth stopping at, either, because there are no shops, no Maori concert group waiting on the side of the road to entertain and, worse still, no hot springs to bathe in. Nothing would register as the cars blur past, not the children sitting on a fence waving, or the old grandfather with his grandson herding sheep apologetically to the side of the road to let the cars through (though why they should be so apologetic is a mystery as they are not the trespassers here), not even the old woman watching from the skyline. The village looks deserted, and it has to be admitted that most of its people have moved to the city, where they are closer to work. Of those that do remain some either commute or else find jobs on the Wi Pere Estate or as casual labourers, shearers or fruitpickers in season. The rest go into Gisborne every second week to pick up their unemployment cheques from Work and Income.

But the village is never without its guardians. Enough remain to look after the hearth, the ancestral culture, and to keep what is known as *ahi kaa*, the flame buring in the hearth. They are the sentinels, the protectors, keeping the watch. They are the constant reminders that the picture is always bigger than it looks, the history much more profound.

Look behind what you see, and there stand the ancestors before us.

Paraki, back in the mists of time, settled at Papuni. He was among the first to come to this land. It was Tui, grandson of Paraki, who struck the ancient boundaries of the land. In genealogy, one of the great descendants of Tui was Ruapani, during the classical period of Maori settlement, and he became paramount chief of Turanga. In him converged all the lines of Maori greatness in eastern Aotearoa. Among those who claimed descent from him were Te Kani a Takirau, Heuheu, Te Rauparaha, Tomoana, Te Kooti, Wi Pere, Timi Kara, Maui Pomare and Sir Apirana Ngata.

Ruapani's story was not, however, as strong or as colourful as that of another great chief, Kahungunu, who lived to the south. Famed for his sexual prowess, Kahungunu passed through Ruapani's land. He established a male line of descendancy which intermarried with Ruapani's line, women chieftains of hereditary title and distinction. The hereditary title, the separate sovereignty over the land, was maintained through these high-ranking women. Among Kahungunu's descendants was Rakaihikuroa, who married Te Orapa and had Tupurupuru. Because the hereditary title lay with Te Orapa, Tupurupuru was regarded more highly than his father. Incidentally, it is through Rakaihikuroa that Te Whanau a Kai link to Mahinarangi and thence to the great queen of Waikato, Te Atairangikaahu.

The migrant king Kahungunu had a grandson, Mahaki, who proved equal to Kahungunu in terms of fame and power. He superimposed a tribal territory, in his own name, over the lands of the original settlers. The eldest of Mahaki's sons was Ihu, and Ihu's son was Kaikoreaunei. It was this son whose name, shortened to Kai, eventually attached to Te Whanau a Kai. His full name is interesting because it symbolises his status: it means 'I am Kai with nothing' (*kaikore* 'without food, or landless'; *au nei* 'that's me'). But because he was male, people began to assume that the son's tribe, Te Whanau a Kai, was a subtribe of his father's tribe, Te Aitanga a Mahaki. The error is easy to understand. To this day fathers and sons are still regarded as more important than mothers and daughters. However, Kai's two wives, Te Haaki and Whareana, were actually the ones who counted, by virtue of their descent all the way back through Tupurupuru to Ruapani to Tui. Kai was from the migrant line; they were not. Because of this, the people of Te Whanau a Kai say, 'Although our tribe bears the name of Kai, son of Mahaki, we are not a subtribe of Mahaki. All Te Whanau a Kai are also of Te Aitanga a Mahaki; but not all Te Aitanga a Mahaki are Te Whanau a Kai. We are a separate tribe and, although our tribe bears a male name, our tribal identity comes to us through the women. When Kai married them they in no way gave up their rights of hereditary title — their rights to hold the land based on continuous occupation and ancestry — to their husband. Therefore, wherever we stand within our boundaries we have a direct connection to the ancestors who were first on the land. We have stayed. This land is therefore ours.'

What were the tribe's assets? The 1869 sketch map of the Poverty Bay District, which shows details of the Poverty Bay Deed of Cession, has written on it 'Whanauakai [sic] Tribe, in possession of 215,000 acres; a block that begins from the Waipaoa River near Patutahi, covering the Kaimoe, and extending to Moanui in the North and across to Maungapohatu before returning to the Waipaoa River a small way downstream.' Straight lines apart, the area described approximates that of the lands of Te Whanau a Kai today.

Within this area, the tribe was a complex entity made up of a number of individually settled subgroups including Ngati Maru, Ngati Hine, Ngati Rua, Te Whanau a Kai of the Waituhi Valley, Ngai Te Pokingaiwaho, Ngati Paeko and Ngati Te Ika. The traditional resources were birds, fibre, root crops, fruits, freshwater fisheries — all the bounty of a fruitful land — but we also had access to the sea between Awapuni and Te Wai o Hiharore where we fished and harvested shellfish including mussels and clams. We had distinct and older origin than our allies. We kept possession since the first settlement of these lands. We lived in ancient settlements throughout our land.

One of our ancient settlements was Waituhi, an aggregation of strongholds and one of Te Whanau a Kai's most populous sites. We built a number of hilltop fortresses, now only serrated silhouettes like staircases to the sky. We constructed river fords across the Waipaoa. We lived in small houses thatched with reeds and nobody questioned that this land was ours.

This is how we began in that time before the coming of the man we called the *Pakeha*. He was without tattoo, without sacredness, and he rendered all things common. He had eyes that were blue and skin that was white.

He changed the world.

CHAPTER THREE

Charlie Whatu's truck disappeared round the corner. Crouched in the drain, two girls listened until the sound of the truck faded into the distance. Hana Walker clambered back onto the road.

'Come on, Janey,' Hana said. 'I'm not going to wait for you all day. It's cold up here.'

Janey Whatu stared back, frightened. 'Is it really safe? That was Dad's truck. Do you think Dad saw us? You said we'd get back before him and Mum got home. They're going to find out I'm not there. What am I going to do?'

Hana was shivering from the cold and was in no mood to deal with Janey's problem. 'For goodness sake,' she answered, 'how do you know they'll even look in your bed? If they do, bluff your way out of it. Tell them you've just been to the lav.' In Waituhi there was no such thing as modern plumbing, just a smelly longdrop with spiders and cockroaches to keep you company while you sat there trying to think of perfumed bathrooms and flush toilets.

'In my best clothes?' Janey wailed. 'Dad'll never believe that.'

'Janey,' Hana snapped. 'Shut up, get out of the ditch and let's start walking. If you don't I'll drag you to the longdrop and drop you in it myself. Now let's go.' She started off down the road. 'Well? Are you coming?'

The two girls were fifth formers at Gisborne Girls High. George Karepa had asked them to represent his side of the family by being the flower girls in the wedding party. Janey loved being a flower girl but Hana had scowled all the way through the ceremony. The problem was

17

the dress. Lime green against brown Maori skin? Not a good look; whatever way you cut it, you or the dress looked sick. Not only that, but Hana had been trying to score some alcohol all night. With her auntie Maka tiko bum — an endearing nickname, referring to the fact that Maka's face looked like her posterior — peeping around the corners with her googly eyes? No chance. And when the dancing started, the music was so slow, it was so embarrassing to watch all those adults making fools of themselves on the floor, and the boys? Oh, puh-lease. So Hana told Janey she was getting out of there and going to a real dance party at The Club. Nobody would notice they'd gone and their parents would assume they went home with some relative or other.

'How will we get home, though?' Janey asked, unsure.

'Watch,' Hana answered, 'and learn.' When the dance was drawing to a close — at midnight, for crying out loud — she peered through the blue smoke and flashing lights of The Club, trying to pick out likely boys she could promise everything to and who would be stupid enough to assume they'd get it. She saw Darryl, a Pakeha boy who she knew had a car. Bright red, pennants flying from the aerial, and with the dubious boast on his back windscreen: B I I G. She ran her fingers through her hair — copying the gesture of gorgeous girls in the movies — and winked at him. Janey was agog when Darryl ambled over with a mate.

'Are you two girls by yourselves?' Darryl asked.

'Not any more,' Hana answered.

They danced. Or rather, Hana and Janey danced while the boys jiggled and jerked to the music. Neither of them had any rhythm whatsoever. After the DJ racked up the decibels and destroyed everyone's eardrums for the rest of their lives, Hana asked Darryl to take them home.

'No problem,' Darryl said.

Hana gave him a passionate kiss. As they got into the car, Hana whispered to Janey, 'When I tell you to run, *run*.'

The trouble was that the instruction came earlier than Janey — or Hana — had anticipated. At the wooden bridge outside Patutahi Darryl pulled over and pulled out his penis. His mate did the same. 'Okay, girls, enjoy,' Darryl said, the smug shit.

'Run!' Janey yelled, without waiting for Hana to give the order. She'd never seen a penis before, and two waving and twitching like that absolutely terrified her. Darryl, of course, wasn't giving up quite so easily and he took off after them. But when Hana picked up a rock and looked like she would throw it at his car he screeched on the brakes. Have his paintwork scratched by a crazy sheila? No way.

'Enjoy your walk home, bitches,' Darryl yelled.

'Oh, what's wrong with you now, Janey Whatu?' Hana snapped.

'Look at my dress,' Janey wept. 'There's mud all over it.'

'It wasn't my idea to jump in the drain,' Hana said. She saw the funny side of it and giggled to herself. But Janey finally got to her.

'I only came with you as a mate,' Janey snivelled. 'I wish I'd stayed at the wedding.'

'Yeah,' Hana answered. 'So do I.'

Silence fell between them. They passed Pakowhai with its church in the paddock. All the anger of being young, trapped and having to live in Waituhi spilled over.

'There's nothing for me here,' Hana said to herself. 'Is that what cousin George discovered? Is that why he never came back?'

All around her, old wooden houses on either side of the gravelled road. As soon as she could, she would get as far away from this place as possible. And nobody would be able to stop her.

Nobody.

CHAPTER FOUR

Miro Mananui woke with a start. The Matua, the Mother, of Waituhi, she was always conscious of the things seen and the things unseen of the world — and something was tapping at her dreams, 'Let me in, let me in.' She rose from sleep and felt the flutter of wings across her face. Her first thought was to reach across the bed and make sure her husband, Tama, was all right. Yes, he was sleeping on his side, turned away from her. Just to make sure he was still alive, she prodded him with a finger. Tama snorted with irritation, farted, and moved away from her.

Relieved, Miro settled back into the pillows. 'As long as you can pass wind, you're still here,' she said to herself. Even though Tama was only forty-nine he hadn't been too well lately. Ever since he had caught bronchitis last year — all that sleeping on damp floors while escorting her to land-rights discussions at meeting houses throughout the country — he'd had trouble with his health. Miro had got a fright when, on waking one morning soon after a return to Waituhi from Taranaki, she thought Tama had died. Mouth wide open, not breathing. Face grey. Body cold. She reached for a handmirror and put it over his mouth to see if it would mist. Panicking, she rolled up one of his eyelids. His eye stared back at her.

'What the hell do you think you're doing?' he asked.

'Oh,' she answered lamely, 'I was just wondering when you would wake up.'

Tama had looked at her thoughtfully. 'Stupid woman,' he said, 'still thinking about sex at your age.'

Miro settled back into the pillows. The tang of Tama's fart was part shellfish and part sea roe, and reminded her of the huge feast at George Karepa's wedding last night. She'd told Tama to lay off the sea roe. Mind you, she couldn't talk. Partial to whisky, she'd obviously had too many nips because although she tried to go back to sleep it eluded her. Instead, Miro turned her thoughts back to the wedding, and a great sense of triumph settled on her. After all, there was some satisfaction to be had that no function involving Te Whanau a Kai could take place without her. The younger generation often forgot her hereditary title but, last night, she was given the place of honour among them. Throughout the evening she was proud that people acknowledged her by calling her by her honorific: *Matua*, parent. This was as it should be: Miro's genealogy, her line of descent, placed her in the ranks of the queens. By virtue of her descent from Kai's first wife, Te Haaki, she could trace her family tree in a direct line to Ruapani. Nobody, not even her younger brother Arapeta, was more senior than she was and, last night, she had enjoyed watching his discomfort and that of other male chiefs, as they all had to acknowledge her status. When she stood up to give the opening speech and prayers, she knew that they were enraged. Within Te Whanau a Kai she was the one who always spoke first, and she knew that none would dare challenge her.

A smile played across Miro's lips. 'You're grandstanding,' Tama had scolded her, 'you're showing off.' There was a certain element of truth in that. Most of all she was maintaining her position in the political framework of the otherwise patriarchal Maori world. With some sharpness she had reprimanded Tama for his opinion. Even he was of lower status and he did not understand that she had to maintain power, hold the control and keep reinforcing her leadership. If she didn't, she would lose the autonomy of her decisionmaking on behalf of the tribe. She trusted her own decisions more than those of any of the male chieftains. Woe betide the tribe if one of them wrested that capacity to be the decisionmaker from her.

Realising she couldn't get back to sleep, Miro went down the hallway to make a cup of tea. She saw Charlie Whatu's truck stop opposite her house where Sam Walker lived just behind Maka tiko bum's place. Who was that in front with Charlie? His wife, Agnes, and was that Maka? Sam got off the truck and seemed to be inviting the others on the back to join him. With a sigh of resignation Miro watched as Mattie, of course it would have to be Mattie, took up his offer. Mattie lived with Miro and Tama, worked for them too, but they hardly ever saw her. Those no-hopers Hine and Jack Ropiho got off the truck also, Hine shooing her son, Boy Boy, off to stay with his Granny Heni today.

The curtains in the window frame fluttered against Miro's face. She saw that Mattie was looking directly at her. 'You can't possibly see me, here, missy, where I am standing,' Miro said. But she knew, even as she had the thought, that Mattie sensed she was there. Mattie's look was confrontational, questioning: 'I know you disapprove of me, you old bitch, and I know I should come home, but it's my life and I'm living it.'

Miro closed the curtains. She recalled George Karepa's shocked face, last night, when he saw Mattie at the wedding reception. He hadn't expected her to be there. He was even more shocked to find that she was living in Waituhi. He stared at Miro, suspicious that she had something to do with it — the last time he had seen Mattie was when he left her in Auckland three years ago. While people were dancing, he came up to Miro and she knew he wanted to get to the bottom of it. Instead, she deflected him by saying, 'Come and see me tomorrow before you go. I need to talk to you.'

'I don't know if I can,' George answered. 'I mightn't have the time. Hayley and I have to catch a plane tomorrow afternoon.'

'There's always time,' Miro reminded him, 'to see your Matua.' She wanted to talk to him about coming back to Waituhi and taking over the leadership. If he was also curious about Mattie's being here and if that helped to tempt him to come today, so be it.

Miro boiled the jug and added gumboot tea to the pot. Such concerns as the political and economic wellbeing of Te Whanau a Kai were never far from her mind: trying to keep the tribe together, trying to keep the land together, trying to find somebody of the younger generation to take the people into the future. It was true what people said about Maori being a people who walked backwards into the future. All her life Miro had done this because, above all else, she knew that she had an implicit contract with the past. For her the past was not something that lay behind her. It lay in front of her, a long line of ancestors to whom she was accountable. When she stood before God, her great fear was not his divinity, but her Maori ancestors who would be standing with him. They would ask the hard questions:

'Under your custodial care, Matua, has the tribe prospered? Have your hands nurtured the seed of our ancestors? Have you assured their future by anointing a successor to look after them when you pass through the vale of tears and join us?'

Miro stared at the ceiling. How would she answer her ancestors? She could feel their presence crowding around her. Without realising that she was doing it, Miro started to moan — for she was in mourning. She was in mourning for her great-nephew, George, who was now lost to her, gone into the dark stomach of the world. George was the grandson of her elder brother, Arapeta, and because she and Tama were childless, he had been given to them as an adopted son — a child of their own. As he grew up, it was clear to all that Miro was grooming him for tribal leadership. The trouble was that sport and pretty girls got in the way. Instead, George became one of Gisborne's most famous sons: a league player, making big money in Australia. No doubt about it, Miro was proud of him. Who wouldn't be, seeing him standing there before his people clutching his pretty Hayley, whom he'd met in Sydney, as if she was the prize for having made it to the front rank. The whole of Gisborne had been there last night to celebrate his wedding, even the mayor, as if George was a modern-day gladiator being crowned with the laurel leaves of victory. When George flashed his smile at everyone, thanking 'My Matua, Miro, for making me who I am today,' she knew he meant it. She caught a glimpse of the boy George had been, barefoot and loving, and she thought to herself that Waituhi hadn't done a bad job on him after all. Was it her imagination or had George carefully beamed a smile across his shoulder to where the local news cameraman could take it all in — all this sincerity of a handsome young man for a tribe he hardly ever came back to visit? Oh yes, the boy had grown into a charming self-aware man with the world at his football boots. Some people might think it arrogant to be so self-aware. As far as Miro was concerned it was simply a case of survival. When George had presented his profile to the camera he knew exactly that it would reflect his charisma. Why waste it, however, on a career as a sportsman?

'That's not who you were supposed to be,' Miro said. 'League is not going to last all your life and I'm not giving up on you without a fight.'

Brooding like this, Miro Mananui finished her cup of tea. She went back to the bedroom. The tapping sound again. A branch, rapping at the window. How many times had she told Tama to trim the trees back? She got out of bed and went to the window to look.

Something shimmered on the other side of the glass.

As soon as she saw it, Miro knew what it was. She felt her heart give a momentary sharp pulse and tried to steady it; sometimes it was better to sleep as long as you could, and not get up in the morning. She opened the window to take a closer look. Outside the window was a tree, and the wind was rustling the leaves like a portent. The wind was cold and Miro shivered. She saw the owl.

'*Tena koe, ruru*,' Miro said. 'Hello, messenger.'

It was perched on a branch within the foliage of the tree. When Miro greeted the owl, it stepped out into the light. Its cryptic colours had kept it well camouflaged. The sun fired its beak and brown plumage and flashed on its white streaked feathers. Its powerful feet dug into the branch. With such a beak and claws, it could kill quickly.

Like Mattie Jones, the owl stared at Miro with provocation. Its eyes grew large and binocular. Miro thought of Maka tiko bum, who would have been screeching with hysteria by now because the owl was always a harbinger of ill tidings or death. But Miro did not have the same fear. As the Matua of Waituhi she expected to be told or warned of events that would impact on her people. For her, the owl was simply a messenger of the gods.

The owl bristled. Grew large, ominous. Screeched out a name. At the sound, Miro bowed her head in acknowledgement. 'Thank you for bringing me your message.' The owl looked at her for a moment, and lifted on silent wings. One moment there. Next moment gone.

'Are you all right, Matua?' Tama asked. After all these years, the man most intimate with her still called her by her rank. Not 'dear' or 'love' or 'sweetheart' for those were common names, without sacredness.

'Yes, husband,' Miro answered. 'It's just that I have a lot to think on. Nothing for you to worry about.'

'I don't know why you say that,' Tama said grumpily. 'All our lives together you know you have your job and I have my job. I know your job is to look after the tribe; well, my job is to look after you, and to try to take as much as I can from your shoulders.'

'I know,' Miro answered. The acceptance in her response of Tama's role in her life was not without guile; sometimes he needed her affirmation and she gave it knowingly. Her husband had such goodness in him. Youth still blessed his appearance; he had the look of vitality, his hair only lightly touched with grey, his face not yet lined. Sometimes, when Tama needed her, she still marvelled at the strength of his thighs and the solidity of his loins as he rode deeply inside her. At such times, when he gave up his long sighs of pleasure to the night, she was pleased that darkness clothed her with kindness so that he could not see that she was old, dried up and without — an old-fashioned word — comeliness. For Miro was sixty-nine, and Tama was twenty years younger. A generation younger. Oh so young, so beautiful was her man.

In the early days of their marriage, Miro knew that people talked and laughed behind her back. They thought the marriage was an obscenity and that Tama, gorgeous in his masculinity, must have been tricked into it. There must surely have been some duplicity, to have resulted in this unnatural joining of such a young man with an old woman. The fact that no children came out of the marriage only confirmed its unnatural estate. Over the years, however, the talk, the laughter, the jokes had diminished. By sheer willpower, Miro had subdued all who criticised her. With a glance she could kill any reference, no matter if spoken in jest, to the relationship. The one voice that eluded her was the mocking, accusing voice that sometimes spoke inside her.

She might be Matua, but Miro Mananui had never been a beauty. Where others girls were lithesome, she was ugly, heavy and squat. Her face was broad and dark, and its only redeeming feature were eyes of extraordinary depth. People feared those eyes because Miro had the gift of prophecy, of second sight, and could see things in other people that they didn't want her to see. Yet above all treasures, the gift of beauty, and youth also, Miro Mananui would have greatly desired to give Tama for all that he had sacrificed in marrying her.

Whenever her thoughts plumbed the utter darkness, Miro would wish with all her heart that she could give back to Tama the life she had taken from him.

'Do you want us to say morning prayers?' Tama asked. He was already rummaging on his side of the bed for the Paipera Tapu, the Holy Bible,

God's word as given unto the prophet Te Kooti Arikirangi, whose teachings they followed.

'Yes,' Miro said. She knelt on the floor and accepted the book which Tama gave her. He was yawning, scratching his armpits, focusing on the words through the glasses he had bought from the cheap rack at the chemist shop.

'*Kororia ki to Ingoa Tapu*,' he began. 'Glory to Your Holy Name.' He made the sign of the upraised hand. It was the first prayer of the day.

CHAPTER FIVE

From the kitchen window Pita Mahana saw two girls passing by and recognised Hana Walker. 'Up to your tricks again,' he muttered. Hana needed a good boot up the behind but she was Daddy's girl and her father, Hepa, would be soft on her. She'd probably spin some story about why she was home so late and he'd believe her. Who was the kid with Hana? Looked like Janey Whatu.

'Pita? Are you there?'

Pita held the telephone closer. It had woken him with its ringing. Miriama told him not to answer it. Maori weren't as polite as Europeans, who at least waited until you had your breakfast before telephoning. 'Only Maori ring at this time of the morning,' she warned, 'and they always want something.' She was right.

'Who's that?' Pita asked.

'It's Wayne here,' a voice answered. 'One of our shearers hasn't turned up. I was hoping to finish the shearing today. Can you come out and take his stand?'

'Give me a break, cuz,' Pita groaned. 'Me and Miriama only got home a couple of hours ago. Isn't Sunday supposed to be a day of rest?'

'Not for us hard workers,' Wayne said. 'I really need you, bro. Jim Franks put in a nightpen and he's counting on us to finish his ewes by lunchtime. Baling the wool should take us to mid-afternoon. The trucks are coming at four. All my shearers are here except young Jacob. I want to keep on the good side of Jim. I'm counting on him to renew our shearing contract for next year. Times are hard.'

27

'You're at Mairangi Station? Way the hell out there?' Pita asked. Times were always hard. The future was always uncertain. In such uncertainty you went where the almighty dollar was and you paid obeisance to the White man who possessed it, for he was king.

'Yeah, I know. I didn't know who else to ring. Never mind, you go back to sleep.'

'No, we'll come,' Pita said. 'I'll bring Waka with me. He'll appreciate making some extra cash. You got enough women to handle the fleeces? I know Miriama will love to help out.'

'Thanks, Pita. The more hands we have the better. I'll go back to the shed and start cracking my whip. Everyone is half asleep this morning. I was at George's wedding too, but I'm raring to go.'

'Tell me that at morning tea break.'

Pita Mahana was descended from one of the great families of Waituhi. Originally followers of the Ringatu religion, they had been ruled over by Riripeti Mahana nee Pere. Through her, the family had become the leaders of the Ringatu movement and politics in the valley. When Riripeti embraced the teachings of the prophet Te Kooti Arikirangi, she set her family on a collision course with destiny. She sought in every way possible to achieve sovereignty for the faithful, the remnants of the Te Kooti followers.

As long as Riripeti was alive, the Mahana family maintained its ascendancy. She came to her fame during the 1918 flu epidemic when she built her hospice, the romantically named Te Waka o te Atua, the Ship of God, which saved many lives during the flu. From that time onward she maintained a powerful position in local and national politics. By the 1950s, however, in failing health, she saw her power ebbing away. When she died in 1957 she was not to know that her husband, Ihaka, and eldest son, Te Ariki, would strike mortal blows to the Ringatu leadership she had so carefully nurtured during her turbulent life. Ihaka became a Mormon and the family joined him in the new religion. Te Ariki tried his best to maintain the family's role in Ringatu politics but lacked the charisma and intelligence that Riripeti possessed.

Now it had all come to this. The Mahana clan had exploded under the pressure of competing ambitions, jealousies and enmities. They had been displaced to the margins. They had become a dysfunctional family, individualised and, like Pita Mahana this day, living on the edges of a world which was common, without sacredness. They had fallen from grace, fallen from greatness.

Pita put the telephone down and walked back to the bedroom. Miriama was waiting, her arms folded. 'So who would love to go shearing?' she asked, having heard every word of the conversation. 'I told you not to answer the phone.'

'It's only till lunchtime,' Pita answered. By Jeez, Miriama was still a beauty. Her hair might be grey but her face was still beautiful with the clear skin and strong cheekbones of her own tribal Tuhoe people. Thirty years ago, when he was twenty, he had met Miriama at a dance at Te Whaiti. She'd been eighteen. Their romance had been short and sweet because they'd been struck by lightning — 'Lust more like it,' Maka tiko bum said at the wedding in her usual droll manner — and he had brought his bride back to Waituhi.

'Well,' Miriama said, 'no use making out if we have to go shearing today.' Her tongue was definitely in her cheek. 'You better go and tell Waka he's coming shearing with us.' She motioned to the sleepout where all her boys had grown to manhood, and went to the bathroom to get dressed.

Watching her, Pita recalled their life together. In the early days the babies had come just about one every second year for the first fourteen years. Miriama's womb was fruitful and Pita had been a healthy sire — 'Too healthy,' Maka tiko bum would have said — after all, they hadn't had television in those days to keep him otherwise occupied. After Waka was born, Miriama had her tubes tied. It was either that or persuade Pita to have a vasectomy; like all men, the idea of a knife anywhere near his groin made him feel faint. That was twelve years ago and you'd think that not having more kids would mean life would be easier. No way. Over all those years, Pita Mahana slaved his guts out to support his family. Uneducated, he was qualified only for labouring jobs: sometimes scrubcutting, sometimes fencing. In summer, he and Miriama joined the Mahana Two shearing gang. After the local shearing was finished in the district, the gang went down to the South Island to shear there. Occasionally they went to Hastings to pick fruit. Lately, there had been no jobs for him over the winter.

29

Pita heard Miriama give a small cry, 'Oh.' He walked to the bathroom and found her doubled up at the washbasin. She was clutching at her left breast. When she saw him she stood and hid her pain.

'I'm all right,' Miriama said. 'It's a woman's problem.' Pita never liked to know about such things — her time of the month and all that. Sure enough, he blanched, turned and went out of the house to the sleepout.

Like Pita, Miriama was also thinking of their life, but she was more concerned about how it was right now, in the present. Pita had been unemployed for three months and, although Miss Zelda at the Patutahi General Store agreed that Miriama could run up an account, it was getting pretty high. The job at Mairangi Station would be handy for a few bucks to help clear the debt.

On top of everything, Miriama had secretly gone to her doctor to ask about the lump in her left breast. Doctor Hewitt told her the lump was malignant. 'You have breast cancer, Mrs Mahana,' he said. He told her it was linked to her heavy smoking. 'If we remove the breast you may have a chance of survival.' The problem was that Miriama had known of three close friends who had breasts removed — but they still died. The local advice was that if death was going to happen anyway, better to have a longer life by keeping your breast than a shorter life by having an operation.

'When do I tell Pita?' Miriama asked herself. He already had enough problems to think about. He would never admit it, but the man who could once shear 300 sheep a day with ease, now found it a struggle. His back was giving him trouble and the kids still depended on him for financial support. Four of the boys were married, with hire purchase or mortgage payments. Not to worry, because there was always Dad to borrow from. Always Dad if their bedroom suite or car was to be repossessed. Why couldn't they live a simpler life! Once upon a time four walls and a roof was all you needed. Today you had to have wall-to-wall carpets, the most expensive wallpaper, a freezer, all the knick-knacks of modern living. It was so tempting to sign on the dotted line, promise to pay so much every month, and when you couldn't keep up the payments, Dad always helped out. Just like now, helping out his cousin Wayne at Mairangi Station.

'No,' Miriama said to herself, 'now's not the time to tell Pita about my problems.' Like all women, she placed her man first and put herself on hold. Pita would never cope with the news of how ill she was. Doctor Hewitt had given her pills for the pain and, for the moment, they gave her respite. When things got really bad, then she would tell Pita. Meantime, there was time enough, time enough.

Miriama heard Pita banging loudly on the door of the sleepout. She opened the window to ask what the fuss was about.

'The door's locked,' Pita said as he banged on the door again. 'Open up, Waka, I know there's somebody in there with you. Open this door and be quick about it.'

Whispered voices sounded behind the door. 'Go away, Dad.' The door opened. Waka stood there, frightened. Behind him, on the bed, cowered a young girl.

'Oh no,' Miriama said. It was Ani Jackson, one of Kepa Jackson's girls. There was bad blood between the Mahanas and the Jacksons.

'We're going to get married, Dad,' Waka blurted out.

Pita looked him over, not knowing whether to laugh or cry. Sixteen years old, this son of his. 'Well,' he said finally, 'if you want to get married you better come out to work. When you've got enough money to buy your girl some pants, then you can get married.' He strode back into the house — and saw the frustration on Miriama's face.

'All our sons have taken after your side of the family,' Miriama said. 'You're all a wild bunch. All you Mahanas should have been drowned at birth.'

'Don't start blaming my side of the family,' Pita answered. 'I seem to remember a Te Whaiti girl who was running wild until I made a good woman of her. What are you crying for? Plenty of time to cry when Waka and Ani start bringing the babies home for you to look after. That's the time to cry.'

He didn't understand at all that Miriama was weeping not because of the grandchildren but because she would not be there to see them, to hold them in her arms, to watch them through all the years of their growing up.

A noise sounded behind her. Miriama looked round. Ani Jackson stood there with her young, oh so foolish and young son. 'Leave us,' Miriama said to Pita and Waka. 'You men have done enough.' She opened her arms to Ani. In Ani's eyes, bewilderment. It was always a bewildering time for a girl who had been made a woman by a man. 'Are you all right?' Miriama asked Ani. 'There's no need to be ashamed.'

'But I am ashamed. What will become of us?'

Miriama began to talk to Ani about love, about life, about love and life between a man and a woman. The older woman advised. The younger woman lit a cigarette and listened. The cigarette disturbed Miriama because of what Doctor Hewitt had told her about the dangers of smoking; she would have liked to tell Ani to put the cigarette out, but she did not. The conversation was both sad and joyful: sad because the girl was no longer a girl and joyful because now she was a woman.

'Pita and I will speak with your father,' Miriama said, 'and Waka will ask for your hand in marriage. Then you will come and stay in this house and begin your life with my son. And you will be as a daughter to me also.'

At her words, Ani began to shiver. This made Miriama recall how she, too, had shivered during her first talk with an elder woman after she had been with a man — not Pita, though he had thought she was a virgin when they married. What was it that the old woman had said to her?

'Woman was made of Adam's rib and, when she tasted of the Tree of Good and Evil, she took the burden of man upon herself. This has always been the lot of all women.'

A sudden riff of pain jagged through Miriama's body. She steeled herself against it and, when it had subsided, welcomed Ani to the world of women.

'Daughter of Eve, welcome to the world of man.'

CHAPTER SIX

————— 1 —————

The old home town looks the same as I step down from the train,
And there to meet me is my mama and papa —

Sam Walker's home was a tin shack behind his Auntie Maka's house. Listening to the carousing that was coming from the shack, Maka couldn't help thinking about how Sam was wasting his life away. How many years ago had it been since he asked her if he could stay in the shack? 'Auntie, Dad won't have me in the house,' Sam had said. Hepa always had high expectations of his kids, particularly Sam, the eldest, but Sam just wasn't a chip off the old block. Maka had taken him in, knowing that it was better all round if Sam and Hepa had space between them — lots and lots of space actually, preferably in a different galaxy. Already Hepa was blaming Sam for being a bad influence on the apple of his eye, his daughter, Hana. But Hana was walking on the wild side without anybody's help, thank you very much.

'I wonder if Hana managed to sneak in the window without Hepa knowing?' Maka asked herself. She had eyes in the back of her head, did Maka.

Maka saw Sonny Whatu coming out of the shack, opening his trousers and letting fly against a wire fence. 'Hey, Sonny,' she yelled, 'that's an electric fence so watch out you don't fry your thing.' The fence wasn't electric at all, but her warning had the desired effect as Sonny sprayed himself with his piss. Scowling darkly, he went back inside the shack.

'That bitch,' Sonny swore as he stepped across Hine and Jack Ropiho and took a pew.

Originally, Sam's shack had begun life as an open courtyard with a dirt floor and roofing iron across the top where Maka cooked over an open fire. That was when the kitchen in the front house was needed for another bedroom for all Maka's kids. Her husband, Haami, solved the problem by throwing the stove out the back, running electricity from the house by a cable out a side window and enclosing the courtyard with more corrugated iron. Haami also threw Maka out there too when she had grown too old to be attractive sexually but still had her uses as his cook. He was an abusive man with a vicious temper. Always out of work, he took his boredom and frustration out on his wife and daughters, Mabel and Polly. When he started to look for a sexual substitute and began to target Mabel, Maka gave the girls money and told them, 'Get out of here. Get away, and don't come back.' The best years of Maka's life began only after the bastard died. She cried crocodile tears at his funeral and, once she had buried him, she moved herself and the kitchen back into the house again. All the time she was shifting the stove back she kept thinking, 'Yeah, you bastard.' Having the kitchen inside was spitting in her dead husband's eye.

Inside Sam's shack the air was hazy with cigarette smoke and stale with the smell of sweat.

'Where's Mister DB gone?' Hine Ropiho asked. She poked at Jack, to see if he had stolen her beer. 'Mister DB's gone home to Mrs DB,' she pouted. 'Hey, Sam, have you got any Mister Vodka or Mister Whisky?' Did Charlie Whatu really think they'd stop partying because he wanted to come home early? Nah! Good old Sam for telling everyone to come around to his place.

With a grunt Sam got up from the old couch and kicked at a refrigerator. 'Never was allowed to do that in Dad's house,' he laughed.

It was dark inside the shack, but enough light streamed through the open door and between the curtains of the window to light up the room. The noise as Sam took hard grog out of the refrigerator made Mattie Jones murmur in protest.

'What did you say, you stupid bitch?' Sonny Whatu asked. He was still brooding over the way Mattie had chopped at his windpipe and was just waiting for the chance to get one back on her. She was lying semiconscious, her hands limply outstretched across the table where beer bottles shone in the light. Her head rested on the tabletop, her face bloated with beer and fatigue.

'Leave her alone,' Sam told him. 'And what's wrong with the music, Blacky? Come on, man, if you're too stuffed to play the guitar give it over here.'

'Be my guest,' Blacky answered. He gave the guitar to Sam who tuned it to his satisfaction and began to strum away their blues. The music filled the big room, big and dark and cluttered with rusted pots and pans. From the ceiling hung a rusting tilly lamp. A big black pot was still suspended from a wire hook in the unused fireplace. Beneath it, empty beer bottles and cigarette cartons were stacked. In the middle of the room the long table, where Mattie was lying, was stained with candle grease and food. Beyond, Sam had rigged up a canvas partition, and behind that was the door to his bedroom. Next to the bed was a chest of drawers with a broken mirror on top. The cupboard where food was once kept was bursting with clothes. A few pictures cut from magazines were sellotaped to the tin walls. Sam's life had all come down to this: a room to live in and mates to drink with. Welcome to his world.

Sam began to sing, and all the pain of broken dreams and unfulfilled hopes came tumbling out of his guts. Good old Sam, yeah, good old Sam. No party was complete without him. A pub without Sam was an empty one, yeah. Wherever he was, that's where the fun was. Where the laughs were loudest, the fights fiercest, that's where you'd find him. Wherever somebody was smashing the body off a beer bottle, ready to wield it against all comers, right in the middle you'd find Sam.

Sam, good old Sam. A chip off the old Walker block? Nah, not Sam. Not like that stuck-up father of his, Hepa Walker, Mister Walker Sir. Not like that brother of his, Frankie, who made his father so proud when he graduated from Police Academy. No, Sam took after the bad Walker side of the clan, bro. Dad tried to turn him into a good little soldier, the littlest corporal, and for a while there it looked like he might make the grade. Handsome once and young, Sam tried to walk as his old man walked. But he knew exactly what he was, a no-hoper, and that nothing he could do would ever change that. At high school his lack of will, self-determination and discipline started to come through. He dropped out. Began to move with the wrong crowd. He couldn't bear to see the contempt in his father's eyes so he left school and pissed off to Wellington. He met up with some Black Power boys, found himself another family, got himself a patch. Did some jobs as a drug courier, sorted out some witnesses in a murder case so they wouldn't testify, ran protection against a rival skinhead gang and was one of the boys.

But one day Sam got caught in a sting organised by the cops, and his own brother was in on the police operation. The police raided one of the houses where Sam was dealing in stolen goods. He tried to get out through a back window but all exits were sealed by the squad and, at eighteen, Sam ended up singing the old jailhouse blues. Did his dad help him when he appeared before the courts? Sam's lawyer told Hepa that Sam's sentence might be reduced if Hepa put in a good word for him, seeing as Hepa was so highly thought of, being an ex-military man and all. But what did old man Hepa say at Sam's trial? 'I have tried to bring up my son to be a law-abiding citizen and a credit to the community but he has failed all of us. A prison sentence would enable him to repay his debt to society and, perhaps, might show him the error of his ways.'

Sam went down, bro. Two years in a juvenile facility. When he came out, the judge, on Hepa's recommendation, put him in the legal custody of his dad, told him not to leave Poverty Bay and to report regularly to his parole officer in Gisborne. It sounded good, but Hepa was only thinking of himself and his reputation. Waituhi was as good as any prison and Hepa was as efficient as any jailer. Sam was his prodigal son and Hepa wanted him where he could see him, where Sam could not embarrass him with any more criminal convictions. But would Hepa let him in the house? Nah, he might make off with the family silver, mate.

Good old Sam, doing time in Waituhi, relishing the irony of his existence in a sentimental song, an anthem to the family.

Down the road I look and there runs Mary,
hair of gold and lips like cherries.
It's good to touch the green, green grass of home —

A sliver of light stabbed at Mattie's closed eyes. She winced and moved her arms. A bottle upturned and beer flowed out, trickling through her hair. The beer followed the curve of her neck and spilled onto her dress. Mattie frowned, moving away from the spilt beer, and the light struck her closed eyelids again. In that halo of haze and amid the beer bottles gleaming, she suddenly awoke. For a moment she was still, gaining strength. She brushed her wet hair back from her forehead.

'Where the hell am I?' Disoriented, Mattie stared at the same old crowd of losers: Sam Walker, Hine and Jack, Sonny and Blacky. When she realised where she was, she gave a bitter shrug. Somehow or another, she always ended up trashing herself at Sam's place, her own personal twilight zone. She wanted to laugh but that damn song that Sam was singing was taking her back, taking her away, taking her to a place where she'd once been happy in George Karepa's sweet and loving arms.

Three years ago, Mattie was a young woman who had left Christchurch and her mother Gladys — solo mother, living on the unemployment benefit, with other mouths to feed, hell, Mattie's going was no loss — to take up a job in Wellington. She lived with Auntie May in Naenae for a while and worked in a car factory until Auntie May accused her of stealing some dollars from her purse, the old bitch. Mattie found a flat with two other Maori girls, Whetu and Marama, in Newtown and got a new job working in the laundry at Wellington Hospital. She worked long hard hours and lived only for the weekends when she could party. She was vivacious, fun-loving and popular. The first time she set eyes on George Karepa was when she and Whetu were eating fish and chips. There in the sports sections of the newspaper wrapping was George's photograph. He had made his reputation playing provincial rugby but had just switched to league. The headline accompanying the photograph read: KAREPA SIGNS WITH WARRIORS.

'What a spunk,' Whetu sighed. Some men were lookers, and George was a handsome son of a bitch. The photograph showed him with his shirt off and his musculature was spectacular. As a league player his position was halfback. He was reputed to be fast, opportunistic, slippery behind the scrum, and he could make the perfect feint. He'd had a dream season playing representative rugby and already had a following among the fans.

Mattie thought George was much too pretty until, surprise, surprise, she, Whetu and Marama went to a party at Wilson Street and there, drinking with some boys from a local football club, was the man himself — and he was more of an animal than she had expected. He saw her, grinned, and came over to do her a line but she cut him short. 'It's my mate, Whetu, who wants a date with you, not me,' she said. That surprised him — he always thought a lot of himself and was accustomed to women wanting to go to bed with him — but he made an act of it, clutching his chest and falling to the floor, yelling, 'Is there a doctor in the house who can heal a broken heart?' When there were no takers, Mattie helped him up. 'Well,' she answered, 'I work in the laundry folding sheets and sewing ripped pillowcases, so I guess I'm the best offer you'll get.'

Mattie groaned and tried to bite back the memory. Harder. Harder. Until blood seeped from her lips and she swept her hand across the table in anger. Glass shattered, beer spilled. She pushed against the table, trying to stand.

'Hey, lighten up, lady,' Blacky yelled.

Mattie gave Blacky the stare. 'Fuck you,' she said — but her thoughts were not on Blacky. Even when George made a play for her that night he already had a girlfriend, Joyce, who kept his apartment clean for him and regularly offered her body as collateral services. Mattie was not to know, was she? George asked if he could take her home that night and she said, 'I never go home with anybody on a first date.' He was a charmer, he looked at his watch and said, 'All rightee, the first date has just ended and the second date begins now.' Even as she was walking out the door with him Whetu warned her, 'Don't do this, Mattie. George Karepa's big trouble. Stay clear of him.' But Mattie thought she had the control — and that Whetu was only jealous. 'Don't worry about me,' she had answered. 'I'm not planning to fall in love with him. I just want to fuck him, and then you can have him.'

Yeah, right. After a week with him Mattie wanted to climb inside George's skin and stay there forever. From the beginning the chemistry had been strong, something to do with skin on skin, with the ruthlessness with which a man possesses a woman.

Joyce, of course, found out. Not that Mattie gave a fuck about Joyce. Mattie went to watch George playing Saturday league, and Joyce came through the door of the clubrooms. 'Is this your new bitch?' she yelled at George. 'Are you the new bitch?' Joyce asked Mattie. 'Yeah, well, there's a long line before I got him, bitch, and there'll be a long line after you've had him.'

And Mattie remembered the day she moved into George's apartment. The sheets were still warm from where Joyce had slept. George swept her into his glamorous life as the girlfriend of the league star: parties, dances, all the stuff that surrounds celebrities. She was the trophy girlfriend, just as Hayley was now the trophy wife.

They lasted eight months, George and Mattie, and they were great months. Better to have eight great months than thirty-eight bad years like Maka tiko bum. Sometimes, eight months were better than a lifetime. But George was a star and Mattie was just the star's girlfriend. There were times when she didn't play the role well and didn't know the rules. She wasn't sophisticated enough, she didn't suck up enough and she was too intense.

'You frighten me sometimes,' George said. 'You're getting too deep into me, you're too much for me to handle.' Mattie had a physical and mental toughness that no other girlfriend of his had ever possessed. More than that, he worried about becoming her obsession.

At that time of his life and career, however, it wouldn't have mattered what Mattie was like. Joyce had been right, of course. George was a serial woman-loving man. Any woman in George's life was there only on a temporary basis. Was it his fault that Mattie, who should have known better, fell so hard for him? Whetu tried to warn her, 'Mattie, he's met somebody else.' Mattie refused to believe her. Sure they'd been fighting, and sure George had accused Mattie of being possessive, but she believed that she was as much in his skin as he was in hers.

George stopped coming home. Born under the sign of Saturn, mercurial and passionate, Mattie went crazy waiting for him. She hadn't realised until then that she was in a dependency relationship, and much of her anger was directed against herself for being such a fool. She waited through the nights. Waited through the days. Waited through the weekends. Alone. Always alone. She didn't realise that this was George's way of getting out of relationships: he simply opted out, didn't show up, didn't force a decision by making his decision. Sooner or later the other person got the idea.

'I must have been thick,' Mattie used to say to herself afterward. In the end she did what Joyce had done before her — she went looking for George. Not to ask him to come back but, rather, just to take some kind of revenge on him for doing this to her. She asked his mates if they knew where he was. 'George? No, don't know where he is,' they said, their eyes looking into the darkness at her. Stupid bitch, couldn't she take the hint and take a hike? They closed ranks around George, protecting golden boy. Eventually, she found him. Ironically, he was at the clubrooms after a Saturday game and he had his latest squeeze with him. Her temper got the better of her. She slapped him twice, punched him in the stomach and, when he was down, kicked him in the crotch and knew he'd be pissing blood for weeks. Of course his latest girl tried to stop her, but she went down too when Mattie got her by the tits and twisted.

'No matter who you end up with, George Karepa,' Mattie told him, 'you'll always belong to me. Always. Whether you like it or not, I'm there forever.'

As charming and as self-aware as ever, George had simply shrugged, smiled, tried not to wince as he stood up, refilled his glass of beer and, shaking his head, said to his mates, 'Women.'

Even then, Mattie had known she was pregnant. She moved out of George's apartment and back into the flat with Whetu and Marama. She never told George about the baby and she made her mates promise not to tell him. Why did she have it? Who knows. Who knows what a woman thinks when she decides to have a child even though the man in her life has ditched her.

Miro Mananui and Tama turned up on Mattie's doorstep in Wellington a month before the baby was born. Whetu had telephoned Miro after despairing about Mattie: she wouldn't go back to Christchurch and Whetu and Marama couldn't keep on supporting her.

The only other person they could think of was Miro. After all, she was George's Matua.

When Mattie opened the door to Miro Mananui, she thought Miro was one of the ugliest women she had ever seen. She mistook Tama, hat in hand, for Miro's son. She saw an old woman with glowing eyes waiting like a squat, dark toad.

'When the child is born,' Miro said, 'it will be the first of its generation. I will not allow the child to be lost to the tribe in the great poisonous garden of the world. Although you are a Gentile, you are coming home with us. You will have your baby with us.'

Not a request. Rather, a command. But also something else: as was Maori custom, Miro wanted to adopt the child — rear it and take care of it, and it would live in her house and bring joy to her and Tama's lives. In those days, Miro didn't give a damn about Mattie or what would happen to Mattie. Whether or not she stayed or went was not her concern — but the child would stay.

Without power, Mattie had no option. She had not realised this ugly old woman's calculated reasons for bringing her back to Waituhi. On the other hand Miro, also, was not to know the complicated reasons why Mattie said yes to her offer. For both women, the baby would be a wild card — the Joker of the pack — to be played if ever and whenever it suited them.

Mattie's head was whirling. In Sam's shack, she swayed uncertainly. 'Do you have to sing that fucken song?' she screamed. Sam laughed at her and kept on singing. Mattie threw a beer bottle. Lucky for him, Sam saw it coming and deflected it with an arm. The bottle spun through the air and there was a yelp as it hit Hine Ropiho on the side of her face.

'What the hell did you do that for?' Jack asked Mattie.

Mattie had been running far too long, away from her memories of George Karepa, away from acknowledging that she still loved him, but no matter how fast she ran those memories always caught up on her. She stumbled to the door. Sam grabbed her round the waist.

'Stay with me, Mattie,' he said. They'd slept together a couple of times. It meant nothing. Just two people, wanting only to find some remembrance of times past, getting some kind of animal gratification out of it.

41

'Keep your hands off me,' Mattie said. She pulled open the door and staggered out into the sunlight. The brilliance struck into the darkness behind her eyes, uncovering her pain. She shaded her eyes from the sun and began to run home. The trees cast shadow across her face, slash, slash, slashing like scars.

Yes, they'll all come to meet me, arms reaching, smiling sweetly.
It's good to touch the green, green grass of home.

CHAPTER SEVEN

The sun, lifting high across the Waituhi Valley, flooded the landscape with daylight. Charlie Whatu and Agnes, having finally got to bed, pulled the blinds against the sun. Schoolgirl Hana Walker had no intention of going to sleep; still dressed in the clothes she was wearing last night, she dreamt the daydreams of the young who always thought that life was a movie and everyone had the right to a Hollywood happy-ever-after ending. Tama Mananui was attending to the tree branches that Miro had been on him to trim; she was on the telephone to an elder from the allying Waikato tribe who wanted her to attend a meeting about their land claim. Tama heard a commotion coming from Sam Walker's shack. From out of the shack Mattie Jones came running. She climbed over a fence, running, running, running, and didn't even see him as she swept past. Nor did she take any notice of the Matua as she slammed the door shut to her bedroom. Since coming to Waituhi with Tama and Miro those three years ago, and since the birth of her child, everything had gone wrong for her. One of these days she would get away from what she was running from.

The sun made for the only place in the valley still shadowed — a knoll where an old homestead stood, starkly silhouetted against the sky. Not for long. The daylight slashed at the homestead and, like a bright guest, entered therein.

The old homestead.

The light from the bright morning sun flashed in Annie Jackson's eyes and she winced. She saw Pita and Miriama Mahana's car travelling down the road.

'There they go,' Annie said to Kepa. 'Even though it's Sunday the Mahanas are shearing while we sit around on our bums.'

'Are you trying to wind me up?' Kepa asked. Mentioning the Mahanas was like waving a red flag to a bull. 'Sunday's supposed to be a day of rest. I'd rather sit around here than shear all day. Bugger that for a joke.'

'Wouldn't be so bad if it was only Sunday you sat around on,' Annie returned. 'When are you going to find a job, eh Kepa? When am I going to see some money from you? I'm starting to forget what a dollar note looks like.'

'It's brown like your arse,' Kepa answered.

Angrily, Annie Jackson stared at her husband. But before she could answer back she noticed that Pita and Miriama's car had turned in through their gate and was coming up to the homestead. And who was that in the back? Waka and — oh no, her daughter Ani.

'What's Ani doing with the Mahanas?' Kepa asked.

Sensing trouble, Annie cast a warning glance at Kepa. 'I'll do the talking,' she said.

Then through slanting sunlight, Pene came laughing. Pene, eight years old, the youngest son. 'G'morning, Ma. G'morning, Dad.'

'What are you so happy about?' Kepa growled.

Pene just grinned until he was all teeth. He kissed his mother.

'About time you were out of your pyjamas, isn't it?' Annie asked. 'And you better get your Nani up for his breakfast, eh?'

'Okay, Mum.' Pene skipped from the kitchen, back to his room. Outside, Pita and Miriama's car arrived at the door.

'Don't forget,' Annie said to Kepa. 'Let me handle this.'

In the car, Pita and Miriama sat looking at the homestead.

'God, look at the place,' Pita said. He hadn't been here for years. His mouth was dry and his heart was beating fast with emotion. A profound sense of regret and sadness settled on him. In the old days the homestead had been an imposing villa built in the style of a grand bungalow: large, single storey and having a verandah entirely circling it. The front entrance led to a huge and spacious drawing-room with a timber ceiling. The ceiling was crisscrossed with black beams so that, in the evening, when the lamps were lit, the shadows linked one with the other like the

44

stations of the cross. The beams had been decorated with religious carvings, the runic characters of the Ringatu religion. Two large windows let in the dawn every morning.

'The bell is still here,' Miriama said with awe. She pointed to the side of the front entrance. 'I can still remember the ringing of the bell.'

Whenever the bell was rung, the faithful assembled and waited. They came crying against the enslavement of Pharaoh. They waited for the woman who gave them hope and inspiration, the woman known as Riripeti Mahana, whom some called Artemis. For this was where Pita's mother had lived. From this homestead, she had ruled their world, and Pita himself had been born here. Riripeti was the Ringatu priestess in the valley, providing charismatic leadership for a people who trusted totally in God to deliver them from bondage; she was his proxy on earth. Known famously as the Matriarch, her symbol in Maoridom had been the black spider with a red mark on its back. She wielded her beauty with a great sense of drama; in accents of majestic pride she uttered the prayers of the day. In the Waituhi Chronicles she represented an alternate history to the tribal history of the valley. From this homestead, all sought her succour and were given it.

'I can still remember the holy days,' Pita said, looking back along the road. 'Mum would be getting dressed and we would be on the verandah, watching the processional of the faithful coming to worship God. In the summer, from far off you would see spirals of dust, and know they were coming.'

No longer. The verandah was gone; most of the eight bedrooms were boarded up. The two sacred windows were cracked and broken. Even though the bell still remained, it was silent. Bereft of its priestess and her followers, the homestead that had been such a prized possession had fallen into disrepair.

'Well,' Miriama said as she got out of the car. 'Let's get this over with. Waka? You and Ani come with us.' There was a flash of light as she shut the door of the car.

Pene raced down the long hallway of the homestead towards his Nani's room. He saw light flashing from the room and, tiptoeing to the doorway, saw that it was reflected from a piece of crystal suspended from

45

the ceiling by a piece of string. He had bought the crystal from the flea market in Gisborne, knowing that his Nani would like it. Nani was watching the light as it flashed onto the walls of the room like a rainbow. He reached for it, an avid glow on his face, trying to catch it as the crystal curled and twisted.

'Good morning, Grandson,' Nani Paora smiled. He reached for the light again. It was part of the game with the boy.

'You're too old to catch the light, Nani,' Pene laughed. 'You're not fast enough. Shall I catch it for you, eh? I'll catch it. I'll catch it.' He darted around the room, hands outspread, following the sunlight as it ebbed and flowed with the patterns made by the fluttering crystal. Nani Paora grinned, pleased that Pene was enjoying himself. Pene jumped and brought his hands together with a sudden clap. He glanced at Nani Paora and whispered: 'Quiet, Nani, you must be quiet or else the light will get scared and fly away. Shhhh. Shhhh. I'll bring it to you. Shhhh. There it is. See, Nani? See the light?' And it really did seem as if there was a small ball of light shimmering in his cupped hands. Shimmering, scattering ribbons of colour, becoming brighter and brighter.

Nani Paora looked at the light and his face softened. It was so beautiful.

'I let it go now?' Pene asked.

'Yes, Grandson,' Nani Paora nodded. 'Otherwise the day may not prosper.'

Pene lifted the light to his lips, blew gently, and the light floated softly away like a glowing dandelion-seed. There was silence for a moment. Then Pene grinned, 'You want to get dressed now? You know what day it is, don't you.' The two looked at each other as if sharing a secret.

'It's the day for the Parade,' Nani Paora whispered.

'Okay,' Pene answered. 'Put your arms around me, Nani, and hold tight. You holding tight? Okay! Shift your legs onto the floor. One leg. Now the other one. There we are. Can you stand up, Nani? I'll take your pyjamas off you quick or else you'll get cold, eh. Let's put your clothes on.'

Averting his eyes out of respect, Pene slowly and gently clothed Nani Paora's withered loins. He was awed that Nani Paora was the oldest living member of Te Whanau a Kai, a Maori Methuselah, the only one of his generation still living. He was an ancient relic, like a giant whale stranded in an alien present. He came from a different time and a different, strange, almost incomprehensible age of rebellion and resistance that had occurred long, long ago. Across the dim mists of his mind, the memories of that time sometimes flickered like shadows, vaguely stirring, slowly gathering and suddenly breaking through. When it happened, the old man would chant and, through his chanting, invoke a dreamtime and an age lost.

Pene lived for those times when Nani Paora made his invocations for, when they occurred, the veil between the past and the present became transparent — and could be stepped through. If you believed enough, it could happen. Nani Paora had made Pene believe. Living on the threshold of life and death, of past and present, he had the power to go back and forth across it. It was only to be expected that he would take Pene with him, walking hand in hand through the village, into the enfolding past that was before them.

'Come, Grandchild, follow me.' The light would dim, then brighten upon another day. The village was a nest of small thatched houses. The hills were overgrown with scrub. Along the road a procession of people were coming, laughing and singing. As they passed, Nani Paora and Pene joined them. Before the procession was a painted house; it was under construction, and young men were painting it and women were sitting in the sun weaving mats for the opening ceremonies. Smoke curled from the cookhouse beside it. Children ran through the grass. Old men stood around a pit steaming with food. Women gossiped in the sunlight. Nani Paora talked with them while Pene played with the children. 'They are building the meeting house for the prophet,' Nani Paora said. 'They do not know that he will not come.'

Another time, when Nani Paora again took Pene through into the past, a magnificent woman came to greet them. She wore long veils and there were pearls in her hair. The tattoo on her chin was like the soft green swirls of a calm river. Nani Paora went down on his knees before her, clasped her hands and kissed them.

'Do you still serve me faithfully, my disciple?' the woman asked.

The pain of the question was too much for Nani Paora to bear.

'Leave my Nani alone,' Pene said.

The woman smiled a radiant smile and patted Pene on the head. She turned to Nani Paora.

'Continue to await the return of the king,' she said.

Pene finished dressing Nani Paora. He heard raised voices. Dad was arguing with the visitors. 'There we are, Nani,' he said. 'All dressed. Come now. We have some breakfast. Come.'

Together, they went to the kitchen.

'I blame you for this, you bastard,' Kepa Jackson swore at Pita Mahana. 'Your son is like all of you Mahanas, cocking his leg like a dog and spilling his urine on all who cross his path.'

In the kitchen, Annie and Kepa Jackson had been told about Waka and Ani. Nobody was happy. Kepa was ballistic and Pita would have dropped him had not Miriama stepped in his way.

'Grow up,' Pita said to Kepa. 'Nobody's to blame. Our son acknowledges he was wrong in sleeping with your daughter. Your daughter didn't exactly say no when Waka took her to bed.'

'You watch your mouth,' Kepa answered.

'Stop this,' Miriama said, trying to prevent the argument escalating out of control. 'The main issue is that our children want to get married and if you allow this' — she made her entreaty to Annie Jackson — 'then I would be happy to accept Ani as our daughter-in-law.'

'I won't have that boy in my family,' Kepa thundered. 'Nor will I agree to this.'

At that moment Pita looked up and, from out of the past, he saw Pene bringing the old man whom he knew as Tamati Kota — for that was who Nani Paora really was — along the hallway.

'Tamati Kota,' Pita whispered in awe. He went down on bended knee before him. This was the same Tamati Kota who had been the great disciple of Riripeti, her priest and right hand of God. In the old days, Tamati Kota had served Pita's mother faithfully. He had taken upon himself the new name of Paora — after Christ's disciple, Paul, who had suffered his conversion on his way to Damascus — as a cloak to mask his earlier history in secrecy. Indeed, not many people talked about Te Kooti or Riripeti. Even in Te Kooti's own village, his name was mentioned only by the few. Sometimes it was as if all that history had never happened at all.

'Greetings, old one,' Pita said. Even though Tamati Kota looked like any old man, you only had to look into his eyes to see the spirit of God still resided in him.

'Greetings, Pita,' Tamati Kota answered. 'Please get up. It is I who should be kneeling. After all, you are descended from she whom I served.'

Pita stood, and helped Tamati Kota toward the kitchen table. He ignored Annie and Kepa. At such a moment of revelation, the Jacksons paled into insignificance. They were of no account, being merely caregivers, nesting like starlings where once hawks had resided.

With disgust Pita heard Kepa talking to Tamati Kota without sacredness. 'How are you today, old man?' Kepa asked. 'You have a good night's sleep? You enjoy the wedding last night? I saw you looking at all those young girls.'

Tamati Kota grinned. 'Hey,' Kepa laughed, 'the old man understood!'

'Of course he did,' Annie sniffed. 'He's not dumb, are you, old one?' The old man continued to grin. Annie put a plate of corned beef and watercress in front of him. She tied a towel round his neck. 'Here's a spoon, old one.'

Tamati Kota began to eat. Slowly at first, but then more quickly. 'Nani likes watercress, doesn't he, Mum?' Pene laughed. 'Just look at him hoeing in! He's scared the food will run away, aren't you, Nani!'

'Let's get out of here,' Pita said to Miriama. The sight of the old man, reliant on such irreverent caregivers, embarrassed him. It was incredible that Tamati Kota still lived. To the pride of his place in tribal history had been added the prestige of his years. All Pita could think of was that this man, Tamati Kota, had once been the helpmate of Riripeti, an icon of resistance. Just before she died, Tamati Kota had gone with her to Wellington, to petition Parliament for land confiscated wrongly after the Te Kooti Wars. The petition failed. It was the same Tamati Kota who had tried to negotiate the best outcome when her succession was the subject of a court wrangle between her husband, Ihaka, and eldest son, Te Ariki.

'Something bothering you?' Kepa sneered. 'Well, you Mahanas had your chance to look after the old man but you didn't take it. If you don't like the way me and Annie do the job, tough. At least we love the old man, which is more than you Mahanas ever did, trying to kick him out of this house.'

Pita's face became strained with grief. The court wrangle had been over land which Riripeti had left in her will to her grandson, Tamatea. Both Ihaka and Te Ariki as husband and eldest son had fought the will. They won. They then fought for possession of the homestead which Riripeti had left to Tamati Kota. She must have known that only he who served her could be trusted to retain it for Tamatea, whom some called Beloved of Artemis. Ihaka and Te Ariki lost. The entire Mahana clan had therefore hardened their hearts against Tamati Kota and repudiated him.

'I'm so sorry,' Pita said to the old man. He felt an overwhelming sense of shame that his family had treated Tamati Kota with such contempt. 'I will visit you again soon.' It was time to put that history right. He pressed noses with Tamati Kota. 'May God be with you,' he said.

'And God be with you, also,' Tamati Kota answered. 'I remember you so well, Pita Mahana. Riripeti always made room for you near her chair where you liked to sit at her feet.'

And then it was time for the Parade.

Annie Jackson saw Pene whispering to the old man and knew what was up. 'Nani's finished all his breakfast,' Pene called. 'Me too, and I've licked my plate clean. Can we go on our walk now?' He looked so eager, shifting from one foot to the other, couldn't wait to get going.

'What about doing your dishes first?' Annie asked.

'Oh, let the boys out,' Kepa said. 'We can't keep them cooped up all the time.'

'Yeah, and I suppose you'll volunteer to do the dishes if they don't,' Annie said. 'All right, Pene, but don't think you can get out of doing the dishes all the time. And you better mind your Nani. Don't walk him off his legs like you did last Sunday. And don't you dare leave him by himself to play with your mates. You stay with him all the time, you hear?'

'I promise, Mum,' Pene answered. 'Come on, Nani,' he whispered urgently. 'Come on, before Mum changes her mind.' They left the table. Pene led Nani Paora outside. Annie smiled as she overheard Pene giving instructions.

'Hold your leg up, Nani. Not that one, the other one. This shoe is for your left foot not your right foot. Don't you know which is your left? No, Nani, give me your *left* leg! If you think I'm going to put your right shoe on first, you're out of luck. I'm the boss, not you. I don't know why you are so dumb, Nani. Right, now don't move yet. I have to tie your laces up. Boy, you're hopeless. How come you can't tie your laces yourself? Even babies can do that. There! All done. Now come on, Nani. Come with me, Nani.'

Annie watched from the window. Every Sunday, Pene took the old man on the Parade. It was Pene's fanciful term for the walks around Waituhi that he and his Nani took together. The old man seemed to enjoy it — you could never tell what he was thinking these days — and it was a good way to get him out of the house and into the sun. Old man Paora and Pene were just a couple of kids. It was great that Pene loved him so much and didn't mind having to look after him. She smiled as Pene guided the old man around the potholes of the drive.

'Nice day, eh Nani. See the sun? Isn't it bright! Makes your eyes watery looking at it, eh. Watch out for that big rock. You might fall down and break your bones. Big rocks must just love you, Nani. They must want you to fall down, eh. I don't know, how come you got soft bones? My bones are stronger than yours.'

They reached the main road and Pene looked back. Mum was still watching. Pene's grin flashed in the sun. He waved and then lifted his Nani's hand to wave too.

'Wave to Mum, Nani. Wave your hand.'

Hand in hand, Pene and Nani Paora walked slowly away from the homestead. They reached a bend in the road and, finally, disappeared from Mum's sight.

'Okay, Nani,' Pene whispered conspiratorially, 'let's get away from here.'

Tamati Kota pulled aside the curtain between the present and the past, and they were *in*.

PART TWO

Children of the Israelites

CHAPTER EIGHT

A boy and an old man walk the proud land. They walk through a landscape that is both real and unreal, tangible and intangible, a land made up not just of what you see but what is unseen, a land which has an official history and one that is covert.

The official history of Waituhi comprises only a few paragraphs of description within the larger tourist guides of Poverty Bay: WELCOME TO GISBORNE, FIRST TO SEE THE SUN; the reference is to Mount Hikurangi, on the coast, which is reputed to be the first place on the earth to be lit every day by sunlight. In smaller type, alphabetically listed, you would find something like this:

'Waituhi (18 km, valley inland from Gisborne City): close to Patutahi, which has a store, petrol station, golf course, farmstay, country retreat, tavern. The road through Patutahi continues as Lavenham Road to Waituhi where magnificent Rongopai meeting house can be viewed, before continuing to join State Highway 2. Rongopai is a very large meeting house built in 1888 [some guides say 1883] and has a remarkable painted interior where Maori decorations and motifs show a strong and unique European influence. Permission is required before entering the meeting house. 12 km up the Wharekopae Road is the Rere Falls, a good place for a picnic. A further 3 km takes you to the Makaretu Scenic Reserve and the Rere Rockslide. Take a tube or a bodyboard for summer fun.'

The covert history, however, is a secret inventory, carried within the village mnemonic and accessible only if you know the password, crack the code, decipher the cipher. What you would discover is that the paragraphs of official description are a detour. You have to look behind the words, look through and beyond them to see what is really there. What you will find is another Waituhi, one that was from the very beginning a centre of active resistance to the White man.

On a bright, clear day, if you look eastward from the top of Tawhiti Kaahu — where Takitimu meeting house stands — you can see flat-topped Maungatapere arising from the plains and, further out, Young Nick's Head cutting whitely against the blue of sea and sky. If you had been standing there at around two o'clock on 7 October 1769 you would have seen an extraordinary apparition: the arrival of a huge white-winged bird, the *Endeavour*, captained by a man called James Cook. His sailors looked like goblins, and when they rowed their boats to shore they must have had eyes at the back of their heads because they rowed with their backs to the land. The Maori thought they were bringing a cargo of gods; if so, they were death-dealing beings. Captain Cook claimed New Zealand for the British Empire. The event was also distinguished by the murders of six Maori, the wounding of three others and the taking captive of three prisoners before the *Endeavour* weighed anchor two days later.

First contact was not auspicious. After Cook came whalers, not only of British descent but also Spanish, Portuguese, Italian and black American (as many Maori genealogies today verify), who lived among the Poverty Bay tribes. Following them came flax traders during the world flax boom, tree fellers, evangelists and, finally, settlers and farmers. By the time the Treaty of Waitangi was signed between the British Crown and some Maori chiefs at Waitangi, 6 February 1840, accommodations were being made between Maori and Pakeha in which Maori agreed that Pakeha could come to land and Pakeha — or so Maori thought — acknowledged that Maori would retain their own sovereignty or intrinsic rights to culture and land.

Some hope. After all, as Mr (later Sir Donald) McLean reported in February 1851, Poverty Bay, including the lands of Te Whanau a Kai, was a fine, rich country, with 40,000 acres of deep alluvial soil: '. . . A Veritable Paradise for Pastoralists.' The land was rich and fertile, in pleasing contrast to the barren Wharerata Ranges which enclosed the Bay. You descended from the ranges and obtained a splendid panoramic view of the lowland and the glittering blue-green sea curving like a sickle toward the harbour. The plain was intersected by three rivers which struck their serpentine course through handsome clumps of white pine and native forests and beside numerous wheat cultivations and groves of peach and other varieties of English fruit trees. The botanical intertwining of foreign flora with native flora was indicative of the blending that was taking place among Maori and the White man. Traders with blue eyes married Maori wives and had their half-caste children. Captains of seafaring ships soon found that Maori were setting up their own fleets once they acquired the technology. Maori were very quick to learn and take on the agricultural skills that would enable them to grow crops and fruits to sell in the growing market centres of Wellington and Auckland. When the evangelists from the Anglican and Roman Catholic churches began to seek flocks, they found amenable and docile sheep who wished to come to God — and who, in turn, aided the missionaries in the razing of Maori effigies and pagan practices. Pakeha sold guns to the Maori so that they could defeat their tribal enemies and be kindlier disposed to them.

In the ebb and flow of Maori and Pakeha relationships some of the Maori tribes of Poverty Bay accommodated the White man more than others. The situation was not cut and dried. Within Ngati Porou, Rongowhakaata, Te Aitanga a Mahaki and Te Whanau a Kai there were some Maori settlements which became known as rebellious or unfriendly, and those which were considered to be loyalist or friendly: domesticated, acculturated, absorbed into a Western ethos. It was not unexpected that the loyalist settlements were those who unwittingly abetted the missionaries in obtaining Maori souls for the Christian God. By 1841, only a year after William Williams set up the Poverty Bay station, Maori people were attending services in their thousands — 3200 at Waiapu and Tokomaru, 2500 at Uawa and Turanga. Three years later, it was estimated that 4300 out of the 6000 inhabitants of East Cape and Waiapu, 2300 out of the 4000 at Uawa, and 6000 out of the 10,000 at Turanga and Mahia were Christian; the White man used the Bible as a sword to split the people. Te Whanau a Kai, also, accepted the presence of missionaries but, as pressure on Maori grew to part with their land, they adopted the concern expressed by Rongowhakaata chief, Raharuhi Rukupo: 'The missionaries came to clear the path for the soldiers who in turn came to clear a path for the land-grabbers.'

By the 1850s, Pakeha settlers required more land, and at a rate of acquisition faster than the Maori were prepared to sell. Increasingly there were quarrels and armed raids over land and business transactions. Throughout *Aotearoa*, New Zealand, Maori tribes began to say, 'Enough is enough.' The decade of the 1850s therefore opened with symptoms of unrest throughout New Zealand, particularly in the Ngapuhi of the north, the Taranaki peoples to the west and the Tainui confederation to the northeast. For a time the people of Poverty Bay presented a remarkable picture of resilience as they attempted to fight their exploiters. 'The natives,' the Rev. T.S. Grace wrote in his report to the Church Missionary Society for 1852, 'have attained a [business] intelligence beyond what might have been expected in so short a period. Their motto is now: "Ploughs, sheep and ships," to establish a civilisation like unto that of the Pakeha. I had had much conversation with some of them individually, but now they appear in a body to lay hold of these ideas with a giant grasp, and, so far, I must say they have continued to work them out with a steady determination such as I never thought them capable of.'

The Pakeha colonisation of New Zealand was relentless. At the time of Cook's arrival, estimates of the Maori population stand at 100,000. By 1858, the New Zealand census revealed that there were already more White settlers than indigenous dwellers. The weight of the invasion impacted on Maori. In 1860 the White settlers viewed the setting up of a Maori king in the Waikato as an affront to the British monarch and to their power. With relentless speed, what the Pakeha called 'the Maori Wars' and then 'the Land Wars' and are now known as 'the New Zealand Wars' (the Maori call them 'the Pakeha Wars') broke out. They began in the Taranaki and then the Waikato. One of the movements to spring up in resistance was the powerful religious Hauhau sect. The White settlers called the Hauhau fanatics who spread anti-Pakeha ferment. When they came to Poverty Bay they found their main adherents among the Te Whanau a Kai and their Rongowhakaata kin.

On 15 March 1865 a Hauhau contingent brought news of the bitter struggle in the Taranaki. They came across the hills from Tuhoe to Patutahi where a fortress, Pukeamionga, was built to receive them. A totem was set up — a tall pole, eighty feet in length and crossed by yardarms with two curved knobs representing two gods, Ruru and Riki, and topped by the Hauhau flag. Rope streamers descended from the totem. The faithful took them into their hands because this was how Jehovah's angels entered their bodies if they believed in Him. As they chanted they marched around the totem, their eyes fixed with a steady gaze upon the totem itself. Round and round and round, the pace increasing, the hundreds weeping for the loss of the land and the people. 'O Lord God, give us deliverance.'

For most tribes, the coming of the White man to Poverty Bay was suspect but was regarded, on the whole, as benign. Te Whanau a Kai were more resistant. They were like a small independent state on a map that could otherwise be coloured the red of the Union Jack. For them, the White man was malign; he was a toxic being.

Yet, to look at Waituhi in the bright sun today, you would see none of this history of rebellion and resistance. Instead, what you would see are people who appear to be living happily off the land and as a family one with another. But look in their eyes and you may catch a glimpse of the fierceness with which they nurture that age-old spirit of resistance and liberation, a return to a sovereign position before they were stripped of their dignity. They nurture a pride and an obstinate belief that there must be possible a redemptive outcome for the people and a rightful reparation. There must surely be, somewhere, justice.

Yes, once they were proud possessors of all this land and in control of its destiny. Of those who are left in the village, there are still a number who cherish the land, their culture and their liberation. Once, the people who felt this love for the people and the land sprang from the soil in great numbers. It is good that some remain to carry on the fight, for if they don't, what hope is there for survival? Without the land, they are nothing. Old houses rot in the fields. Starlings and sparrows have their nests in them. The cornices of the verandahs are spun across with spiders' webs. The wood is riddled with borer. Mice breed in the straw-strewn wind-invaded rooms, scratching sharply at the ripped and yellowing wallpaper. Yes, without land the people would have no capital or economic principal to invest. All that would be left would be pieces of a broken biscuit. Tribal life and family life would continue to splinter, and the people would continue to leave for better money and a better life. There would be nothing for them here.

Let a leader of Te Whanau a Kai — Wi Pere, the parliamentarian who thought to fight the onslaught of the Pakeha from within the corridors of the New Zealand Parliament — have the last word on the fatal nature of the Maori–Pakeha conflict. In the late 1890s, when the Maori population hovered around 40,000, he welcomed the Waikato king, Mahuta, to a seat in the Legislative Council. Mahuta had given up the whole of the King Country to Pakeha settlement, for this dubious reward. Wi Pere related the following fable:

'There was a certain owl,' he said, 'who lived in the darkness and fastnesses of the forest. While in his protected surroundings he was one day attracted by the joyful crying of the other birds outside the forest. "Oh!" thought the owl, "what a lot of good things there must be there." He flew through the trees, but on reaching the forest edge his eyes were blinded by the light and he was obliged to perch on a tree. A man saw the owl and took a firebrand in one hand and a stick in the other. As he neared the owl it prepared to fly, but the man blinded the bird with the firebrand and stunned it with the stick. He then put it in a cage and made an ornament out of it.'

Wi Pere put out his arms to King Mahuta and, his voice tinged with great irony, resumed this fable about the failure of leadership to maintain a sovereign position for the Maori people:

'Welcome,' he said. 'The owl is you, and we, the Members of Parliament, are the other birds. The man is the Prime Minister, the firebrand is the bundle of notes for your salary, the stick is your oath, and the cage is the House of Parliament.'

A century later, the people still live in a state of limbo.

CHAPTER NINE

George Karepa's dreams were disturbed by dark wings and the harsh cries of a nocturnal bird hunting for prey. An owl was after him. Panicking, he began to run away from it. But the owl passed over him. Caught up in its turbulence, George was dragged along behind it and across the landscape. The bird circled the dawn sky above Waituhi, pausing above one house and then another.

'No, not that one,' George moaned, his head threshing the pillow.

Inexorably, the bird made its way across paddocks toward Miro Mananui's place. Miro was in the sitting-room, talking on the telephone. Her husband, Tama, was cutting some branches from trees growing too close to the house. George tried to signal him, to warn him that the owl was approaching. Tama looked up — and into George's eyes. Quick as a flash, Tama lifted his clippers and began swinging them at the owl. Only it wasn't the owl but, rather, George. Fighting for his life, George woke up.

'George!' Hayley cried out. 'It's me.' He had backhanded her in his sleep. Eyes wide with shock, she sat up in bed, edging away from him.

'Babe, I'm so sorry,' George answered. In a whirl Hayley stepped out of bed, walked quickly to the bathroom and slammed the door. George followed her. She was rinsing her skin, peering closely at her face, wondering if it was bruised. 'Great, just great, George,' she said, 'one day of marriage and already you've slapped me around.'

'Let me see,' George said.

Hayley looked at him with those clear, penetrating green eyes. God,

61

she was so *flawless*. From the moment he had first met her he had wanted her.

'Honey, it was an accident.'

'What's going on, George?' Hayley asked him, pushing him away. 'Ever since we came to Gisborne you've been so wired.'

'It's nothing, babe.'

'Nothing?' Hayley smoothed moisturiser over her reddened skin. 'Don't tell me it's nothing.' What a relief, the mark of his hand was already fading. 'I didn't get this for nothing. What's the problem? Where are these nightmares coming from?'

'I don't know. From unfinished business at *Waituhi*, I guess. The Matua asked me to go out there today. Maybe I can sort it out when I talk with her.'

'You're going out there?' Hayley asked, surprised. She looked at her wristwatch: nine o'clock. 'We're supposed to be on a plane at four this afternoon.' They were connecting in Auckland to a Sydney flight. That was home for Hayley. Although her father was from Te Arawa he had migrated to Australia years ago. He got a job in Australian broadcasting and Hayley had followed in his footsteps. She was a television presenter on a multicultural television channel.

'Plenty of time to do a quick trip,' George answered.

Hayley was angry. 'Well thanks for inviting me to go with you.' She pushed past him and back into the bedroom.

'Babe, it's just family stuff. I didn't think you would want to come.' He went to embrace her. All his life he'd dreamed of women like her. Pretty women, women who looked good, smelled good, made you feel good.

'Don't mess me around, George,' Hayley said. 'Is there something you don't want me to find out?'

Hayley was stronger than people thought. She might appear to be compliant and come across as just another pretty face, but she was a survivor. She inherited her survival skills from her father and, like him, she was not about to let anybody, least of all George, jerk her around. People thought Hayley was some kind of airhead bimbo, but nothing was further from the truth. She knew what she wanted, how to get it and, more important, how to keep it.

'No, there's nothing like that.' George tried to charm her into acceptance, smiling his easy smile, stroking her with his fingertips, making her shiver. 'I've got no secrets from you.' As soon as he said it, he thought of Mattie. How come she was living in Waituhi? He didn't give a blink as he looked into Hayley's eyes. Mattie wasn't a secret exactly; Hayley knew there had been girlfriends before she came along. George hadn't mentioned that Mattie was one of them, that's all.

Secrets? Hayley shivered. Everybody had secrets. Although she had a way of finding out other people's secrets, she kept hers to herself. That was the way you played this game. You pretended you were innocent, even though you were just as guilty as the other person. You used your innocence as part of your power. It was the best way to make the other person feel that they weren't good enough for you, as if they felt they owed you more than they were giving.

'I'm not a fool, George Karepa,' Hayley said, her eyes wide, penetrating — innocent. 'Don't treat me as if I don't have a brain.'

Not even a day married and already they were playing games with each other.

CHAPTER TEN

──── 1 ────

Flick. Flick. With each flick of her hand, Hana Walker sent the light cord swinging in a wide arc above her bed. It had been so easy for her to get into the house without Mum and Dad knowing she'd been out all night. It was always easy to sneak in. Just lever up the window and hop through. Nothing to it. She'd done it plenty of times. Something to laugh about.

Hana was lying on top of the quilt, still in her party clothes. She wondered if she should bother to change. What was the use? In half an hour, Mum and Dad would be calling for her to get up and get ready for church. She'd have to go, naturally, and sit there dutifully between Mum and Dad, listening to the priest and moving her lips to the hymns. There was no chance of escaping. None at all. The only way you lived your life was Dad's way.

As she thought of church, Hana's anger began to shake her apart. She didn't like the idea of being trapped in somebody else's reality. She started to dream — not Waituhi dreams, but white-girl dreams, fantasies based on magazines and movies. Like all such dreams, they replicated an idealised European teenage world. Hana's bedroom walls were covered with pictures of rock stars ripped from magazines, showing the kind of lives they were living. Her radio was always on full blast, for only when it was on loud could she fill the silence that surrounded her. She read all the popular young girl style and fashion books and, when she looked in the bathroom mirror, vainly tried to impose on her own face the same European look. With her mascara, lipstick, powder and comb she tried to obscure the way she was and create the way she should be: blonde rather than black, high cheekbones, the eyes of a temptress and the slim body of a model. To go with her fantasy there was always a boy — preferably blond, tall and blue-eyed, as exemplary in looks as the girls who were her models.

Hana dreamed of leaving Waituhi, leaving school, leaving, just leaving. Any other place was better than being here. Whenever any of her older cousins living in Auckland or Wellington returned to Waituhi on a visit, Hana projected all her fantasies of the parties, movies, people they were meeting and fun they were having onto them. They fed her envy — toll operators, postal clerks, train conductors, engineering apprentices, shop attendants all — for they, too, were still in pursuit of the dreams they had dreamt when they were fifteen. They told her of the fantastic times they were having. When they left, Hana wished she was going with them. There was nothing here for her. Getting away from the village was like a fever. One of these days, she'd make it. Roll on that day. She saw herself being discovered by some entertainment producer who would make her into a rock star. She'd come back by helicopter, dropping in on the olds, and they would be so proud of her. Just on a visit, mind, the shorter the better. Such dreams of the successful return were always integral to Hana's fantasies. She needed them to justify her wish to escape from her reality — and from herself.

'Hana? Already dressed?' With a start Hana saw Dad standing at the doorway. 'You're up early, aren't you? Put the kettle on? Mum will be up soon to make breakfast.'

Hana looked at her father and, for a moment, the words that she most wanted to say to him almost came out. 'I can't be who you want me to be. I can't make you proud because I'm not like Frank, who made you proud by being a policeman. That's not me. I'm like Sam, weak, a failure, a coward, a no-hoper. I'm not who you think I am.' But the words died on Hana's lips when she realised that what she really wanted to say was, 'I hate myself, Dad. I don't want to be Hana Walker. I don't want to come from Waituhi. I'll find somebody else for you who does, and they can take over this body and you won't know the difference. Don't worry about me. I'll be long gone. I'll be somebody else. I'll have somebody else's face. I'll have stolen somebody else's body and be living their history, their life and their dreams.

'Please let me go before I break your heart.'

————— 2 —————

Dreams, dreams, even Hepa Walker had a dream.

Hepa was a man who occupied a position of prominence in both Maori and Pakeha society. Yet, to judge from his early life, you would not have thought his present prestige possible. Born in the village, he was the third son of a large family with little status. No silver spoon for him. His boyhood was filled with hardship. His father pulled him out of school because he needed the boy to help him in scrubcutting. Even if Hepa had remained at school, his academic achievement would have been mediocre. At eighteen, Hepa had a shearer's handpiece shoved into his hands.

The Second World War interrupted Hepa's progression towards a labouring life. He swapped handpiece for rifle and went to fight overseas. Like many other recruits he wasn't expecting much of himself and neither were his commanding officers — but war had a habit of finding people out, turning the tables, and Hepa and his superiors discovered his skills as a strategist. Before long he was organising Maori Battalion deployments. His promotion to lieutenant in the Maori Battalion was rapid. He got on the good side of the great Maori Battalion leaders like Colonel Arapeta Awatere and Hemi Henare. He counted among his mates Tawhiwhi Meha, Tuta Wirepa, James Henare, Wi Huata and George Marsden. He was well liked by his men because, like many other Maori commanders, he led from the front. Fearless and bold in battle, he distinguished himself during the Crete, North African and Italian campaigns.

Hepa may have begun the war as a foot soldier but when the war ended he returned to New Zealand as a leader. On Colonel Awatere's recommendation, the Ministry of Defence offered Hepa a job as a Maori liaison officer, and he accepted it. Thrust into the limelight at a time when New Zealand and Maoridom were looking for Maori leaders, he found himself assuming a wider role as a national spokesman on Maori affairs. He joined an influential network of Maori men working within the infrastructure of Government — Maori Affairs, Education, Broadcasting, Social Welfare and Internal Affairs. He and the others, including John Waititi, Matiu Te Hau, Bill Parker, John Tapiata, Bill Tawhai and Winiata Smiler, were actively involved in strategically deploying programmes for the advancement of the Maori people. He walked with parliamentarians like Eruera Tirikatene-Sullivan and Ira Ratana, and there was talk of his being nominated for one of the Maori seats. The catchphrases were integration and assimilation, and their bible was the Hunn Report. Hepa embraced the fervour of the 'We are all one people' doctrine.

Had it not been for the death of his father and the need to take over the family farm in Waituhi, Hepa might have risen to the heights of national Maori politics. Mind you, living in Waituhi had not prevented him from maintaining his role in public affairs. He now worked for Gisborne City in the city's planning office. There, he continued to strategise and to dream.

Yes indeed, Hepa Walker also had a dream. It was a dream of a bicultural country of Maori and Pakeha, in which Maori succeeded on Pakeha terms: let us all be one people. There was nothing wrong in that, but could it really happen? Would the Pakeha in power allow it?

Hepa walked back to the bedroom. He was in a thoughtful mood. His wife, Dinah, had just finished ironing his shirt. She dressed him, buttoning the shirt and brushing him down.

'Something's wrong with that daughter of ours,' Hepa said. 'Something's bothering her. I've sensed it for some time now.'

'Hana's growing up, that's all,' Dinah answered. 'She's becoming a woman.' She reached for Hepa's favourite tie and began to knot it in the military style. She'd been doing it all these years; it was second nature to her.

'Do you think I'm hard on her?' Hepa asked. He stepped toward the mirror and appraised himself critically. In the mirror he saw Dinah looking at him — as if she was afraid.

Dinah paused, measuring her words carefully, 'As hard as any father who has an only daughter.' She hoped that Hepa would let matters pass but he caught the meaning.

'Then you do think I'm too strict,' Hepa said.

Dinah gave a slight smile. 'You're not strict, dear. But Hana's not Daddy's girl any longer and you're too ambitious for her.' She was still in her petticoat and made a show about needing to get dressed herself for church.

'Is that wrong?' Hepa asked. 'All I want is for her to get a good education, have a good career and marry the right person.'

Dinah chose a formal suit from the wardrobe and put it on. She turned so that Hepa could zip it up. They'd had this kind of conversation before about Hana, and Dinah never won. The trouble was that Hepa thought he could secure the children's futures as easily as he organised a battle plan.

'Dear, you have some kind of ambition for Hana,' she said finally. 'But is it her ambition too? You pushed Frank and, well, Frank always did what you wanted him to do. You pushed Sam and that wasn't a success. Just be careful with what you want for Hana.'

Before Hepa could reply, Dinah left the room. His thoughts kept bothering him. Becoming a leader had not been easy but male Maori society had embraced him in the brotherhood and he was now accepted in the front ranks of Maori society. He and Dinah were welcome and respected guests at meetings and other large gatherings throughout the country.

Goddamn it, he'd also managed to make it into the brotherhood of male Pakeha society too. It might have taken him longer — he had no business education and none of the qualities, social and personal, that were required to operate in Pakeha society — but by sheer perseverance and self-education he had managed to foot it with the best of them. Oh, of course there were still some in their Old Boys clubs who patronised him. They tolerated him; he was quite a fine chap really. Anyway they needed a Maori to sit with them at their official ceremonies — opening a new post office or school — and to appear with them in the social pages of the local newspaper. One had to remember to include a Maori on any guest list, for the Maori were important to the community, and wouldn't Maori be proud to see how well they were becoming integrated into society? Not only that, but Dinah, who was Pakeha and blonde, was living among them and she couldn't be abandoned altogether.

Hepa allowed himself a smile of triumph. He now socialised with the best of them. He played golf on Saturdays, drank wine in the best restaurants, attended the best church, and was on first-name terms with the district elite. In every way, he was a success. He knew some of his own people thought he had become 'just a brown Pakeha'; brown on the outside but with a white soul. He also knew that some people thought that marrying Dinah was all part of the plan: marrying a Pakeha was the fast way for a Maori man to improve his status. But it wasn't as logical as people thought to assume that if you walked into a Pakeha life you walked away from a Maori life, or that having a Pakeha wife meant achieving an automatic upgrade. Crediting yourself in the European world did not mean you debited it somewhere in the Maori world — though sometimes this was the cost if a Pakeha partner demanded you choose to live white or leave. No, what it usually meant was that you had to show the Pakeha that you could do better than he could. You ran twice as fast to reach the same spot. You paid your dues.

Hepa Walker had reached a level of achievement that any man would have been proud of. He had remained Maori, but he had also managed to succeed in Pakeha society. If he could do it, so could others. The answer, as he saw it, was in education. Through education, Maori would start moving up from lower class to middle class. Frank was proving the theory right. So would Hana.

As for Sam, the oldest, he was a bad seed and he had lazy Maori blood in him. Planting him in good earth would not redeem him.

'So why should my hopes for Hana be wrong?' Hepa asked himself. 'She'll thank me in the long run.'

The Maori race was a proud race, but they lived a Pakeha life now. The sooner more Maori realised this the better. And if the Pakeha way, the 'you have to get on' way, came at a price, the risk was worth it.

As a leader, Hepa's role was to bring Maori to this realisation, even if they didn't like it or want it.

CHAPTER ELEVEN

Tama Mananui heard the telephone ringing in the house and, through the sitting-room window, saw Miro answering it. Some nuisance was wanting the advice or assistance of the Matua. No sooner had she put the telephone down than it rang again. Three calls in one morning. What was this? A telephone exchange?

Muttering to himself, Tama finished trimming the branches of the trees outside their bedroom and put away the ladder. He saw Hepa and Dinah Walker and their daughter Hana driving past on their way to church. Over recent years the people of the valley had become either Mormon or Anglican, splitting their ecclesiastical allegiance between an American seer and the British queen. The Walkers were Anglican, but originally their family had been Ringatu adherents. 'They now worship the very Crown we fought against,' Tama muttered to himself. He took some ironic pleasure from the fact that the Anglican Church had been established by a king, Henry VIII, for the sole purpose of legitimising his divorce from a royal wife he later beheaded. 'And they called us savages,' he said to himself.

'Husband?' Miro called. 'Have you finished your work?' She was dressed in hat, coat and gloves. Must be something urgent. When the Matua wore gloves it meant her hands had work to do. With those hands she delivered babies, blessed the sick, did her sacramental work, closed eyelids at death.

Tama washed at the pump. 'What's up, Matua?'

Miro was biting her lip with nervousness. 'That last call was from Arapeta,' she answered. 'I want you to drive me to his place. He wants me to do a ritual of protection for him.'

'More prayers?' Tama asked. 'Will I have to wait for you?' He and Arapeta Mahana, Miro's younger brother, didn't get on. From the beginning of their marriage, Arapeta had made it very clear to Tama that he considered his sister had married beneath her status.

'Yes,' Miro answered. 'George called too. He's coming out at lunchtime. I told Arapeta we have to get back as soon as we're finished with him. He's thankful we can come. He's in a bad way, husband.'

'Did you tell Mattie about George coming out?'

'No,' Miro said. 'She's asleep,' she continued, her lips curling with disapproval. 'Not only that, but if she knows, she might take off. Let's tell her later.'

'I'll get the car,' Tama nodded. He didn't bother with putting on a jacket — after all, Arapeta never invited him in. Anyhow, this was brother–sister business. Better to let them speak in private and wait in the car until it was over. If Arapeta was in a bad way, his past misdeeds must be coming back on him.

Tama and Miro took the road to Manutuke. The Matua didn't drive, which suited Tama because he loved driving her car and, anyway, it was one of his jobs to be her chauffeur. Whenever the telephone rang and the Matua needed to be driven somewhere, he drove her. Apart from keeping the house running, a big enough job on its own, and keeping the Matua happy (sometimes, man, could she have one of her tantrums and require lots of loving and pampering to bring her down), driving her places was the third most important job in his job description. Tama loved the driving because it got him out of Waituhi and, for the time they were on the road, he was the one in control. He was the one driving Miss Miro. She trusted him to get her there, wherever 'there' was. Other people might think he was inferior to the Matua but, on the road, he was the boss.

Tama began to hum to himself. The Matua had told him, while he was cutting the branches, that they would be going to a meeting at Ngaruawahia. The prospect of a long weekend away, spending the time jawing with his mates while the Matua went about her important business with the Tainui elders, made him jaunty. The car began to weave all over the road. Just as they were approaching Patutahi, Tama saw they had caught up to the Walkers. A gleam came into his eyes. He didn't think the Matua would notice when he put his foot on the accelerator and, just before they reached the hotel, he passed the Walkers.

'You racing-car driver, you,' Miro said as Tama roared through the township and took the road to Arapeta's place. 'The faster the better, husband,' she continued, shivering. 'Arapeta is going up the wall today.'

Was he what. When they reached Arapeta's and were pulling through the driveway, Miro could hear her brother yelling before Tama switched off the motor. She rushed to the house, met his distraught wife Florence at the doorway, and smelt the familiar smell of fire and brimstone.

'The door won't open,' Florence cried. 'Please do something.'

Miro tried the doorknob. It was hot, but her gloves protected her. She tried again. Still no luck. She had to use all her strength before the door sprang open. 'Brother, are you all right?' Miro asked.

The room was Arapeta and Florence's master bedroom. Something or someone was in there with Arapeta. Whoever it was had run rampage through the room. A full-length mirror was cracked into a thousand pieces. The huge oak dresser was on its side, the contents scattered everywhere. Other furniture was either broken or overturned, and all of the photographs in frames were shattered. Fearing the worst, Miro entered. The stench inside was overpowering. It was the smell of rotting flesh.

'Sister, you've got to help me,' Arapeta jibbered. He was pressed against the bedstead. His eyes were popping from their sockets and sweat was streaming down his face. Terrorised and burdened with guilt and sin, he pointed at the three dead people who were sitting on his bed, waiting for him. 'Tell them to go away.'

When she saw them, Miro felt a sense of contempt for her brother. What did he expect? The three dead spirits were people he had cheated in his life. Auntie Bobbie was smoking on her foul pipe of tobacco. With her was the old man Hopalong, who used to have the land by the bridge until Arapeta persuaded him to deed it over, and a fierce warrior with a bulging stomach. Those like Arapeta in whom guilt resided deserved to be traumatised when the dead made calls on their conscience. Even so, they had no business here.

'Not you three again,' she said.

This was what she did, the *Matua*. Not only did she look after the physical welfare of her people, she was also charged, by virtue of her special powers, with their spiritual welfare. How had she put it to Tama? 'The Pakeha only have a one-dimensional view of health and wellbeing,' she said. 'We know that health depends not just on looking after the *tinana*, the body. It also requires us to look after the *wairua*, the spirit. We have to think of the *hinengaro*, the mental health, too. Then there's the *whenua*, the land and the world we live in. All these aspects must be in the right relationship: the inside with the outside, the person with his tribe, and all of us with our history. If one of these things is sick, then everything will be sick.'

Standing outside, leaning against the car, Tama didn't have to go in to see what the Matua was doing. He could visualise her already at work, sprinkling holy water over Arapeta to give him protection. He could tell from the rise and fall of her voice, its various tones of entreaty, force, authority and pleading, that she was finding opposition. No doubt the spirits, whoever they were, were wanting to take payment from Arapeta now and not wait until he came to them at his death; the Matua was trying to find diplomatic ways of negotiating around them. Shaking his head, Tama saw the Matua as clear as day as she walked around the room chanting a prayer and eating crumbs of bread — for eating food was a way of returning the paranormal to the normal. He could tell from the cajoling way she was talking that she had found a way to persuade the restless spirits to forgive her brother for his wrongdoings — and to wait, for he would be theirs soon enough.

Although goodness resided in the Matua, it found no home in her brother. Arapeta had stolen land from others in the tribe. He had used his tribal position to take what others had earned with the sweat of their brow. He had even cheated his own sister of her birthright. Their father, Claude, had always favoured Arapeta but their mother, Mariah, was insistent that at his death, their children would inherit an equal share of the family property. Mariah was a strong-willed woman, fighting for Miro's rights, and she firmly believed her husband was wrong in favouring one of his children over the other. 'The inherited title lies with the women,' Mariah reminded him. She died when Arapeta was twenty-five and Miro was nineteen. Claude followed her shortly afterward, while Miro was still a minor. Arapeta became Miro's guardian with trust over the land and shares owned between them.

Miro had been content to let her brother handle her affairs. She loved him deeply and trusted him implicitly. However, when she came of age she discovered that Arapeta had sold her land to local farmers, leaving her with only the shares in Maori land in Waituhi. From somewhere inside her Miro discovered the same fighting spirit that her mother had possessed. Miro drew on it, using it to assert her independence. She took her business affairs out of Arapeta's hands. In particular, she forced him to compensate her by giving her a document, in writing, which gave her full and total rights to any land that might be theirs in any future action to retrieve land confiscated at nearby Patutahi. Arapeta laughed as he signed the document. He considered he was actually giving her nothing. The Pakeha were never going to give that land back. Hell would freeze over first.

'Matua, why do you still persist with him?' Tama had asked Miro.

'Arapeta is my brother,' she answered, 'and I must forgive him his manipulations and his greed. I will not turn from him nor will I allow him to go into the darkness before his allotted time, no matter what he has done or might do in the future.'

Tama heard a high-pitched, strangulated squeal come from the house, the kind that comes when your nuts have been grabbed and twisted. It was Arapeta, and the turning point had been reached. Even though the Matua could forgive him and prevent him from being troubled, she could never stop the other people — now dead — whom he had cheated. If they now pursued him, so be it. He thought of the other terrible act that Arapeta had done: burying his son in an unmarked graveyard on his farm where nobody would know his son's secret. *No, Sam, not everlasting darkness.*

The house grew silent. Tama heard Florence weeping and the Matua talking to her. He heard Arapeta thanking his sister.

The Matua appeared at the doorway. Tama saw she had lovingly taken the ghosts into her. At times like this, weighed by the burden of their souls, she looked older to him, and he felt a sense of revulsion that this old woman was his wife, his partner to whom he had cleaved all his life. Immediately ashamed at his thoughts, he prayed for forgiveness.

'Husband, succour me,' Miro said.

This was the part Tama always feared. Which ghosts were they? Some were easy to cope with but others were really difficult, kicking the shit out of him as she transferred them to him. Even so, he overcame his fears. When Miro came to him, he put out his arms to her and embraced her. He shuddered, his body rippling with violent spasms, and he began to foam at the mouth. The dead came into him, wrestled him, tried to find evil in him where they could reside. Tama recognised Auntie Bobbie immediately; her vile-smelling weed made his nostrils crinkle and, as usual, she bit him on the bum as she left him. The other two were harder to handle. Being male, they tried to find a way to get at him, to find some chinks in his defences. Instead, as usual, they found only innocence and, acknowledging this, glided through him and went back into the earth.

Miro recovered. She looked at Tama as he regained consciousness.

'Thank you, husband. Bobbie and her mates only wanted to have a little fun, reminding Arapeta of what would be waiting for him when he crossed over.' She tried to find humour in the situation, but Tama was still not back with her. She remembered the owl and grew suddenly alarmed, looking for signs that he had not suffered too much. With a sigh of relief she saw that he had earthed himself well, standing square to the earth and with shoulders to the sky.

'Another one you owe me,' he joked as he recovered.

This time, getting rid of the spirits had been hard, so hard. They had sensed the slight revulsion he had earlier felt about the Matua. Ah well, he'd have to try harder. To love harder.

After all, it was his job.

CHAPTER TWELVE

Rongo Mahana shut the gate and walked back to the pick-up truck. On the skyline he saw Paora with the boy, Pene, waving to him. Smiling, he waved back. He was just about to step back into his truck when he heard a voice calling to him.

'You're up early,' Maka tiko bum said. She was sitting on her front porch having a smoke. 'No rest for the wicked, eh?' She laughed her earthy laugh and winked.

'Are you talking about you or me?' Rongo answered. 'Can't sleep?'

'My head hasn't even hit the pillow yet,' Maka moaned. 'How can I when Sam, Hine, Jack and God knows who else are still partying in the shack?' She made one of her eyes swivel in its socket and check out yet another person coming out to water her garden; this time, it was Blacky. 'You'd think they would have had enough from the wedding reception last night,' Maka continued, 'and Hine Ropiho has a cheek sending Boy Boy to Granny Heni's.' Heni was like Maka and had an eye affliction too; she was blind. 'Don't you worry though, Rongo, I'm going to fix them. When they've finished their party and think of getting some sleep I've got all my pots and pans ready. I'm going to bang them and clang them and smash them together and then I'm going to shout all over God's heaven.' She gave a raucous peal of laughter. 'Oh, and by the way, you better get ready for another wedding. My nephew Waka and Annie Jackson's girl. The world wags on, eh?'

Nodding, Rongo got into the pick-up truck, started it up and drove down the muddy track leading from the road to the potato paddock. The car lurched and slid in the mud. 'My goodness,' he grumbled, 'I'd better come out next week with some gravel and fix the track. You'd think my other brothers and sisters would keep the place up. Surely they can't be all that busy. Fences broken. Scotch thistles all over the place. Potholes.' He swerved to avoid one. 'Ever since me and Huia left here, the place has been going to the dogs.'

Rongo and Huia Mahana lived in Gisborne, in a tidy wooden house in a tidy wooden suburb. Like others in the Mahana clan, following Riripeti's death their lives had been individualised, split away from what had once been a solid core based on *whanau*, on extended family. They had lived in the city for three years now. It was Huia who decided on the move, saying, 'There's nothing here for us, and anyway it would be better for the kids if we moved to the city. They'll be nearer to school, nearer to the library and —' but she didn't say it, just thought it — *maybe they'll find good lives again.*

Huia also had another reason for moving. She wanted her kids to get the best, whatever that was, and be nearer to civilisation. She hadn't slaved all her life for nothing, out in the paddocks picking maize all day for fun. She'd done everything for her kids. Suffered for them. Fought for them. And she'd keep on fighting for them. Because she'd known what it was like to go to school in rags, to know nothing and have nothing, and to be laughed at for being so poor. She'd known it all, known it all. She was making sure that her kids didn't feel the pain and the humiliation of having to sign their name with an 'X' on their pay slip to confirm they'd received their pay — as she once did, until she taught herself how to write her signature — or of not understanding the words when some smart person arrived at the door to sell them a set of encyclopaedias, because they didn't know how to read. She had educated herself, was in the process of getting their kids educated and, as she used to say to Rongo whenever he got in the way of her beady eye, 'You're next, husband.' The Mahana family were on their way back up in the world, their part of the family at least.

'Even so,' Rongo smiled, thinking about Huia, 'why do we keep on coming *back*?' Why couldn't he break the emotional link between him and Waituhi? He came here almost every week on some pretext or another. And Huia sometimes came with him, to bend beside him in the fields. Yes, there was no doubt about it; some day, maybe when the kids had found their own way in the world, he and Huia would return. Huia was just kidding herself when she talked about the city. Waituhi was their home. This was their heart. As Huia once admitted as they sat having a break from planting the potatoes for the season, 'Old habits die hard.'

And then there was Riripeti's millennial dream to be taken up again.

Rongo stopped the pick-up truck at a corner of the paddock. He got out and took some sacks from the back. The paddock was planted with long rows of potatoes, a few rows of pumpkins, cucumbers and marrows, and tall maize glistening yellow and green in the sun. A big paddock, stretching back to the road. One of four paddocks in the village which was all that was left of the Mahana land. 'May as well get started,' he said to nobody in particular. But he couldn't help remembering that not many years ago Riripeti got all the Mahana clan together at a family meeting, organised the buying of seed and then, blessing them, sent them to do the planting. She fixed the time the old way, calculating by the shape of the moon and the position of the stars in the night sky.

The planting was a good time. A family occasion. The men would be in front, planting the seeds. The women would follow, watering the seeds. The younger members of the family would come after them, folding the seeds into the earth. Although it was hard work it didn't seem to take long, because everybody was too busy laughing and gossiping and chucking off at each other to think of how strenuous it was. 'Hey, Cissie, cover that seed properly with the dirt, eh?' 'Worry about your own seed, cuz, and while you're at it, don't you know how to plant in the straight line?' 'Who says I'm not planting straight? It's the furrows that are crooked.' 'Don't blame the furrows, eh? Blame the drinking last night. And tell that son of yours he only has to dig a small hole for the seeds. Does he think he's digging all the way to China?' So it used to go on all day. The laughter, the light-hearted exchanges, sweat flowing healthy and well. The constant bending into the planting. At smoko times, the clan rested beneath a willow tree and ate bread and drank clear water. Then back to work again until night fell.

Sometimes, the planting would take a whole week, depending on how many paddocks the clan had decided would be planted with seed. One week among the very few weeks that all the Mahana families became one family. A happy week of shared muscle and sweat.

Afterward would come the waiting time. The waiting for the maize and potatoes to grow. The Mahana clan was rostered by Riripeti to work in the paddocks, weed the growing plants and water them. Once the crop was ready, it was all hands to the work and the fulfilment of family reaping the riches of shared labour. And Riripeti would come among the workers, praising and blessing their work, and leading all in a prayer of thanksgiving.

'Glory to Your Holy Name, Amen.'

That was then.

This was now. Today, Rongo Mahana had come for the year's harvest. He came with spade in hand to the paddock. Last planting season, Rongo Mahana planted the paddock by himself. On this day he had come alone to the harvest. There was no sense of fulfilment.

'Times are changing,' Rongo muttered. He threw the sacks on the ground. He sat on one of them and unlaced his shoes. He put his boots on. With the spade gripped in his hands he pushed into the earth to uncover the potatoes. They clung to the roots of the upturned plants. He bent and pulled at the potatoes, his fingers searching the soil for any others which had not been exposed by the cleaving spade. He piled them in the furrow between this row and the next before thrusting the spade again beneath the next plant in the row. Spade turning earth, body bending and fingers scrabbling in the dirt. Spade cleaving earth, body attuning itself to the rhythm of the work. Plant after plant being upturned. 'Good spuds, these,' he said, praising his work. Losing himself to the rhythm of the spade. Trying to forget being alone in the digging. Moving up the row, leaving potatoes strewn in the furrow. His heart was racing, the sweat beginning to bead his face. An aching began in his bending body. Alone in the paddock. A solitary speck amid the expanse of furrows cut into the earth. Alone under the hot sun.

The spade slipped. It cut into the roots of a plant and sliced into the potatoes beneath. Frustrated, Rongo grasped them and flung them at the sky. He cursed the sun for being so hot, so all-seeing, so unyielding in that bright sky. 'Damn you,' he shouted to nobody and nothing in particular.

The rhythm of this man to the land was destroyed.

*

A big clan, the Mahanas. Once they had a purpose in life. Riripeti and the Ringatu religion had given them that purpose: to serve God, the people and the faithful. Once the religion went, everything else went. Of the entire clan, only two families remained in Waituhi, Pita's and Teria's, Rongo's brother and sister. The rest, like Rongo, were scattered throughout New Zealand. There, in the land of the White man, they were at the mercy of the Pakeha. They were like the Children of Israel, living under the rule of pharaoh in the cities of the Egyptian kings, slaves in the shadows of the pyramids. The cities were seductive and sybaritic. They offered jobs and money. Once you were there they were difficult to escape from. They bound you to them with contracts — high mortgages or steep rents, hire-purchase payments and threats of repossession. They asked more of you: more of your money, because you bought things you did not really want. Once you were caught, you could never escape. Whether slave or free man, you could never find your way back.

The Pakeha life ate everything up. It was voracious. Hungry. It stopped at nothing. No matter who you were or what you were, if you were in its path, you would be eaten.

Rongo chastised himself. 'Can I really put all the blame on the Pakeha life? Nothing lasts forever. The gate to the way we were is already shut behind us and we cannot get back in. We just have to make the best of it.' He thrust the spade into the earth again, looked for an example of self-blame — and found it in the planting. 'After all, Teria promised to come to help me. But did she? No. And did Pita? No.'

On that first day of the planting there had been no sign of either his brother or his sister. Rongo couldn't wait any longer. He had felt the earth crying out for seed, the womb of the land waiting to receive its seeding. He had felt the yearning of the land for peace, for it had become accustomed to the rhythm of the yearly work. There was a crying out of his blood too. The rhythm of the land and the rhythm of his blood were one and the same and had to be appeased. And he had started the planting, thinking that maybe Teria and Pita would turn up eventually. He got going because when the time came for planting you had to plant before it was too late. No good planting late — it put the growing out of rhythm. There was a time for everything: for planting, for harvesting, and if you missed it you were done for. In the old days people died of starvation if the sweet potato did not come to crop. Unplanted land did not bear fruit.

The sun sprang quickly in the sky. Still nobody. And Rongo realised that it was all over, all over. He couldn't blame the others for moving from the village and destroying the rhythm of the land. He couldn't blame Teria for not being able to come — she already had enough trouble on her plate — nor Pita and Miriama for being away shearing. If he was to look closer to home, what about his own son Tama, who had gone to Wellington to work? No, nobody to blame but himself for waiting, for being so stubborn. For hoping.

On that planting day, something had nagged at Rongo and wouldn't leave him alone. Something about the way things were supposed to be. The ancient gods of the Maori — Tane, God of man, forest and birds; Tawhirimatea, God of the winds, Rongo ma Tane, God of peace and agriculture; Tangaroa, God of the oceans and all therein — had not given unto man their bounty without strictures. Everything was connected. Man had a reciprocal responsibility with his world. There was a cycle of birth, death and replenishment which had to be maintained. There was also an implicit contract with the soil, with all things animate and inanimate, that had to be respected and honoured. It was not a contract given either to abuse or to play with. Arrogant man had set himself above nature; the relationship was not something about which either had any choice. They were contracted to each other. Man, by not respecting the contract, was in danger of killing both his world and himself.

Rongo Mahana had made a promise to the land that day. 'When the time comes for harvesting, I'll be back,' he said.

'And here I am,' Rongo smiled, patting the land. He had fulfilled his promise. The time for harvesting had come — and here he was. The belly of the land was swollen and ready to deliver. He was the midwife, the orchardist, the agriculturalist, come into the bountiful garden.

Rongo looked back over the rows of potatoes he had harvested. Not too bad for an old man, and the spuds were good this year. How many sacks should he fill today? Better dig up as much as he could before he switched across to that part of the paddock where pumpkins, cucumbers and melons were wasting. 'Better keep working,' he laughed. 'Times may have changed, eh, land! Me and you are getting old. But my goodness, we're not giving up yet, eh? Let's see what else you have for me.'

And when you are dead, Rongo Mahana? the land asked. *Who will maintain the contract which Riripeti made and which is for the benefit of all? Who will maintain the cycle of life between man and nature? Who will render unto me?*

Rongo plunged his hands into the earth.

'Oh, Riripeti,' he said, 'forgive us.'

CHAPTER THIRTEEN

——— 1 ———

'Come, Nani Paora.'

Pene and Nani Paora were on the Parade; Nani Paora preferred to call it 'Te Haerenga', The Long Walk. They were walking along the road from the old homestead, near Taumata o Tumokonui, toward the hill, Tawhiti Kaahu, where Takitimu meeting house was. Wouldn't you just know it — Nani had already been diverted. He slipped through a fence and made his way up the side of the slope to a wild patch of scrub.

'No sooner do I take my eyes off you for a second,' Pene scolded, 'than you run off.' Arms akimbo, he was a little frowning boy stamping his foot on the ground. 'Come down from there. Come down this minute.' Do you think Nani would obey? Nope. He disappeared into the scrub. 'Oh no,' Pene groaned. He ran up the hillside and confronted the tangled mess, trying to find a way in. Very soon he was in thick gorse, and Nani Paora was nowhere in sight. Just as Pene was ready to give up he found the old man. Nani Paora was putting something in his mouth.

'Nani,' Pene yelled. 'What are you eating?' He scrambled quickly through thorny branches. Who knew what berries or seeds Nani had picked. 'Spit it out. Let me see it. You might get poisoned.'

Nani Paora did as he was told. He spat a mashed up, purple pulp into Pene's nice, clean hands. 'Oh, gross,' Pene winced. He brightened up when Nani Paora opened his mouth to be inspected and poked out his tongue. 'You've found a patch of wild blackberries, Nani,' Pene said.

'Sweet,' Nani Paora answered. He picked more fruit from the patch and passed them to his grandson.

'They taste all right,' Pene said. 'They are all right!' Very soon his mouth was red with the fruit. He made a mental note to tell Dad about the blackberry because, like gorse, it claimed the land as irrevocably as the Pakeha; the annual cutting and burning could stop it from spreading, but the roots were tenacious and, having invaded the earth, only came back. 'A few more handfuls,' Pene said, 'and then we'll go. Otherwise, you'll get sick.'

What was this? The old man had gone to ground. Quickly, Pene dropped down beside him. He was just about to ask another question when Nani Paora put his left hand firmly across Pene's lips.

Nani Paora pointed through the blackberry and gorse entanglement of the thick scrub. 'Be on guard,' he hissed. 'Soldiers.'

The soldiers were heading for the fortress which Te Whanau a Kai rebels had built as their fighting centre in Poverty Bay. It was November 1865 and a lot had happened since the Hauhau had visited Waituhi earlier that year in March. When the Hauhau crossed over from Opotiki, the response from the Pakeha settlers was paranoia, fear and military action. Under the leadership of Colonel Fraser, a quick punitive eight-month campaign began against the Hauhau and those who supported them. The campaign comprised the Pakeha Wars in Poverty Bay, and the principal opponents of the Pakeha were Te Whanau a Kai.

Tamati Kota took his hand away from Pene's mouth. 'Don't move,' he said, as the soldiers passed them by. 'Be silent.' He pressed some berries on Pene's face and smeared them like war paint.

The soldiers were a squad of Hawke's Bay Colonial Defence Forces. They were laughing and boasting because, after some months when the military campaign hung in the balance, they were gaining the upper hand on the East Coast. Henare Potae and loyalist Ngati Porou forces were helping them. 'But the Poverty Bay Maoris still have to be brought to heel,' one of the soldiers said. He stepped so close to Pene that the young boy's heart almost stopped. He could smell the soldier's tobacco and sweat. What would the soldier do to him if he was discovered?

'We'll do it, boyo,' another soldier laughed. 'Hirini Te Kani has now declared himself to be on the side of the Crown and Rongowhakaata loyalists have joined him. We have the rebels already on the run. They may have bivouacked at Waerenga a Hika but the battle goes against them.'

The soldiers faded into the green and sunlit bush. Tamati Kota made a sign to Pene. 'Let's go,' he said. 'Let us follow.' They slipped out of the bush, shadowing the soldiers.

Pene's heart was beating fast. All his senses were alert as he and Tamati Kota tailed the soldiers. He was so caught up that it was a surprise to find himself at Huiatoa, on the left bank of the Waipaoa River. Not a great distance away, as the crow flies, was Waerenga a Hika fortress.

'Our people are inside and under siege,' Tamati Kota whispered. 'We must join them and help them. Let the soldiers go ahead. We'll swim the river and approach the fortress from the other side.' He slipped down the bank and into the water.

'I can't swim,' Pene said.

'Can't you?' Tamati Kota answered, his eyes twinkling. 'What kind of grandson are you? Neither can I. Lucky for us, the river is not deep.'

Waerenga a Hika fortress stood on the banks of the old riverbed. It was close by the mission station, abandoned since April by Bishop W. Williams on account of sinister rumours that the local Pakeha would be massacred.

'We're here, Pene,' Tamati Kota said. 'This is where it happened.'

In front of the mission station was a quickset hedge. Between the hedge and the fortress lay a flat, open space about 150 yards deep. The main defence system of the fortress was a double palisade, about twelve feet high. The uprights were stout logs, between which sharp stakes were interwoven. On the outside was a twig-woven apron, designed to deflect bullets into the air. Thick scrub stood to the north of the fortress. Almost a thousand rebels, most of them Te Whanau a Kai, manned the fortress. Tamati Kota saw some of them getting water from the lagoon at the rear.

'Stay down, Pene,' Nani said. He took his bearings from the sun. Sniffed the air and smelt death on its swirling currents. 'Alas, we are too late,' he cried. 'This is the sixth day of the battle.'

The rebels had already taken a beating. The first Pakeha attack began on 13 November. 'Go straight at 'em!' instructed Major Fraser. On the second day some of the troops gained the upper rooms of the nearby bishop's residence and those of the girls' school as vantage points from which to fire into the fortress. The Military Settlers entrenched behind the hedge facing the fortress were at the ready. The Forest Rangers took up a position on their left, and the Hawke's Bay C.D.F., flanked by Ngati Porou loyalist troops, on their right. Lieutenant Wilson, with a party of twenty Military Settlers, made a sortie to command the water supply. On the third day, between 150 and 200 rebel reinforcements under Anaru Matete managed to get into the fortress from the rear and to help in its defence. The fourth and fifth days were characterised by a fierce battle for victory.

Suddenly, there was a lull. 'This is our chance,' Tamati Kota said. The rebels raised white flags as tokens of surrender. 'We can run through the lines of soldiers and join our fighters.'

It was too late. Although a white flag had been raised, a six-pounder howitzer from the *Sturt* rained its shots into the fortress. Three shots were fired from the howitzer, each making a breach. A white flag was raised again.

Tamati Kota stood and raised a wild cry of anger and passion. 'Take heed,' he said to Pene, 'this is the lesson of the day. See how the Pakeha treated us?' He gave a sign and, taking Pene's hand in his, pulled him across the threshold from the past back to the present. One minute there, the next minute gone.

The bush melted around them as if they had never been there.

--------- 2 ---------

The wild blackberries were the great discovery of the morning.

'That was *good*,' Pene said. He was washing Nani Paora's face at the Pouarua Stream trying to get the red stains off. No such luck. 'Looks like those stains are there to stay,' Pene added. 'Mum's not going to like that at all.'

Nani Paora was still staring into the past. One hundred and thirty Maori were killed or wounded at Waerenga a Hika. Over 800 surrendered to the troops. It was the deciding battle in Poverty Bay. During the struggle, seven fortified positions were destroyed, 223 Maori were killed, close on 1300 rebels surrendered or were captured, and 600 stands of arms were given up.

'We're being watched,' Nani Paora said. He saw wide, binocular eyes staring from out of the hole in a tree where the owl was raising its young. Five weeks had passed since it had incubated its clutch of two eggs but it still brooded and guarded them. For a moment both owl and Nani Paora took up defensive positions, alert, ready to defend.

Pene brought the old man back to attention. 'Let's keep going,' he said as he pulled Nani Paora onto the road. There, he took charge. 'How am I going to get you to behave?' he asked Nani Paora. 'I know.' He pretended he was an army bugler blowing a bugle to call soldiers to arms. 'Ta tum ta tara ta tum ta ta *ra*!' Yay, Nani Paora got the idea and stood up straight. 'All present and correct?' Pene asked. Nani Paora snapped a salute, his feet together, his head up. Pene took a twig, put it under his left armpit and pretended he was inspecting Nani Paora on a regimental parade ground. 'Okay, Private, what have you to say for yourself? Late on parade and look at the state of your uniform. And where's your rifle, Private? You left it in the barracks? You could be shot at dawn for that, Private.'

'What are you saying?' Nani Paora asked, puzzled. 'What's your problem?' Sometimes his grandson made no sense.

'Just follow my orders, Private,' Pene answered. 'By the left, shoulder arms! Qui-ck march!' Whistling *Oh Susanna*, Pene marched Nani along the road. 'Oh I come from Alabama with my banjo on my knee, I come from Alabama my true love for to see. Oh Susanna, oh don't you cry for me, for I come from Alabama with my banjo on my knee —'

They were like toy soldiers marching along the ridge, keeping step to fife and drum, heading for Tawhiti Kaahu. Once, a meeting house called Tawhirimatea had been built on the hill. Ninety years ago it was burnt down because it was believed to be haunted, and in its place a new meeting house, Takitimu, was built. When they reached Takitimu, Pene called, 'Platoon, halt.' Nani Paora peeled off and sat in the grass, exhausted. 'You're not supposed to do that until I give the order to fall out,' Pene complained.

'What do you think I am?' Nani Paora said. 'I don't want to play being a soldier for the Pakeha.' With that, he sprinted up the grass and past Takitimu. Pene looked at his disappearing Nani with a smug look on his face. 'As it happens, Nani, that's the way we were going to go anyhow.'

It was Pene's custom, once they reached Tawhiti Kaahu, to choose to do the Parade along either one of two routes. Nani Paora had followed the first route up Tawhiti Kaahu to the village graveyard, where he liked to pay respects to the dead. Once that was done, they followed the ridge as it curved left through scabbed, scrubby farmland. The walk kept them both high in the sun, which meant that Nani could look across the landscape and, at the same time, get a suntan. From there, he could point out to Pene the landmarks of the tribe. The ridge paralleled the road and circled back on it where Rongopai meeting house was. The Parade always ended at Rongopai.

· Pene followed after Nani. Up the sunlit slope he went. The sun sparkled on the hillside and Pene flung himself on the ground. Looking across the slope he saw that the sparkling light was coming from long, glistening spider threads, gossamer strands strung from blade to blade. Whenever a breeze blew across the hill, spiders would take the opportunity to unhitch from the grass and go springing through the air. They were like circus aerialists snaring the sun, spinning out their threads, thousands of spinning threads, spinning, spinning, spinning: *Wheeee*.

When Pene looked up, Nani Paora had already unlatched the gate to the graveyard, closed it, crossed over the threshold and, looking at Pene, closed that too. 'Don't come in,' he said.

'Suits me,' Pene sniffed. He was never comfortable in the graveyard with his Nani. Although he wouldn't admit it, he was always jealous of those other people who Nani liked to talk with.

Nani Paora walked slowly among the graves, marked and unmarked, and the pain and the sadness rushed out of him in a passionate outburst to all the loved companions of his youth. 'Why me, you fellas?' he asked. 'Why have you left me behind so cruelly? Is there some reason? Was I the strongest, you weak beggars? You think I'm the strong one, is that it? You think it's been easy for me to bury you all? Useless beggars. You could never do anything for yourselves.' He sighed and panted for breath. 'Well, even the digger has to die some time,' he said at last. 'You all better move over and start thinking of making a place for me. Don't think I'm staying longer than I have to while all you beggars are enjoying your reward.' He saw the woman with pearls in her hair whom he had loved and served, and was ashamed of his petulance. 'Forgive me, my lady,' he said, as she smiled her glorious smile. 'Once I have given the keys of the kingdom over to the king who is to come, I long to join you.'

'If it be His will,' Riripeti answered, 'you, Tamati Kota, will have a chair with me at the table of the Lord.'

The sun sprang high in the sky. 'Still talking?' Pene yelled. 'Maybe I should have taken you the other way today.' Nani Paora was definitely not playing the game, and he was pretending to be deaf. 'Aren't you finished yet?' Pene asked, impatient. He was fidgeting, ready with the water to wash Nani's hands when he came out. When Nani finally came to Pene, the young boy immediately felt bad about being so impatient. 'Are you all right, Nani? I didn't mean to stop you from saying hello.'

Nani Paora gave a mournful sigh. He washed his hands. Then, 'Gotcha,' he laughed. With a jaunty step he proceeded up the ridge, away from Tawhiti Kaahu.

'You old teaser!' Pene laughed as he chased after him. He picked up a fallen branch, and using it as a rifle, shouted, 'Bang!' Next minute, Nani Paora had picked up a rifle too and was shooting back, 'Pow pow!' They chased each other through the bush, sighting and firing, 'Boom! Pow pow! Bang!' Rifle tight into shoulder. Sighting down the barrel. Squeezing off the trigger. 'Pow pow! Bang! Boom!' Pene thought it was all just a game but shadows were gathering. Darkness came across the hills. The dark clouds were to the southwest, and as soon as Nani Paora saw them he halted the game.

'More soldiers.'

The moment expanded around them, and Nani Paora looked into another fortress. This time it was not Waerenga a Hika but a clifftop fortress: Ngatapa. Nani Paora saw that it was too dark, too dangerous to go there. Although the boy wanted to cross the threshold, Nani Paora gently restrained him.

'Not this time, Grandchild,' he said. 'Best to watch.'

'Glory to Your Holy Name,' Tamati Kota began. 'Do you know what happened after Waerenga a Hika fell in 1865, Grandchild? The Government, still fearing the possibility of further Maori uprisings, deported rebels taken prisoner at Waerenga a Hika to the Chatham Islands without trial. In particular, they wanted to get the more troublesome rebels out of the way while their land confiscation policy was settled. The Chatham Islands were inhospitable, bleak, cold, and some twelve days' sail from Poverty Bay southward, but our people were told that if they conducted themselves well they would, at the end of two years, be set at liberty. Seventy were in the first party sent away in March 1866. They were followed by three further groups of prisoners — forty-five in the second, 116 in the third and fifty-six in the fourth — comprising men, women and children, escorted by thirty guards.'

Tamati Kota was peering into the past, looking for a certain man among the prisoners and, when he saw the man, his voice became hushed with veneration. 'Among the prisoners wrongfully imprisoned was a man who was no ordinary man. Can you see him, Grandchild? The one languishing in his cell? His name is Te Kooti Arikirangi Te Turuki. And look — the spirit of God has appeared to him in that place of desolation.'

And the spirit of God came in a cloud of blazing light. The spirit aroused Te Kooti from his sleep and said to him . . . 'Arise; I am sent by God. Be not afraid, for your cry has come unto God, and He has given heed to your crying. Hearken; and I will strengthen you and make known to you the words which I spoke to your fathers, to Abraham, Isaac and Jacob, and to their seed even down to David.' Transported, Tamati Kota pressed Pene's hands so hard he hurt them. 'The spirit moved Te Kooti to study the psalms,' Tamati Kota said. 'Te Kooti also studied the books of Joshua and Judges. He composed scriptural verses and began to hold religious services among his fellow prisoners two times a day. So it was that while in imprisonment Te Kooti ascended unto his true purpose and established the beginnings of our Ringatu faith, of which I am the remaining priest.

'And the prisoners,' Tamati Kota continued, 'were able to find succour in their long travail. They looked forward to release, for eventually they served their two years, illegally detained without trial, on those barren windswept Islands. However, although they behaved in an exemplary manner, at the expiration of two years they were not let go. That was when Te Kooti began his dreams of liberation, not only for himself and his followers but also for the Maori people of Aotearoa. If Pharaoh would not let him go, would he ever let the Maori people go? Fired by sadness and anger, the spirit moved Te Kooti on 4 July 1868, to seize the schooner, the *Rifleman*, which was landing supplies on the

Islands. All together, 163 men, sixty-four women and seventy-one children were on the schooner making their dash for freedom; three men and one woman had remained behind. When Te Kooti arrived twelve days later at Whareongaonga, the East Coast, on the evening of 10 July, he was ready to begin the Lord's work.'

Major Biggs, accompanied by Pakeha militia from the military garrison at Matawhero, were waiting to arrest Te Kooti and return him and his followers to prison. 'The Pakeha did not see that the Lord was in the prophet,' Tamati Kota said, 'rather, they saw an escaped prisoner who had now become a religious fanatic, leading a fanatical band of followers. Te Kooti and his followers began their running battle from the moment they landed when Major Biggs asked them to lay down their arms and surrender. The prophet's reply was, "God has given us the arms and we are not going to give them up at any man's bidding. We wish to go our way unmolested." That's when the Te Kooti Wars with the Pakeha began. In July 1868 Major Biggs and Colonel Whitmore went relentlessly in pursuit of the prophet. Battles took place at Paparatu, Te Koneke and the Ruakituri. The prophet and his men were victorious and, in August, they ascended to Puketapu mountain where they established a base of operations. The paranoia of the White man reached new heights and he became increasingly nervous of Te Kooti and the revenge he might take on the innocent settlers of Poverty Bay. Thus, in October 1868, the Government assembled a large native force at Wairoa to make an assault on Te Kooti's stronghold. Realising that he would be pursued forever, the prophet had no option but to protect his people.'

With sorrow in his heart, Te Kooti sent a message to the Government. 'Friends, I agree that we fight, for I have been followed up by you three times. I will fight you in November. That is when the trouble will arise.'

'With this resolve,' Tamati Kota continued, 'the prophet came down the ancient Tuhoe track where it descended to the Hangaroa River. His destination was the Matawhero military garrison. If Biggs wanted a fight, he would be given a fight. On 9 November 1868 Te Kooti deviated from the ancient track along Repongaere Lake and followed the banks of the Waikakariki Stream to the Maori settlement at Patutahi. From there he proceeded along the western side of the Waipaoa River down to the lower ford at Matawhero. He began his attack at 3 am on 10 November and Te Kooti was triumphant. No quarter was given —'

And Pene *saw* the prophet, Te Kooti Arikirangi Te Turuki. The prophet was calling to him, saying, 'Come through.' Images of blood, axes, fire, rifles, death, the awful carnage of the Matawhero attack, exploded around him. Tamati Kota said, 'No,' and pulled Pene back. But in that moment, Pene glimpsed the bloodshed and deaths of Major Biggs and those defending the garrison: twelve militia attached to the Defence Forces, seven wives, nine children and five half-caste children. One minute there, next minute gone. Just like that.

'Come back from the threshold,' Tamati Kota said. Although he would gladly have gone through to Te Kooti, it was not the place for the boy. 'Return to me.' It was a strong command, for Pene was shivering and in the grip of the seeing. Pene snapped out of it, his face pale and shocked. Even so, it took some time before Tamati Kota was able to really calm him.

'This is what war is like, Grandson,' Tamati Kota said. 'In war there are only the living and the dead.' He had to remind Pene, however, that while the Te Kooti action at Matawhero was considered a massacre, atrocities occurred on both sides. 'But what you are seeing is just one side of the war,' he continued. 'Now look upon the other side and the vengeance that the Pakeha took on Te Kooti and his followers.'

Oh yes, for there *was* vengeance. Nobody could let such an act against the Crown go unpunished. A military force under Lieutenant Gascoyne including also 270 Kahungunu, sixty Northern Kahungunu and 100 Rongowhakaata began their pursuit of Te Kooti and his followers to bring them to Pakeha justice. European Volunteers and 376 Ngati Porou amplified the numbers. On 4 December the *Sturt* arrived with Colonel Whitmore, Major Fraser and seventy members of the Artillery Corps, whose equipment included six artillery pieces. 'The Gravedigger Has Arrived!' placards in Poverty Bay announced.

'Te Kooti went to ground at Ngatapa fortress,' Tamati Kota said. 'The Pakeha came and began his siege on 27 December.'

And this time Tamati Kota could not prevent Pene from crossing the threshold. The boy saw that the fortress was at the top of a mountain and comprised three compartments, one behind the other. You had to get through one before you could attack the next. It had steep flanks and the colonial forces were having trouble storming the defences because of fire from the Maori defenders. At the rear was a cliff.

A chain of small forts had been built up the Ngatapa Valley. In all Colonel Whitmore had 700 troops and his equipment included two cohorn mortars capable of throwing shells into any part of the fortress. The day was 4 January 1869 and the mortars had done their job; fifty-eight dead bodies testified to the terrible havoc they had wrought, double the number killed at Matawhero, surely a just compensation. The defenders were driven back from their outer trenches. When dawn came, the colonial forces entered the fortress. But where were Te Kooti and his men? The attacking force found only women, children and the old men and the wounded they were caring for.

The Ngati Porou loyalists asked the prisoners, 'Where are your men? Which way have they gone?' An old woman among them pointed to flax ladders, tossed over the rear cliff. Far below the flimsy lifelines, thick bush.

'They escaped in the night,' the old woman said with scorn. 'They are already gone to a place where you will never find them.'

'And neither will you, old woman,' a soldier said. With that, the soldier ordered the troops to line the prisoners up along the cliff where the ladders tossed and swayed.

The old woman took Pene by the hand and pulled him with her. Tamati Kota tried to stop her, but the old woman gave him a look of rebuke. 'Let the boy see, priest,' she said. 'Don't sanitise the history.' She turned to Pene. 'When the soldiers fire, I will protect you so that you will not be shot.'

Pene felt the wind as it struck the cliff and curled over the lip of the bluff into the fortress. There were forty prisoners in the first line to be shot. Resignation was written on the faces of the old men. The younger prisoners were quivering, not knowing what death was like, and their hearts were bursting with fear. The women were weeping, not for themselves, but for the children who were to die that day. Two of the women had already turned their children away from the firing squad, facing them toward the open space of sky and the valley below, saying, 'Look to the west, for our prophet and our people have gone that way, and there they pray for us who have protected them in their escape.'

Another mother had her hands ready to put across the eyes of her child and clasp him to her when the shots rang out.

'Will we not be spared at all?' Pene asked.

'No,' the old woman said. 'The time has long passed for clemency. The Pakeha will not stop until he has everything. It is his nature. And we have had a bounty placed on us. Twenty pounds for every rebel head. If we must be killed let us go singing to our deaths so that our Lord will hear from a long way off that we are coming.'

It all happened quickly after that. Pene looked for Nani Paora — but he was not there. The old woman and the people with her were singing and preparing to go to their Maker. Some of them had been together at the Chathams and they remembered the harshness and privation of their time in exile.

'Better to die in our homeland than in the prison of the Pakeha,' one of the men said.

The time had come. The firing squad raised their rifles. The sun glinted on the long barrels. The women began crying and the children, not knowing why their mothers were crying, began to scream. The old woman was angry with them and whispered to everyone, 'If we are to die, let us all fall over the cliff so that the soldiers will have a harder time collecting our scalps. Better to fall than to have your head taken by the Pakeha. Come closer,' she urged them. 'Come closer to the edge.' She laughed at one of the soldiers and said to him, 'Hey, Pakeha, one last smoke on your pipe, eh?' The soldier passed the pipe to her. She drew deep upon it and, while the soldier's attention was diverted, pressed Pene behind her skirts. 'Don't be afraid,' she whispered.

The shots rang out. Pene screamed. 'Nani Paora —'

The sound was shocking, echoing and echoing across the valley. The prisoners jerked and danced to the obscene song of the bullets.

'And now we go to our Lord in Paradise,' the old woman smiled. Blood sprayed and gouted from bodies and limbs and heads ripped by the bullets. They began to fall, pitching over the cliff, 120 men, women and children, crowding the air in the long slow dive into death.

Tamati Kota reached for Pene and caught him before he fell. The child was still. His eyes rolled into his head, the whites showing like the eyes of a corpse. Although Tamati Kota knew he should have been more careful, another part of him was saying that the old woman was right.

'Yes, Grandchild, you look,' Tamati Kota said. 'You see. You listen. You watch. You feel. Only then will you know. Where does the power of the White man come from? It comes from Satan.'

He pressed hard on Pene's temples and made a pass over the boy's body. Pene became limp. His eyes fluttered open and he stirred. From far away he heard the voice of Tamati Kota calling him back.

'O God,' Tamati Kota prayed, 'if our hearts arise from the land in which we now dwell as slaves, and repent and pray to Thee and confess our sins in Thy presence, then, O Jehovah, blot out the signs of Thine own people, who have sinned against Thee. Do not Thou, O God, cause us to be wholly destroyed. Wherefore it is that we glorify Thy Holy Name.

'Deliver us, O Lord.

'Amen.'

CHAPTER FOURTEEN

The sound of Charlie Whatu snoring was like an engine revving up, coughing into silence and revving up again. Agnes made herself immune by putting cotton wool into her ears. Smiling, she dreamt of wearing a bikini and speedboating on the blue waters near Nadi off the coast of Fiji.

Charlie wasn't the only one snoring his head off. In the bunkroom, Mana and Victor were making a ruckus. They had also been farting all night. Luckily, Sonny was partying over at Sam Walker's; Sonny had the stinkiest farts of all.

'Time to abandon ship,' Andrew Whatu, the youngest son, said to himself. He slept in the same room as his brothers and had been trying to keep his ears and nose closed against Mana's snoring and Victor's withering stench. He should have kept his eyes closed too. As he opened them he saw Mana's underdungers on the floor — with skidmarks on them, whoa — and Victor's dangly bits hanging over the side of the bunk. Not a pretty sight.

Andrew shuffled into jeans and T-shirt, found his boots under Mana's pillow and Mana with his nose in them; Mana always slept arse up and head down on the floor. On his way out Andrew tried to open the window because, apart from fart smells, the room stank of toe-jam.

'You want me to freeze to death?' Mana yelled.

Victor joined in, saying, 'Just close that window and be quick about it, shitface.'

'Oh, *nice* one, bros,' Andrew muttered. If his brothers wanted to die of toe-jam asphyxiation, fine, go ahead. On he went, past Janey's bedroom. She cocked an eye at him from under a pillow where she was trying to hide from the sunlight. 'Got back before Dad could find out, I see,' Andrew drawled. She moaned and showed two fingers.

The sun was warm. Andrew sat on the steps in front of the house. Even in the open he couldn't get away from the racket. He tried to focus, picked up his *Plain Sailing* English textbook and began to read. Miss Dalrymple had set him and his mates, Simeon and Haromi, an assignment to read a Katherine Mansfield story as punishment for playing up in class; she planned to test their knowledge of it tomorrow. But today just wasn't going to be Andrew's day. Across the fence Blacky had hooked his guitar to Sam Walker's amplifier:

'I have a band of men and all they do is play for me —'

Even the birds were holding their wings to their ears against the noise.

'Oh why was I born?' Andrew yelled to nobody in particular. 'Surely, somewhere, must be a place where people don't fart, snore or play guitars.' Every weekend was the same. When he went to sleep someone was always making loud, horrible noises. When he woke up, they were still at it. You'd think that Blacky would at least have lessons in playing a guitar. Somebody should shoot the guitar, put it out of its misery. Muttering crossly, Andrew gave up all thought of studying, put his textbook aside and resigned himself to failing the test. Ah well, so what was new? His whole week had been diverted by one thing or another. For instance, during library period last week he had come across a reference in a New Zealand history book to a young man named Hamiora Pere.

'Hey, look guys,' Andrew had said to Simeon and Haromi. They had never come across the name of somebody from Waituhi before in a book.

HANGED FOR TREASON

Hamiora Pere, one of the Te Kooti rebels in Poverty Bay, was required to stand trial for high treason at Wellington in September, 1869. He was captured after the fall of Ngatapa. The chief witness for the Crown was Maata Te Owai, who said she was married at the Chatham Islands to Te

Kooti, who had seduced her. She testified that Pere was one of the band which had participated in the Poverty Bay massacre. He had been a prisoner at the Chatham Islands. It was urged in Pere's defence that the rebels were savages who felt that they had a right to repel a foreign foe which had entered into the occupation of their country. Pere said that, in order to save his own life, he had had to stay with Te Kooti after they had returned from exile.

After retiring for only 15 minutes, the jury returned with a verdict of guilty. Mr. Justice Johnston, upon sentencing Pere to death, congratulated him on the fact that the practice of drawing and quartering after hanging had been abolished.

Sobbing bitterly, Pere had to be assisted to ascend the scaffold on 16 November 1869. Huskily he attempted to utter a few words. All traces of nervousness then left him. Standing erect, he repeated in a loud, clear voice the prayers that were being said on his behalf.

'A jailbird,' Haromi said in her usual flippant way. 'That figures.'

Reading about Hamiora Pere had been one diversion. Another happened when Josephine Wilson flashed him a smile during the lunch break. It hadn't been just an ordinary smile either. This one could have come from one of those women who appeared in centrefold spreads of magazines he wasn't supposed to know about.

Now totally sidetracked, Andrew lifted his face to the sun. He closed his eyes and thought of the two subjects that were becoming an interest in his life — girls and sex — and one girl in particular. 'Mmm, Josie,' he sighed. He leant back, moistened his lips with his tongue, closed his eyes and, abandoning all discretion, opened his legs so that the one-eyed monster had plenty of room to move, yeah baby. Allowing himself to fantasise, Andrew began to dream impossible dreams about Josephine Wilson. But as soon as he did that, he realised he was in a no-go zone.

'Who am I kidding?' Andrew asked himself. He was Maori. Josie was Pakeha. Although she had smiled at him, they inhabited two separate worlds. He lived in Waituhi, she lived in the best suburb in Gisborne. His father was Charlie Whatu, her father owned an accountancy firm. He was still struggling at school, she was top of the class in English.

'Don't even think about it,' Andrew's friend, Simeon, had said to him when Andrew disclosed his feelings. 'We're not in the same league, not playing in the same paddock. Not yet, anyhow.'

Not yet anyhow. Ah yes, both Andrew and Simeon had big dreams, bigger than they admitted to themselves. Andrew wanted to be a lawyer, Simeon a writer. To admit how big these aspirations were was to accept the shocking fact that two Waituhi boys had ambitions that were bigger than Waituhi and would take them away from their home town. What would it be like to leave home behind?

Andrew, in particular, had already crossed the threshold and knew he could never step back. Although he was tied up in knots about the prospect, the idea of making it in the legal profession in the Pakeha world drove him forward. He didn't care any longer that he, Simeon and Haromi were the only Maori left in the Fifth Form; he relished the challenge. Nor did he care that the longer he stayed at school, the whiter the world got. Poor Simeon had found that out himself on the last school trip when he had scored the visit to the courthouse. 'Why tempt fate?' Andrew quipped. But although he had joked about it, the truth was that Andrew would have liked to have gone in Simeon's place, and seen a courtroom.

Andrew heard somebody coming up behind him. It was Dad scratching, yawning and burping his way back from sleep.

'Who can get any rest around here with your mother snoring her head off and your brothers joining her?' Charlie Whatu asked. As usual, like everybody else in Waituhi, he plonked himself down beside Andrew without being invited. 'The whole world can see up your trouser legs,' Charlie said.

Quick as a flash Andrew answered, 'Scared of the competition, Dad?'

Charlie roared with ribald laughter. This youngest son of his always surprised him. Andrew had a talented and lively mind that whizzed along at a mile a minute. 'So what's up, son?' he asked.

'Why should anything be up?' Andrew answered.

'I know you,' Charlie teased. 'You're always thinking about something. You want to tell me about it? Not that I'll be able to help much. After all, you're the one with the brains.' Charlie liked to get into Andrew's head. He liked to know what his boy was thinking about. It thrilled him that this son had an inner, intellectual life.

'There's nothing to talk about, Dad. And don't say things like that. About being dumb. You aren't.' Andrew was cross that Dad never gave himself any credit. He always put himself down.

'Come on, son,' Charlie cajoled. 'I can hear you thinking from here.'

Shrugging, because he didn't really know what to say, Andrew asked, 'Dad, do you know anything about Hamiora Pere?'

Charlie hadn't heard that name in such a long time. He backed off fast. 'We don't talk about those things now, son,' he answered. 'They're all in the past.'

After the Te Kooti Wars, Te Whanau a Kai had pulled their heads down and out of sight. Like Esau in the Bible, they drew the animal skins of a larger neighbouring tribe, Te Aitanga a Mahaki, around them so that people would not continue to punish them for supporting Te Kooti. It was not a repudiation of their birthright; rather, it was easier to go underground, take another identity as Tamati Kota had done when he became Nani Paora, and wait for better and kinder days.

Quickly, Charlie moved on. 'Now, son, tell me what's really bothering you?' Could he deflect Andrew's question? Yes.

Andrew, compelled by all his thoughts, dreams and ambitions, unburdened himself. 'Dad, one of these days I think I'll have to leave Waituhi. There's so much I want to do with my life, Dad, but it's all out there —' Andrew pointed beyond the hills of the valley '— and not here. I want to go. I want to be somebody. But I want to stay too.'

Charlie stared at his surprising son. My word, who would have thought that Andrew would turn out to be such a serious boy? 'Son, you have to follow your star,' he said. 'If it leads you away from here, of course you'll have to follow the bloody thing.'

'That wouldn't disappoint you?' Andrew asked. 'If I walked away from here, am I not walking away from everything I am? Here in the valley, it's a Maori world. Out there, it's a Pakeha world. Here I know I'm Maori, but there I don't know who I am. You're so lucky, Dad. You know who you are. You know you belong. I envy you. As for me, I'm scared, Dad, really scared.'

'You envy me?' Charlie asked. 'What the hell for? I don't know anything, son.' Boy oh boy, the things you discovered about your own kids. 'Look at my hands. All they know about is labouring work. Fencing and digging postholes, that's been my life. This head has got nothing in it. These feet will always be stuck right smack in the centre of Waituhi. You shouldn't envy that.'

'But I do, Dad,' Andrew said, insistent. 'You're content, I'm not. You know about life, all I know is from books. Your life is here and you only want to stay here. I don't know where my life will lie. Wherever it is, it will not be as happy as yours.'

Bemused, Charlie shook his head. 'You think I'm content here, son? I stay because I'm no use anywhere else. Whereas you —'

Charlie tried to find the right words. With a sudden sense of surprise, fear and compassion, he realised that he was having a conversation with his youngest son about growing up and becoming who you're supposed to become. For some reason, this particular day had been chosen for a father to soothe his son's fears about leaving home and to tell him, 'Let go, son, let go of us and take your first step into your own self.' And Charlie realised he had to do it right, get it right, and give his son permission to take that step.

He took a deep breath. 'Son, what would disappoint me,' Charlie said with tenderness, 'is if you didn't go.' Oh shit, what was he saying? 'Of course you'll leave Waituhi,' he continued, his lips trembling because he loved this boy. 'No question about it. You've got no choice in the matter because you're different from us. We've always known it, son.' He saw the look of pain on Andrew's face: different. 'You've always liked books, classical music, learning for the sake of learning. Your mother used to ask me, "Where did Andrew get his brains from?" When you were a young boy you tried to hide your ambitions from us, but you can't any longer. So don't think you're the same as us, Andrew, because you're not. You've got a future that your mother, brothers and sisters and I haven't got, as a teacher, an accountant —'

'I want to be a lawyer, Dad.'

'A lawyer, eh?' Charlie asked, his voice breaking. 'Okay, son, don't you even dare to think of becoming anything less, of not claiming a place for yourself in the world. Your mother and I deserve better.'

It was a big speech for Charlie. It took a lot out of him and he was surprised at how emotional he felt. How often did a father tell a son to go for broke? Charlie was a man of few words, preferring to do rather than talk about it. 'You know what your problem is, son?' Charlie asked. 'You think too much.'

101

But Charlie realised there was one last point to make to Andrew. How could he do it? He remembered the ornamental tree at the back of the house. 'Come with me, son.'

The tree was in full bloom, its branches glowing with yellow flowers.

'You know, don't you,' Charlie began, 'that your afterbirth and birthcord are buried here?'

'Yes,' Andrew answered. At birth it was always the custom for the baby's caul and placenta to be buried in family ground. Maori believed that the caul, which was your spirit self, had special powers and that burying it where you were born would ensure you always had a special link with your place of birth.

'Never be worried about leaving home or losing your way,' Charlie said. 'Remember that you will always be attached to Waituhi through your birthcord. You will always belong. You will never be lost to us. No matter what any of us do in our lives, good or bad, if you are born a Maori you die a Maori. Your people will always come to collect you and bring you home.'

Even as Charlie said the words, he felt something kick him in the heart. Mouth dry, he turned to Andrew.

'As to your other question,' he said, 'yes, I've heard of Hamiora Pere. The matters surrounding him are not really in the past. None of that stuff about Te Kooti and what happened is in the past. Hamiora should never have been hanged. The Government demanded its pound of flesh for what had happened around here, and Hamiora was it. We don't know where he is buried. Perhaps, when you become a lawyer, you might be able to find out for us.'

There, it was out.

'Bring him home, son,' Charlie said.

PART THREE

Shout All Over Heaven

CHAPTER FIFTEEN

Te Whanau a Kai pana pana maro
Te Whanau a Kai; we never retreat

Who are we? Let me tell you.

Te Whanau a Kai is one of several tribes of Poverty Bay, on the East Coast of North Island. Rongowhakaata are to the southeast. Te Aitanga a Mahaki are in the northeast. To the southwest are Ngati Kahungunu. To the northwest are the Tuhoe. Ngati Porou, founded by the whale rider, Paikea, take possession of the coast around to the lands of Te Whanau a Apanui.

The traditional lands of Te Whanau a Kai include Patutahi/Kaimoe, Repongaere, Tangihanga, Okahuatiu No 1 and No 2, Wharekopae, Hihiroroa and the Te Wera and Koranga parts of Tahora No 2 block. Te Whanau a Kai land also includes Pouparae, Oariki, Kahunui and Tutoko, these being across the Waipaoa River. Within this huge area Te Whanau a Kai held numerous settlements, forts, meeting houses and graveyards, and within it are located numerous sacred sites and places of historical and cultural significance to the tribe.

Koraetaiao, the Waikakariki Valley, the Papokeka Stream and the northern banks of the Hangaroa River west to Waimaha, the Wharekopae Valley, the Ngutuera River in the vicinity of Houpapa and the Koranga Valley are traditional living areas of members of Te Whanau a Kai, Ngati Hine, Ngati Maru and Ngati Rua. Cultivations, fern grounds and eel weirs were located in and alongside these streams.

Lake Repongaere, the rich lands of the Whakaahu Stream as it flowed across the Kaimoe flats into Pipiwhakao and the swamps of Kaimoe were traditional food-gathering areas for eels, fish and the food of the bulrush shoots; Repongaere was once a swamp inhabited by a large man-eating eel which, when it was caught, swirled about and thrashed so much that it made the lake from its death throes. Sweet potatoes and native tubers were grown in the warmer eastern parts. Purahokongia was a tuber and potato nursery at Te Kowhai near present-day Ngatapa. The heavily forested areas of Tahora and Wharekopae and the lighter forest of Okahuatiu were traditional bird-hunting areas where all kinds of forest, grassland and swamp birds were caught, and also the Maori rat.

A site of particular significance for Te Whanau a Kai is Tokitoki. In ancient times, when Maori voyagers came on canoes to Aotearoa, they established sacred houses of learning so that the worship of the old Polynesian gods could continue. Such a house was established at Tokitoki, close to Patutahi on the Repongaere block. It prospered under a succession of powerful priests until the coming of the White man. Tupai, the father of Matenga Ruta and grandfather of Peka Kerekere, was the last priest. He destroyed Tokitoki when he became a Christian.

Ngatapa and Makaretu fortresses and battle sites are located in Te Whanau a Kai lands and feature in the Te Kooti Chronicles. Other fortresses and battle sites associated with Te Kooti are Te Pukepuke and Okare in the Waikakariki Valley and Parewarewa at the headwaters of the Waitieke Stream of the Ngutuera River. Ngatapa and Kaingaungau were Te Whanau a Kai's only fortified positions in olden times and our people would come to those places from the extent of our lands at Waimaha and the Koranga Forks at the head of the Waioeka River.

The history of Ngatapa settlement is interesting. In 1913 a piece of land was bequeathed to another great resistance leader, Rua Kenana, and his Tuhoe followers, by Heni Te Auraki of Pakowhai — the Tuhoe people have always been welcome to camp anywhere in our lands — but, in 1917, the people were transferred onto the Okahuatiu block where Ngatapa settlement now stands. The first house was built there by Eria Raukura and named Te Ao Aotearoa. The Tuhoe people of Ngatapa settlement are known as Te Whanau a Eria.

Tuhoe and Te Whanau a Kai have always been close: a regular point of entry for Tuhoe into our lands was Rua's Track from Maungapohatu, down the valley of the Hangaroa River through Waimaha and then either (1) along the watershed between the Wharekopae and Hangaroa catchments or (2) down the Wharekopae River. In the old days up to the 1930s Tuhoe horse teams of some forty strong would be spread out over a mile as they trekked into our lands. When the little kids saw Pakeha, they would kick their horses to catch up with the rest; never having seen White men in their lives, they didn't know what to make of them.

Mokonuiarangi is a block of property that was given as a place for anyone working the lands in the southwest parts of our territory. We also gave land to workers in the Hangaroa, Tahunga, Tangihau and Mokonuiarangi area around the time of the 1918 flu epidemic. Nobody currently lives at Mokonuiarangi.

How was the land confiscated? This is the story.

The impact of European settlement on Te Whanau a Kai was similar to that felt by other Maori tribes of Aotearoa; some of them suffered more grievously than we did. As for us, disease, casualties in the fights of the 1860s, and land loss through confiscation all took their toll on the numbers of people who identified themselves as Te Whanau a Kai claimants in the Land Court.

We resisted the White man, for who cannot answer the call of love of country, the song of the earth? Waituhi put itself on the side of the opposition by welcoming the first emissaries advising us to take up arms. We supported Te Kooti, the prophet, when he made a pre-emptive strike against the Pakeha at Matawhero. The Te Kooti followers paid for this military act when they were executed at Ngatapa fortress. They fought a desperate rearguard action against Pakeha pursuit. To escape it, Te Kooti found sanctuary among the Tuhoe people. But government troops followed him there and, between 1869 and 1872, the Tuhoe people felt the brunt of their wrath. Concerning land, it was estimated that 448,000 acres were confiscated from Tuhoe for their part in supporting the prophet. It is an irony that Te Kooti was later pardoned. He died on 17 April 1893. He had a number of successors, including Rua Kenana at Maungapohatu and Riripeti Mahana at Waituhi. Riripeti's great-grandfather, Wi Pere Halbert, told her, 'You will be the one to drive the Pakeha back to the sea.' She never did. Later came Chris Campbell, another messianic leader trying to fulfil millennial dreams of liberation. Those dreams are still dreamed, and some still await the return of the king.

The Pakeha exacted his retribution. It is true: the White man's peace is always more vicious than the White man's war. In June 1869, the Government took 20,337 acres from the people of Te Whanau a Kai, Te Aitanga a Mahaki and Rongowhakaata. It also took 56,161 acres from Te Whanau a Kai alone, including some 26,000 acres taken in error. Those tribes included in the retribution were angered at us for having been ardent supporters of resistance movements and blamed us for being at the centre and the cause of the matters that resulted in the confiscations of their land.

We have never forgiven the confiscations, or forgotten them. In 1878, Riperata Kahutia appeared in Parliament and, on behalf of all Poverty Bay tribes, prayed for the return of the land. Her prayer was rejected. Subsequent petitions were made by other claimants including Wi Pere Halbert. In 1919 the Government appointed a commission of inquiry into our grievances. In 1923 Heni Materoa, daughter of Riperata, represented Rongowhakaata in a hearing of the claim. In 1938 three representatives of Rongowhakaata again petitioned the Government. The Promised Land they variously sought in the past is no different to the Promised Land we are seeking now.

In these latter days, the claim of Te Whanau a Kai is what it always was. We seek reparation for:

1. The Crown's military actions in Gisborne, including the attack on Waerenga a Hika, transportation of members of Te Whanau a Kai to the Chatham Islands, and the executions at Ngatapa.
2. The execution of Hamiora Pere at Wellington in 1869.
3. The confiscation of the Patutahi block by the Crown. In the massive land grab that followed the end of the Te Kooti Wars, Whanau a Kai were among the losers with 57,000 acres taken at Patutahi.
4. The failure of the various commissions and inquiries into Patutahi to provide effective and fair redress for Te Whanau a Kai.
5. The effects of the Native Land Court, Validation Court and Crown purchasing on Te Whanau a Kai interests in Hangaroa–Matawai, Wharekopae, Okahuatiu, Tahora and other blocks.
6. The effects of the East Coast Trust on Te Whanau a Kai.

7. Along with other claimant groups, Te Whanau a Kai has also raised issues relating to the social and economic effects on us of Crown policies in relation to the lands and waters of Gisborne, and the foreshore between.

All peoples have a right to their own nationality. A Maori is a person who has Maori blood, wants to claim Maori ancestry and follow a Maori path. That is our birthright. All nations have the right to their own identity and sovereignty. It is their birthright.

These are the tenets held firm by the survivors. The challenge we make is for all to accept the self-determination we will place on our own destiny.

Te Whanau a Kai are a people who never retreat.

CHAPTER SIXTEEN

—— 1 ——

Midday. Heat waves shimmered across Gisborne city. The sun was at its apex between morning and afternoon.

George drove the car up to the petrol pump. Hayley was sitting next to him. They'd been arguing all morning about whether or not she would go out with him to Waituhi to see the Matua — and she won.

'How much petrol, mate?' the attendant asked. The driver looked familiar. Picture in the paper. The Maori rugby league player, that was him.

'Fill it up,' George answered. 'Check the oil too, thanks.' The garage attendant nodded. He smiled at Hayley but got nothing back in return. He remembered reading somewhere about George and Hayley getting married. Last night, was it? If so, trouble was already brewing in paradise. None of his business though.

George saw a NO SMOKING sign near the petrol pump. He flipped a cigarette from the pack and lit it. 'Rules were made to be broken,' he said, trying to make a joke. Hayley wasn't having any. She was really off her rag.

'That's always been the trouble with you,' Hayley answered. 'The rest of us play by the rules but you don't. You think you can get away with anything. Be careful of what you wish for, George, that's all I'm going to say.'

'Wish for?' George asked. 'Honey, don't be this way.' Hayley was being such a prima donna. 'If you want to come out to Waituhi with me, come. If you don't, go back to the motel and wait for me. Watch some television. Sweetheart?'

Hayley was cross that they were going out to Waituhi. Ever since coming to New Zealand to get married, George's tribe had taken him over. Her father had warned her about it but she hadn't taken any notice until now. 'Being Maori always comes first with our people,' Dad said. 'Once a Maori, always a Maori. That's why I came to Australia. I couldn't hack it.'

'So you don't want me to come with you, is that it?' Hayley answered. 'Well, maybe I shouldn't.' She got out the door and slammed it.

'Honey,' George groaned. Hayley was so volatile. First she was coming and now she was not coming. 'You're making such a big thing of this,' he said. 'All I'm going to do is go out there, talk to Miro and find out what she wants.' He shrugged his shoulders helplessly. He knew Hayley wanted him to talk her into getting back into the car but it would really be better if she didn't come with him. He pressed on before she could have the option. 'All right, babe,' he sighed, as if he was disappointed. 'If you want to stay, stay. I'll be back as soon as I can. Before you know it we'll be on the plane to Auckland and home to Australia.'

'Okay,' Hayley said. George couldn't even hide the relief on his face. 'Do what you have to. While you're away I'll pack and wait for you.' With that she bent to give him an angry peck. George held her tight and turned the kiss into something that held a promise.

'I won't be long, honey, truly I won't. Trust me.' He wanted to find out from Mattie what the hell she was doing in Waituhi. It was better if he did it alone.

The garage attendant returned. He frowned when he saw George smoking but let it go. 'That'll be forty bucks, mate,' he said. Hayley was walking back to the motel. 'Trouble with the wife?'

'Nothing I can't handle,' George answered. He gunned the motor, turned the car on the highway out of town and headed for Waituhi.

The heat waves shimmering, shimmering.

In Waituhi, down in the trees around the Pouarua Stream, a hole appeared in the air and, out of it, the owl came flying.

The owl's young chicks were ravenous. Although the owl was nocturnal and reluctant to leave its chicks, it had been forced out into the daylight to hunt and return with food: large moths, flying beetles, small birds, mice, rats, lizards, anything. Parched by the heat, the owl swooped down to the stream to drink. Sated, it set off. Its cryptic colours were so reflective of the shadow and light that its flight through the trees registered only as a blur of sun. Nor would you have heard it: soft feathers along the edge of its wings muted its passage through the air to a low-decibel *swish*. Reaching the edge of the trees, the owl came silently to rest on a branch overlooking the paddock where Rongo Mahana was standing, stretching his aching back.

'Time for lunch,' Rongo said. His sister, Teria, lived close by and he decided he would make a nuisance of himself by going over and having lunch with her.

Perfectly camouflaged, the owl watched Rongo as he stepped into his pick-up truck and drove toward the road. The owl had exceptional hearing. Discs around its eyes channelled sound to its large ears. As the truck roared away, the owl heard something else. Tracking the sound, its neck turned 270 degrees. It saw a small field mouse, attracted by Rongo's digging, come out of its hole in the field to investigate any potato shards he had left behind.

Launching quickly, a grey shadow low across the landscape, the owl was on the mouse before it even knew it was there. It pounced, and the mouse gave a small squeal of terror as powerful claws dug into its back and lifted it into the air. Still wriggling, it found itself in a nest where the owl's young were waiting. The owl struck the mouse again and again, tearing it to pieces, blood on its beak, and began to distribute the pieces to its chicks.

Mattie stirred in her sleep. Something was pecking at her dreams. At first the pecks were harmless, but then they began to hurt. Really hurt. The binocular eyes of an owl filled her vision, and, next minute it wasn't just jabbing at her dreams. It struck again and again, shredding the dreams apart in an effort to get at her. She twisted away and was falling.

'God, what time is it?' Mattie asked herself. She was in some twilight world made of two parts alcoholic haze and one part sleeplessness. Her throat was parched and raw. She needed a drink of water. Stumbling out of bed, she went to the bathroom, turned on the tap and began to gulp the water down. She drank as if her life depended on it. When she had drunk enough she wiped her lips and, with antagonism, stared in the mirror over the basin. 'Yup, that's you all right,' she said to her image. Battle-scarred veteran of life. Wearing every fight she had ever had with life like a bruise, a cut, a wound, so that everybody would know she was not to be messed with. What you saw was what you got. Not for her the cosmetics of civilised behaviour and educated conduct. Unvarnished, ungilded, everything about her had been pared down by a whittler's knife to pure rage and anger. All that was left was a skull with the screams all trapped inside.

Mattie saluted her image and went back to the bedroom. She was halfway through the sitting-room when, all of a sudden, she looked around her and began to laugh and laugh and laugh. God had played a huge trick on her. He was making her pay for all her sins by keeping her here. She'd be better off in hell.

With grim humour, Mattie looked at what her life had come down to. Three years of a living death in a godforsaken village called Waituhi, at the beck and call of a bitch called Miro Mananui. And that old woman was making her pay. Forcing her to live in this old house that everybody called 'Miro's Museum' because it housed all the treasures of the village: a place of dead things, of artefacts that once belonged to dead people. 'You are my bondswoman,' Miro had once said to her. 'As Sarah did with Hagar, I have taken you into my house, and you will serve me and my husband and do your allotted time with us.'

'What better place could there be for me,' Mattie laughed, 'than here in a house where dead things reside?' Here in the sitting-room was all the village's history, genealogy sheets, names upon names of the dead joined by horizontal and vertical lines, mapping out blood connections as if all that stuff really mattered. Near the window were feather boxes, carved figurines, rippling feather and dog's-hair cloaks, traditional costumes, objects inventorised from a cultural past that nobody any longer valued.

Near the opposite doorway was a big oval photograph, coloured by an artist long ago, of a young woman with a tattoo on her chin; Miro's grandmother and, in her time, Matua. Above the fireplace was the cloak Miro's grandmother was wearing, its feathers dusty and fading. To what purpose were they displayed? In glass cases on the other side of the room were silver trophies and shields, big and small, all shapes and sizes, gleaming in the dim light. All commemorated the times when Waituhi had sent teams around the country to compete in Maori cultural and sports tournaments. All was vanity, vanity. All vainglory. On a side table was the ledger book in which Miro and Tama had been updating the evidence they hoped one day would form the basis of yet another claim for the return of land and reparations for what had happened to Waituhi during the Land Wars. Justice, Justice, *Justizia!*

Why bother? What a cosmic joke. Who were Maori to think that they were owed something for their mere existence, as if somebody kept a record of winnings and losses? Compared to the Egyptians, the Assyrians, the kingdom of the Abyssinian tribes owing allegiance to the Queen of Sheba herself, all of whom had succumbed to desert and desolation, who were Maori but some pathetic tribe lost at the bottom of the world? Cultural memory could only lead to hopeless expectations. Culture was only a cul de sac, a place you escaped to when there was no place else to go.

'I should have got away from you ages ago,' Mattie said to the room.

She heard a noise outside. The Matua and Tama had arrived back from Arapeta's. Tama parked the car and Miro came up the path. She was the last person Mattie wanted to see. These days Mattie tried to avoid her altogether; they were always at each other's throats. Why buy another fight?

It was too late to escape. The door opened, Miro came in, and Mattie turned square on, facing her.

Sometimes, when one person intersects with another, there are all kinds of collisions. Miro was not to know that Mattie was at the depths of Te Kore, The Void, filled with self-loathing and hatred. All she saw was that Mattie was drunk, belligerent, coming out of her corner, and the bell for the next round hadn't rung yet. As for Mattie, she was not to know that Miro's soul was tired — and that the Matua was set on a course of action with George Karepa which depended on Mattie's obedience.

114

'So you're up, are you?' Miro asked. 'When are you going to clean up your act, eh, missy?' She gave Mattie a look of disgust. 'Drunk all day and all night. Sleeping God knows where.'

'What I do in my own time is my own business,' Mattie flared.

'Not when you live in my house, it isn't,' Miro answered.

Tama entered the room. He tried to intervene. 'Mattie, leave us. Matua, you have more important work to do than argue with the girl.'

The Matua gave him a look. 'Don't interfere, husband.' She turned to Mattie. 'You better clean yourself up and get dressed. An old boyfriend of yours is coming out to see us.' It was said meanly and viciously, and Mattie recoiled at the words. Immediately she reacted.

'What do you want me around for? Do your own dirty work.' Mattie turned on her heels, ready to return to her bedroom, to get dressed and get away.

That was when Miro attacked. She moved surprisingly fast for an old woman, rushing through the room, telling the air to move aside and let her through. 'You dare to turn your back on me, you, a Gentile, and therefore below me,' she said. She grabbed Mattie by the hair and pulled.

With a cry, Mattie fell to the floor. Before she knew what was happening, Miro was dragging her screaming through the doorway out into the sunlight. Tama tried to stop Miro but she brushed him aside. 'Get out of the way, husband,' she said.

Mattie's scalp was on fire with the pain.

'Three years I've invested in you,' Miro seethed. 'I brought you into my house, I cared for you while you had your child, I looked after you both, and today I will have payment.'

So much violence was in the attack. Watching, Tama was reminded of the Matua during traditional meetings. You crossed her at your peril. In that public domain, she was ruthless enough. Try to stop her, belittle her or turn your back on her and she attacked. In the private domain, the same ruthless strategy prevailed. Attack was the only way she knew how to defend herself. When she attacked, she possessed extraordinary reserves of mental and physical strength — of intelligence, rather, for the Matua's ruthlessness did not come from some uncontrollable passion. It came from the need to always maintain the control, no matter the situation. Lose it and Miro would cease to be Matua. *Matua tu, Matua ora, Matua noho, Matua mate*; if you want to live, stand, if you want to die, lie down. All that Miro ever knew about was standing. It was as if that was the only stance she could take in the world, as if her fate and the fate of all who lived in her world depended on her. There was always some agenda, some purpose, motivating her ruthlessness. Attack her, place the fate of even one of her people at risk, and she never retreated.

Miro threw Mattie against the outside pump. She held her there and, panting with exertion, worked the handle. The water from the deep underground spring rushed up and out — and Mattie gasped, flailed, trying to get away from the rushing water. Miro kept her head under. 'Sober up, Mattie,' Miro hissed between clenched teeth. 'I'm sick of you always feeling so sorry for yourself. Time to get over it.'

Mattie crumpled, sobbing. Miro left her there and went back into the house, brushing Tama aside as if he was of no consequence. His eyes were filled with rebuke. Hers were still filled with murder.

'You shouldn't have done that, Matua,' he said.

'She didn't mean it,' Tama said.

He went out to Mattie and, kneeling, brushed her hair from her face. He had a towel in his hand. He wiped the water from her eyes and wrapped the towel around her.

'Yes, she meant it,' Mattie said with a sigh. 'And I deserved it.'

Tama saw the Matua had exerted her power, succeeded in imposing it, and brought Mattie to heel. Indeed, Mattie looked at him alarmed. 'I don't want to get you into trouble,' she said. 'You'd better go in to the Matua. I'll be all right. Just leave me for a moment. Then I'll come in and —' Mattie shrugged her shoulders in an ironic gesture '— do as I'm told, I guess.'

Mattie pulled the towel close to her. She was aware that her slip was clinging to her body, showing her dark nipples and her pubic hair. Although Tama was old enough to be her father and the feelings she had for him were those of respect for an older generation, he was still, for all that, a man.

Tama and Mattie were silent. Mindful of her modesty, Tama averted his gaze from her and looked across the landscape. To the west were the hills which separated Te Whanau a Kai from Tuhoe and the People of the Mist. Maybe it was because Tama and Mattie were both outsiders

— Tama from Tuhoe and Mattie from the South Island — and because he needed to find some way of healing the brutality of the moment, that Tama felt compelled to try to explain about Miro, the Matua, the woman whose life he shared as her husband.

'The Matua was thirty-seven when I first saw her,' he began. 'I was a young man, coming on to my seventeenth birthday, and there was a Ringatu celebration, which was being held in Ruatahuna, which is where I'm from. I was in the concert group welcoming the guests to the celebrations. They came from all over: Rotorua, Whakatane, Ohiwa, Te Kaha, Ruatoria, Waituhi, everywhere. I was in the front row, and people say I was handsome in those days. I must have been, for them to comment on it.'

The words were said with embarrassment and self-deprecation. Mattie looked at the old man and, this time, through his years. Yes, he must surely have stood out from the crowd. Tall. Muscular. A smile that brightened the world. The sun happily finding home in him.

'As for the Matua,' Tama continued, 'the trouble was that before she arrived she had already become a figure of fun. She had a nickname, Te Ngarara, The Beast. It was a cruel name to give her, the kind of nickname that fell easily to everyone's lips because the Matua has never been redeemed by beauty. My people of the Ruatahuna Valley sometimes have too ready a wit. Even though their perceptions were correct, over the years those bold enough to refer to the Matua's appearance in my hearing have had to answer to me. I have always protected the Matua's honour.

'What happened to make the Matua even more a figure of fun was that the word got around that not only was she coming to enjoy the celebrations, she was also looking for a husband — and our elders had agreed to honour her request. This is difficult to explain, today, when such things do not happen, but marriages were sometimes contracted between the various tribes for political purposes. They were known as *taumau*, matrimonial contracts. Riripeti, whom some called the Matriarch, was subject to such a marriage when she married Ihaka. In the case of Miro and myself, because Te Whanau a Kai had given some land at Ngatapa to Tuhoe — my people later shifted to the Okahuatiu block — my elders said, 'Yes, in exchange for the great gift of your ancestral land to us, we will allow you to find a sire for your dame.' It was known that the Matua was concerned that she was already moving beyond her child-bearing years and sought lively sperm among the Tuhoe. Our men have always been regarded highly as breeding stock but unfortunately, when the Matua and I got together, my sperm, although they jumped high, were unable to find the fertile pond in the Matua for it had already dried up. I would dearly have wanted to give her a son, and it was not for want of trying.'

Tama gave a slight cough to hide his embarrassment about talking at such a personal level about such matters. Mattie tried to soothe him, saying, 'I'm humbled that you would share such a confidence with me.' She was moved by the antiquated yet dignified manner in which he expressed himself. He said it plainly. He said it without varnish. It came without boastfulness.

'Well, the Matua came and went,' Tama said. 'A number of potential suitors presented themselves. Two were widowers as old as she was, with grown-up children to prove that their seed had not been damaged by the Te Kooti Wars or by the troubles over Rua Kenana, our own prophet of Tuhoe. A few other applicants, again of her age, were presented to her at a dance in honour of all the visitors to Ruatahuna.'

It was not done openly, of course, this series of introductions of possible stallions so that the rich mare could sniff them and see if they were to her liking; everyone at the dance pretended it was not happening. Miro was dressed in blue satin with white gloves and white shoes. She saw some younger, lovely girls giggling behind their cupped hands. She heard one of them say, in mocking tones, 'Oh, she dresses so beautifully to take the attention away from her looks, which are unfortunate, but see, she has such beautiful, tiny feet.' Very soon she heard the comment echoing around her, *But she has such beautiful, tiny feet, beautiful feet, tiny beautiful feet tiny.*

'The Matua is strong and fearless, but she is not without feelings,' Tama continued. 'I could see that she was embarrassed and humiliated. I was with my girlfriend, Rawinia. It was actually Rawinia who had made the remark about the tiny feet. I felt so sorry for the Matua that I couldn't help myself. I winked at her.'

It was such a small gesture but Miro noticed it, like a star, twinkling. She saw the boy from whom it had come. She remembered him.

'After the dance and all the other festivities,' Tama said, 'I went up the back of Maungapohatu with my brothers, where we had a forestry contract. I never gave another thought to the Matua and, anyway, Rawinia was my girlfriend. Apart from which, the age difference was so great that I never in my wildest dreams would have looked the Matua's way. While I was there, one of my elders arrived on his horse. "Boy oh boy," he said, "I'm saddle-sore from riding to find you." He got off his horse and at least he had the courtesy of looking embarrassed about what he was going to say to me —'

'She's chosen you,' the elder said. 'After the dance, she made inquiries about you. She doesn't want any of those old men. You are the one she wants.'

'I was the price to be paid for the covenant between our peoples,' Tama said. 'I tried to get out of it. I was beside myself, and Rawinia was distraught. "Let the Beast find somebody else. Let her take somebody else's man," she screamed. Rawinia divined something evil in the way the Matua had made her choice. "She's getting back at me," she said, "for mocking her about her tiny feet."

'My life really wasn't my own,' Tama continued. 'The elders reminded me of Tuhoe's obligations to Te Whanau a Kai. What could I do? I had the hard word put on me. Even my parents argued with me, saying I should agree to it. In the end, everybody wore me down. I felt I had no choice, no other option, except to say yes. I sacrificed my personal feelings. I sacrificed myself. I came down from Maungapohatu and the next time I saw the Matua was at our wedding.'

As befitting a woman of Miro's tribal status the wedding was large and visitors came from throughout Tuhoe, Turanga, the Bay of Plenty and Waikato. Tama was waiting at the Ringatu church, terror-stricken and sweating, his eyes starting out of his face. Everywhere around him, all he could see were the mocking grins of the wedding guests. They were laughing at him. Making the entire wedding a farce. They had only come because it was the comedy of the year, this unnatural coupling, this obscenity, this indecency. 'I can't go through with it,' Tama whispered to his best man. 'She's so old, I don't even know anything about her, and she is not attractive to me.'

It was too late. Miro came into the church.

'Hori Gage officiated at our wedding,' Tama said. 'I turned and saw the Matua coming up the aisle. She was heavily veiled, clothing herself in the semblance of virginity and innocent youthful beauty. I couldn't see her face or her body. Only her dark shape beneath her wedding veils. But I would have recognised her tiny feet anywhere.'

Such beautiful tiny feet. Beautiful. Tiny. Such.

The memory, after all these years, was still so intense that Tama had to try to hide his emotions from Mattie. His eyes brimmed, his lips quivered. Blindly, he looked around for something to do, something to mask his feelings and enable him to recover. He took a corner of Mattie's towel, dipped it in water, and began to wash her feet with it. The touch was cool, soothing.

The Matua had been compassionate. After the wedding, knowing how upset Tama was, she said to him, 'Although this is our wedding night, I will allow you to say farewell to your childhood sweetheart. Go to Rawinia, I bear her no bad will but, come the dawn, I will be waiting for you and we will begin our lives together.'

'Of course, it wasn't as easy as that,' Tama said, remembering. He and Miro left Ruatahuna the next day to travel to Waituhi where he was put on display as the young stud come to bring Miro to foal. Homesick, despairing, he couldn't consummate the marriage and, although they slept in a matrimonial bed, no blood appeared on the sheets. Three weeks later, Miro took control. 'You are a fool, Tama Mananui. I know you think I am too old for you and I know that because I am called The Beast and because you are so beautiful, people mock us with the nickname, Beauty and the Beast. But I chose you to be my husband because you had the audacity to wink at me — and I thought that you saw beyond my appearance. I see I was wrong. I say again, you are a fool, Tama Mananui, because whether or not I am beautiful is not the point. The point is that I will love you and care for you and give you a life that has a greater purpose to it than anything you have ever dreamed of. At the end of it you will know you have truly lived, truly been given a life and been able to give something back to the tribe. But if you want to go and live a life without courage, selfishly squandering the gifts that God gave you, go to your girlfriend or to any of those young women who would gladly put their slippers in front of your door. Go. I want a man, not a boy. Courage, not cowardice. Go if you wish, be happy in your dull life, and live it meaninglessly.'

'She gambled,' Tama said, 'but you know the Matua, she's always been good at cards. She stacked the deck by reminding me that our union had a larger purpose. She also made me believe that I was being given a choice. I decided to stay with her and, well, we came together —'

Delicacy and fastidiousness marked his choice of words, but what occurred shocked both of them. Entry was difficult. Miro was a virgin with a stubborn hymen which, after years of protecting her, would not give up its long-held duty at its gates. Once opened, however, both found themselves captive to lust, passion and anger.

'Since then,' Tama continued, 'we have grown together.' He wiped Mattie's feet with the towel, drying between the toes. He looked Mattie in the eyes. 'You understand about her now?'

'Understand?' Mattie answered, unsure.

'The Matua is not a person who stands by and lets life happen. She makes it happen. I have learnt to trust that she knows what she's doing — as should you — even though, sometimes, she is so difficult to love.'

Love, ah yes. Tama's girlfriend, Rawinia, straight after their last night together, went to the river and drowned herself.

Miro watched Tama and Mattie from the window. In the sunlight, Tama was washing Mattie's feet as if she was Mary Magdalene or the Woman of Samarra. They looked like lovers. Miro felt a twinge of jealousy, of sadness and regret. When Tama came back into the house she confronted him. Sometimes when one person intersects with another —

'You spend too much time with her,' Miro said. 'Don't take sides. This is just between me and her, husband.'

'Will you cast the first stone?' Tama gave Miro a look that pierced her heart. 'You yourself are not without blame, Matua,' he said.

CHAPTER SEVENTEEN

—— 1 ——

'More sheep!'

It was hot and stifling in the shearing shed at Mairangi Station. Six shearers were at work, skilfully guiding their handpieces through the sheep's wool. The sweat was dripping off Pita Mahana's face as he finished off the penultimate sheep in his pen. He gave the sheep a firm push on its rump and it slid down the ramp. When he stood up he stretched for his towel and wiped his face. Only one more sheep to go and he'd be finished. He looked across at Miriama where she was supervising the women trimming the fleeces. Wayne's women were slack and not taking enough of the neck and skirt wool off the fleeces. Miriama was diplomatic, doing the job herself in her usual unobtrusive way before allowing it to be passed. Already she was teaching Ani Jackson the finer points of wool classing. Pita noticed that Miriama was favouring her left arm. Whenever she extended her shoulders she winced, bent over, and put both hands to her chest. She saw that he was looking and straightened up as if nothing was wrong.

Not far from the table was the wool press. Waka was jacking the press. Every now and then he would grin at Ani. 'Well,' Pita thought, 'time for Waka to graduate from wool presser to shearer. Now that he's getting married, he needs to start making better money.' Waka would be over the moon with the news. He'd been wanting to get onto the shearers' stand all season.

Shaking his head, Pita went into his pen for his last sheep. Once Waka became a shearer he would be a shearer all his life — and while Pita was proud that his son would join him, another part of him was angry that Waka would end up like his father with nothing else ahead of him except another sheep, another shearing shed, another shearing season.

Pita came out of his pen with his sheep. His cousin, Wayne, was shearing next to him. 'I really appreciate your help,' Wayne said. 'I didn't think we'd cut out Mairangi so quickly. Once we've finished these sheep, we're home free.'

'Don't think I'm doing this for nothing,' Pita joked. 'I'm expecting triple pay for working on the Lord's day.'

'Funny you should say that,' Wayne answered. His handpiece was racing. He and Pita were neck and neck, blow to blow. 'The Lord's asked me to give your pay straight over to him.'

'Oh has he now?' Pita asked. 'Tell you what. If I finish this sheep before you finish yours, let's leave the middle man out.'

'You're on,' Wayne laughed. Sensing the competition, the other shearers joined in. Very soon Miriama, Ani, the other fleece workers, Waka and the shepherd were barracking: 'Go, go, *go*.' Pita's handpiece was skimming the sheep like a metallic bird and, luckily, the sheep wasn't giving any trouble. Unlike Wayne's sheep, which gave a sudden kick, startling him, and wriggled out of his grasp. The sheep ran amok down the stand.

'Sorry, Lord,' Pita said, looking to heaven. 'You lost.'

With a cheer the shearing was over. Pita cleared his stand, put his clippers away and began to clean his cutters. He noticed Miriama wincing again and gave her a questioning glance. 'Didn't I tell you, darling?' she pretended, rolling her eyes. 'I'm pregnant.' As if. She'd had her tubes tied last year.

Pita laughed and hugged her. 'By the way,' he said, trying to be casual, 'when we get back to Waituhi, would you mind if we went to see Tamati Kota again?'

'Oh, no,' Miriama answered. 'Ever since we saw the old man this morning, I just knew you wouldn't be able to leave well alone. You had your choice to have him come and live with us. You let it go. All you Mahanas had the choice. When Riripeti died, and he told you all that she had chosen her grandson, Tamatea, to be her successor, did you take his side? No you didn't. Instead, you let your father, Ihaka, take

Tamatea's place. Then you discovered that Riripeti in her will had left Tamati Kota the homestead. No matter that he told you he was keeping it in trust for Tamatea, did you honour her wishes? No, you took a court case against the will. Well the Mahanas lost that case and you've only yourselves to blame for the misfortunes that have ever since dogged your family. Don't forget, either, that Annie's a Kota. It was only right that when she applied to be the old man's caregiver, the court agreed to it.'

At the mention of their names, Pita gave Miriama a grim look. *Nesting like starlings where hawks had once resided.* 'We may have turned our back on Tamati Kota, yes,' he said, conscience gnawing at him, 'but I didn't like what I saw today when we went to the homestead, and the more I think about it, the less I like it. Although Annie might have the law on her side, she and Kepa are not the right people to look after him.'

------- 2 -------

Teria Mahana, sister to Rongo Mahana, stood at the front door of her house. Where the heck were her kids? She shaded her eyes against the sun and saw that they were near Pakowhai meeting house pestering Samson, the old bag-of-bones nag that Maka tiko bum liked to call a horse. Maka had owned that horse for years; she had a sentimental attachment to Samson and wouldn't send him to the knacker's yard to be slaughtered and made into dog tucker.

'What are those kids doing to Samson?' Teria asked herself. Oh no, August was leading him and the other six were riding; no wonder Samson had developed a sag in the middle and his legs were bowed. 'Time to go to the rescue,' Teria said. She breathed deep, expelled and boomed her voice across to them. 'Lunchtime! Come and get it!' It was a big voice which suited this big woman.

The children looked at each other. 'Big Mama's calling, fellas,' August said.

Teria's voice boomed out again like a cannon. 'I said come and get it and if you kids don't come you sure will get it from me.'

The children moaned to one another. Big Mama was always spoiling their fun. 'Better do as your mother says,' August said.

'What do you mean our mother?' June answered. 'She's your mother too.'

Like August, his sister and brother, June and July, had been named after the months in which they were born. The twin boys were Anzac and Crete because two uncles had died there in the Second World War. The two youngest were Daisy and Hope; and Hope declared Teria's hope that she wouldn't have any more children. Seven was enough, thank you very much. Not that Mo-Crack would get much chance at making an eighth, seeing that he was in prison on a drug charge.

The seven children were very similar in appearance. What else would you expect? They'd been mass-produced, following each other so quick and fast that there wasn't time for Teria to give them any individuality in the mix. June, July and August were born one every year, give or take a few months. A gap of two years marked the length of time that Mo-Crack was inside for his first prison sentence (his current incarceration was for his second) but he made up for lost time when he got out — and the twins, Anzac and Crete, arrived. Daisy and Hope followed soon after them. Teria's doctor had told her to call it quits.

'Don't talk to me,' Teria said. 'No sooner do I get out of Maternity than Mo-Crack has me flat on my back again.' She hoped Mo-Crack would take the hint with Hope.

The kids raced to the house. Across the paddock, over the fence and through a flock of grazing sheep they ran, yelling war cries Indian-style that would have scared any mother to death. Teria braced herself to meet them and planted her body firmly across the back door. The screaming and yelling grew louder as the children closed in, ready to scalp her. They burst into the back yard like wild horses.

'Whoa there,' Teria boomed. Stamping and whinnying, the children crashed to a halt. Teria waited for the commotion to die down. Well, whaddya know, they were under control. She gave an angry thought to Mo-Crack; if ever he went to prison again, she was going to plead to the judge that she go there for a holiday and he spend the time raising the kids.

Teria tried to find humour in the situation, but it was no laughing matter. To be frank, it was better for Mo-Crack to be in prison rather than out where he could slap her around and abuse the kids. She was sick and tired of hiding the bruises, nose bleeds, cracked ribs, hurt breasts where he'd twisted so hard — all the items in the usual Battered Wives Catalogue. The downside, though, was being forced into the role of

Maori trash, somebody whose social highlight was to go into Gisborne every week and suck up to some bitch at Social Welfare for some extra dollars. What other option did she have? She was yet another Maori solo mother trying to make sure her kids grew up with clothes on their backs and food in their mouths, so that her kids would escape the cycle of violence and deprivation. If she had to grovel for every dollar, she would grovel.

'No, no, no,' Teria thought, 'I will not feel sorry for myself.' She watched her children seat themselves for lunch — if that's what you called leftover sausages, peas and spud with bread to slop up the gravy. She saw them putting on brave faces, knowing Mum was doing her best, and she was so proud that her children were bloody good kids, and looked after each other — and her. Look at how brave August had been, trying to stop Mo-Crack the last time he had given Teria a fist sandwich. High on marijuana, Mo-Crack came home thinking he was at the gym and his wife was the punching bag. 'Get out of here, August,' Teria yelled, 'and take your brothers and sisters over to the Matua's place.' Instead, August launched himself at his dad and got the same walloping as his mother. The rest of the week, Mrs Perfect Mother kept August home so the local school wouldn't come around to find out where he got his black eyes from. Teria realised she had to turn her life around, but how, oh God, how?

She heard a horn beeping, and saw Rongo turning in at her driveway. 'Your uncle's here,' she said to the kids, but they had already heard the truck, and went rushing out.

'*Kia ora*, Uncle,' August said.

'Hello, boy,' Rongo answered. He was up on the truck, sorting through the sacks of potatoes, marrows, cucumbers — and was that watermelon? 'You and your brothers take this food inside.'

'Brother, you shouldn't have,' Teria said. She was elated, relieved and happy all at the same time. Already, Daisy was saying, 'Can we have some watermelon now, Mum?'

Laughing, Rongo said, 'Sure you can.'

Teria couldn't help laughing too, because it was so good to see the kids laughing. Then she remembered, 'Oh, brother, today was harvest time. I'm so sorry —' She was suddenly ashamed. She didn't deserve this food. She had not been at the planting and neither had she been at the harvest. She wanted to shout at the kids and say to them, 'Put the food back on your uncle's truck.' But she couldn't say that, not with seven mouths to feed, not with seven lives to look after. Instead, she swallowed her pride, kissed Rongo and said, 'We were just about to have lunch. Come inside, brother, and eat with us.' She put another plate on the table. 'All right, Daisy,' she said. 'Your turn to say grace.'

'Our Father which art in Heaven,' Daisy began.

June kicked her under the table. 'Grace, stupid.'

'LordblessthisfoodAmen,' Daisy said.

Everyone tucked in. But, as usual, Mrs Perfect Mother watched and didn't eat because she had become used to making sure the kids ate and, if there were any leftover scraps, guess who was a lucky mummy.

She couldn't help it. All of a sudden, Teria was bawling her eyes out. Weeping a river. Crying a sea. The children didn't know what to do. They sat there, eyes looking down, because whatever it was that Big Mama was feeling, it was all their fault. They knew they were a burden and they tried to like the food she could afford to put in front of them. They never asked Mum for new clothes or toys or all those things other kids had. They were quiet when she wanted a sleep. They tried, they really tried.

'August, you and your brothers and sisters finish your lunch,' Rongo said. 'Your mother and I are going to take a walk.' He put his arms around Teria's shoulders and held her tight. Across the land they walked to willow trees overlooking a stream.

'Brother, how did I get myself into this mess?' Teria wept. 'You and I grew up with a mother in the house, a father in the house, and what have my children got? One parent. When you and I went to bed, we went with full tummies because we were fed, but can I guarantee the same to my children? No, because the breadwinner's a jailbird and I have to depend on a benefit cheque. You and I and the rest of us children, we could sleep and feel safe in the house. What do I do? I spend my nights wondering whether one of Mo-Crack's mates will turn up and kick the door in looking for some drugs or cash that he thinks Mo-Crack stashed away before he got caught by the cops. Or whether some bastard will come creeping through the window and molest one of my daughters while I'm sleeping in the next room.'

Rongo held Teria tight. He didn't know what to say. He listened to the willows whispering their eternal truths and the stream trickling over its stony bed.

'Times were different then,' Rongo answered, struggling to find his own answers. 'God was a guest in our house. He blessed us with love, good health and strength.'

Teria was persistent. 'It's more than that, brother, much more than that. What happened to us? It wasn't supposed to end up this way.'

What happened? Rongo Mahana felt the question kick him in the solar plexus. Oh sis, what answer do you want? Life happened. The Pakeha happened. After the Land Wars and the Te Kooti Wars, the land was confiscated and the Maori as an automatic underclass happened. The great Maori parliamentarians saw it happening — Wi Pere, Apirana Ngata, Te Rangi Hiroa, Maui Pomare — and tried to stop the land confiscations and to get government policies working for Maori rural development. At the tribal level, leaders like Te Puea Herangi, Wi Ratana and Riripeti worked hand in hand to maintain the infrastructural framework of family and tribe by advocating Maori independence: political, economic and cultural sovereignty. But did New Zealand want that? Don't kid yourself.

You ask what *happened*, sis? History happened. The twentieth century happened. The Making of Bicultural New Zealand happened: let's get Maori working with Pakeha and, oh yes, why don't we help them to Be Pakeha. If we assimilate them, integrate them, *voilà*, we won't have any Maori to worry about any more and we'll all have benefited by becoming caramello. The First World War happened and the 1918 flu epidemic that decimated the people. In one fell swoop, a whole generation of leaders went to their graves. The Depression happened. Do you think that Maori, because they were able to fish and grow potatoes and other crops, were not affected by the Depression? Think again, sis.

What happened? The Second World War happened. After the Second World War the rural-to-urban migration began to happen. Guess who started going to the cities, and why? Where else do you go when you have no land? Working for the Pakeha happened. Know any Maori millionaires, sis? Know any Maori who own their own business? And now, who was the great underclass in Auckland and Wellington? And who stayed behind on the broken-biscuit pieces of land that are left? You, Teria, me, and all of us happy-go-lucky, gosh-we're-such-good-singers workers, trying to get by on occasional work as scrubcutters, shearers and posthole diggers. But for how much longer? Even living in Waituhi is becoming difficult. New zoning laws mean we can't build on less than ten acres. When some of the old houses burn down, they can't be rebuilt. And when your house is condemned, Teria, you'll be driven out, forced out onto — don't laugh, sis — a quarter-acre section in the city. If you're finding life difficult here, how are you going to find it there?

And then there's the matter of not being obedient to Riripeti's wishes. Did we bring this upon ourselves, sis? This decline of the family's fortunes that people called the curse, the misfortune of the Mahanas?

'No sis, it wasn't supposed to happen like this,' Rongo said. 'Riripeti would not have wanted it to be like this — but it is. And maybe your question is the wrong question to ask. We should be asking, what are we going to do about it?' Rongo couldn't help pushing the point. 'For instance, why didn't you come to the harvesting today, sis? Where was our brother Pita? You both knew that it was today —'

'I'm sorry, Rongo,' Teria answered. 'I just forgot.' Usually, whenever it came time for planting and harvesting, there was no question that all hands would be to the task — and she enjoyed working with the family.

Rongo tried to be kind. 'Forgetting is not an excuse,' he said. 'None of us should ever forget.' But he wasn't going to join the queue in blaming the victim. 'We have to remember that our people were survivors, Teria. You come from a line of survivors who didn't come all this way by canoe from Raiatea to New Zealand simply so that we could beach ourselves in these difficult economic and political times. Our own journey is as nothing compared to theirs when they left Raiatea to find Aotearoa. We have to find the survivor in ourselves — and go on.'

A noise came from the home. Rongo saw that the children had finished lunch. They came racing out, following August, who had a kite in his hands.

'Teria, you have to find your own way out of this,' Rongo went on. 'You have to rid your life of Mo-Crack.' Teria had made some bad choices, and Mo-Crack was one of them.

Teria looked at Rongo, alarmed. 'How would I get on? Who would look after me and my kids? Who would feed them? With seven kids what chance would I have of getting a job? It's impossible.'

'You have to do it *for* the kids,' Rongo insisted. 'Mo-Crack will probably be out on good behaviour in six months. How long will it be before you're pregnant again or until he starts hitting you?' *How long before he batters one of you to death?* 'You have to break the cycle of dependency you're in before it gets deeper. Do something. Take one step. Then another. Before you know it you'll be on your way, going somewhere. Wherever that is has surely got to be a better place than where you are.'

Teria bit her lip. 'What you really mean is that I should get myself out of the hole I'm in and maybe end up in a better hole,' she joked, cynically. 'I don't know if I can do it, brother.' Silence fell between them, and Teria tried to change the subject. 'All I know is that you're a life-saver bringing the food today. I really appreciate it.' She loved her brother. He tilled and cared for the family as much and as tenderly as he did the family gardens.

'Not good enough,' Rongo answered. 'I'll help you. Come and stay with me and Huia. You've got to make the break. Before it's too late.' As a gesture, he put his hands in his pockets and brought out some dollars.

'I don't need a handout,' Teria flared.

'No arguments,' Rongo answered. 'Take the kids somewhere nice next time you go into Gisborne. Think about what I've said.' He was looking at the kids as they tried to launch the kite into the air. August was in charge, giving orders to his brothers and sisters. He was a good boy. He would look after his mother. He had nothing of the look of the feral children whom Rongo had seen living under the bridges of Gisborne, already on their way to gang rape, robbery and prison.

'What happens to us, sis, is of no account,' Rongo said. 'What happens to the kids, though, that is what matters.'

Watching the children, Rongo was reminded of something that Apirana Ngata had inscribed in a book that a young girl had given him: Grow up, young and tender plant, according to the needs of your time. Master the skills of the Pakeha for your physical well-being. Cherish your ancestral culture of the Maori for your dignity. Have faith in God who is the author of all things.'

And Rongo saw that August was running and running to the edge of the sky, his brothers and sisters running after him. The kite trailed behind, bouncing along the ground. Would the God of Winds be kind? Yes. Just as August was in danger of falling over the edge of the world, a strong breeze came — and the kite lifted.

'We did it,' June laughed.

The kite soared high, its long tail bobbing with coloured streamers. It tugged at the cord in August's hands, wanting to go higher, swooping and curling with the wind currents, dancing in the air.

——— 3 ———

Hana Walker stared out the window of the kitchen. It was almost two o'clock in the afternoon. Some kids were flying a kite. Half the day gone. What a waste of time, spending it at church. Or was it? Even going to church was better than spending the whole day doing nothing in this dump.

The Walker family had just finished Sunday lunch and Hana was helping her mother, Dinah, with the dishes while Dad — the man of the house, natch — read the Sunday newspaper.

The telephone rang. 'For you, darling,' Mum said to Hana. It was Janey, and she'd just woken up. 'Did you get caught coming in?' Janey asked.

'What do you think?' Hana answered. 'What about you? No? I told you not to worry but you wouldn't believe me, eh.' She was already bored with Janey. 'Catch you later.'

So what was she going to do the rest of the afternoon? Nothing except wait for tomorrow. Then the next day. And the day after that. And what would come later in the week?

Nothing. Zero. *Nada.*

Hepa Walker was feeling annoyed. Having enjoyed a good lunch, he was planning on a read of the Sunday paper but, as usual, it was filled with bad news about Maori. He flipped the pages and his annoyance increased. One story was a very graphic criticism of the collapse of Maori leadership — and the criticism was coming from a Maori. 'Once, that leadership kept our own social and cultural structures intact,' the activist said. 'But underneath all the idyllic landscape of rural Maori New Zealand and its strong cultural base — even though a lot of that is crumbling away — the grim reality is poverty and all the side-effects of poverty: depression, abuse, neglect. The scale of the problem is enormous and there is a strong lack of interest or ability among Maori leadership to address it.'

'What the hell do you want, lady?' Hepa muttered to himself; as usual, the activist concerned was another well educated Maori woman, and he always got very angry when they were critical of the job he and his mates were doing for the people. In his own eyes, he was truly trying to make a difference. A self-made man, he never liked it when his leadership was questioned. He also didn't like it when the activists took what he considered to be the other easy way out: blame the White man. It was either Maori leadership or the Pakeha but it was never the Maori themselves.

'Something in the paper, dear?' Dinah asked.

'More of the usual,' he said. 'Leadership-bashing. We didn't fight in two world wars and send this new generation to university just so that they could turn around and blame us. Always ready to blame somebody for their ills, that's their trouble. And if it's not us they're blaming it's the Pakeha we're working with.'

'I wish I hadn't asked,' Dinah smiled. She was accustomed to Hepa's opinions when his passions were involved.

'You saw the way they acted at our education meeting last month,' Hepa continued. 'They talked on and on about educational non-achievement and cultural deprivation. Hell, even I know that.' There were some Pakeha at that meeting and they weren't being shown any respect. Hepa had spoken up on their behalf. 'We may be different races, but we can't get along without each other,' he said. 'We should be building one race, and the only way we can do that is with the Pakeha, not without them. If I can make it on my own merits, so can you.'

What had one of the activists said in reply? 'Sir, just because you are a success does not mean that everybody else will be a success. Also, the way you define success may not be the way others define it. We are coming from a Maori position, not a Pakeha one.'

Nonsense. Success was success. No colour or gender was attached to it.

Oh well, turn to the sports section or the arts section. At least there was a chance of something entertaining to read. What was this? George Karepa's wedding was in the paper. Now there was a boy who was making his mark on his own terms and showing that a Maori could foot it in the Pakeha world. He was a credit to his people, just like Kiri Te Kanawa. 'Among the guests at the wedding were the mayor of Gisborne, the president of the New Zealand Rugby Football Union, the MP for Poverty Bay Gisborne, and local Maori dignitary Mr Hepa Walker.'

Pleased to see the mention, Hepa showed it to Dinah.

And guess who was the lonely little petunia in the onion patch?

Dinah Walker, nee Harrison. Born in Wellington. Educated at Wellington East Girls College. School Certificate: B+ average. Main subjects passed: English, history, geography, phys ed. Trained as a teacher at Wellington Teachers College. Transferred to the Army Education Corps where she met Hepa — and married him just before he left New Zealand for the European Campaign. She was pregnant with Sam at the time and people thought that was why they were married: why else would a pretty Pakeha girl marry a Maori? On her wedding day, which her parents did not attend, her father said, 'I never thought you would do this to us,' as if she was bringing shame on the family. Her mother sighed, 'Well, Dinah, don't expect to bring your tar babies around for us to look at. And if the marriage doesn't work out, don't come back to us. You've made your bed. Now lie in it.'

Of course, Dinah's family all laughed about it now, but it certainly helped when Hepa became a war hero — 'Just like Douglas Bader, dear,' her mum said — and that when Sam was born he was a little blondie boy who looked like any other child in Herne Bay. By the time Frank came along, another blond child, and then Hana — 'Hannah would have been a more appropriate spelling, dear' — all had been forgiven. Hepa's stocks rose higher when he clinched the Ministry of Defence job in Wellington. When he achieved further prominence in Wellington's government circles, it was obvious that he was somebody to be proud of. All the early nonsense was forgotten. Pity about Sam, though — but even as a child he had been a wicked, wicked little boy.

So here she was, Dinah Walker, and she was proud of her life, her husband and her children — even Sam. When he was born one of her great vanities was that he wasn't a chalk-white baby but a lovely apricot colour. She was always quick to defend her marriage to a Maori which, in her day, was not something that happened often. A family story, affectionately told — although it caused a scandal when it happened — involved a certain Christmas gathering of the Harrison clan, when Uncle Angus baldly and clearly asked her, 'So, Dinah, what's it like to be married to a Maori?' Hepa was not there; Sam was a three-year-old and she was carrying Frank, and she wasn't going to take that lying down. 'As I have not been married to a Scotsman, Uncle Angus, or an American, Englishman, Frenchman or Italian, let alone an Arab or whoever else lives in the Gobi Desert —' she took a deep breath '— I have no basis for comparison.'

Yes, one could laugh at such a story, but there were other not so laughable stories. At least the adults could handle the discrimination, but what about the half-caste or mixed-blood children? One day, Hana came home in tears because the neighbours' children had found out that her father was a Maori and they weren't allowed to play with her any more. Then the Maori children found out her mother was a White woman and, guess what, they didn't want to play with her either. Poor Hana, all grown-up now, and already hating herself.

Dinah Walker nee Harrison. Wife and mother, she loved living in Wellington. She was also committed to raising her children in the knowledge of their father's culture. It was only to be expected that she and Hepa would become involved in Wellington Maori Cultural Association and that they would begin to make good friends among the Maori folk. Dinah would have died if Auntie Dovey had asked her to get up on stage and do the poi dance with the women — she tried once and her pois twirled out of her hands and went flying across the hall — but she nevertheless turned into a good provider for the regular bring-and-buys and the housie raffles and could cook a boil-up with the best of them.

The years in Wellington were the happiest in her life. Wellington was a cosmopolitan city where Maori, Pakeha — and Greek, Italian, Islander and other races — commingled. There were the occasional glances of surprise when Dinah walked with the children in the street — Sam lost his blond looks very quickly and became a dark little boy —

but nobody said anything; and in Auckland, Dinah's parents passed this off as Spanish blood from her 'Spanish' husband. Dinah, by that time, had accepted her parents' silly pretences, and anyhow, she was always too busy to bother about what other people might think. Hepa kept on being asked to do more and more representational work — there was even a bit of excitement when he was appointed to the Wellington City Council — and, just at the end of their long stay in Wellington, Dinah went back to teaching. She was in all ways fulfilled.

Then came the day when Hepa's father died and somebody had to go back to look after the family's interests. When Hepa asked her if she would mind going to Gisborne to live, what else could she say but yes? After all, that's what good wives did, didn't they? — followed their husbands wherever they went, the wives hipping the children along with them.

But Dinah had expected they would live in the city. Instead, they settled in Waituhi. Was the move a mistake? No. Dinah was lucky to get a teaching job at Gisborne Girls High School. Every weekday she went into Gisborne, waving to all her neighbours, 'Gidday, Maka, how are you today?' 'Hello, Teria, would you like me to bring something back from Gisborne?' As well, Hepa still required her to accompany him to social events like, for instance, George Karepa's wedding last night. Once a month she went with him to Wellington for the weekend meetings of the Maori Council — and that gave her a lovely chance to see her old friends from Wellington and to catch the latest show.

But in her soul, if Dinah was to ask herself, 'Do I belong?' her answer would be 'No.' It wasn't a matter of being in transit either. It went deeper than that.

One evening, Dinah was talking to the Matua and, God knows how the subject came up, but all of a sudden Miro asked her, 'So, Dinah, when you die, where will you be buried?'

Dinah laughed, surprised. 'I haven't really given any thought to it,' she answered. 'With Hepa, I suppose.' Miro had given her such a *look.*

Shaken, Dinah pondered the question. That night, in bed, she began to sob and sob. Hepa woke up, and it all spilled out. 'By virtue of your blood,' she told him, 'you will be buried in Waituhi, no question. And by virtue of their Maori blood, so will our children, no question. But where does that leave me?'

'Silly woman,' Hepa answered. 'You're beside me now and you'll be beside me when we're dead.' But no matter what he said, she wasn't convinced. Her husband was Maori, her children were Maori, Waituhi was Maori, but she was Pakeha. Her children had all the benefits and rights of being Maori. As for her, she was and would always be an outsider.

Dinah's mother, now dead, had been right. Dinah had made her bed. Now she had to lie in it.

CHAPTER EIGHTEEN

—— 1 ——

Far above, the kite. Far below, the village.

Tossed by the wind, the kite soared high. The expanse of earth beneath it enlarged and the village became a small cluster of houses encircled by green, green farmland. The sun was declining, the mountain ranges darkening. Shadows marked the valleys, and arrows of green patterned those ridges still lit by the light. A car was coming down one of the ridges, winding homeward on a twisting road.

Ani Jackson had her head on Waka Mahana's shoulder. She reached up and pulled a wisp of sheep's wool from his hair. Her mind was filled with dreams of the life she would have with Waka. She'd enjoyed their first day working together. It was like being married. No boredom, no hardship yet.

In front, Miriama and Pita Mahana were still arguing. 'I've made up my mind,' Pita said. 'As soon as we get back I'm going over to Annie and Kepa's house to check up on Tamati Kota. If I find one thing that bothers me, just one, I'm taking him out of there and he's coming to stay with us. And I don't care that we had our chance earlier to look after the old man and didn't take it. I'm taking it now.' He was so angry he misjudged his speed and the car swerved at a corner.

Higher still the kite soared. George Karepa's car approached the small wooden bridge that Charlie Whatu's truck had crossed earlier that day. Sunlight and shadow slashed at the car as it sped towards Waituhi.

Andrew Whatu was on the front doorstep putting on his boots. He saw the kite as it dipped and swerved in the sky. How had August managed to get it up there? The tail was too long, like a sea anchor threatening to pull the kite down. There was also a huge hole in the body of the kite where the wind had torn the newspaper fabric away. The kite flew against all the laws of aerodynamics.

'So did Maori history,' Andrew thought with a sigh. At school last week he had an argument with the history teacher, Mr Green, about what constituted history. He had told a story about two magic kites.

'In my tribe,' he began, 'there were once two chiefs, Kahutapere and his cousin Rakaihikuroa, who was the paramount rangatira at the time. Kahutapere had twin sons, Tarakiuta and Tarakitai, and he wanted to increase their prestige and strength by feeding them on the special birds that Rakaihikuroa raised and kept in his fortress. When Rakaihikuroa discovered this, he became very worried. He had a son himself, Tupurupuru, and didn't like this threat to Tupurupuru's leadership. He spoke with Tupurupuru about it, and they decided to kill the two boys. But how and when?

'The twins were younger than Tupurupuru, just boys really. They were beautiful, youthful and well loved. In those days, one of the sports that young men loved to compete in was the spinning of the tops along an obstacle course. Competitors would hold their tops in one hand, release them, and use whips made of flax to keep them spinning. The courses for the races included jumps or pits or fences, and competitors had to show their dexterity by making their tops leap, soar, spin, pirouette, retreat, go left and go right to negotiate the course successfully. The twins were so adept at the art of spinning their tops and proficient in racing them against other competitors that they had become champions at the sport.

'The night before one of the competitions, Tupurupuru saw his chance to implement his murderous plan. He made himself a double-ended top. Tupurupuru was not as good at the sport but by having a top with two spinning surfaces rather than one he would ensure that he could keep up with the twins. Tupurupuru also built a huge pit at the bottom of the course. Then he challenged the twins to a duel during a practice run when only they were present.

'The twins liked competition, so they accepted. They didn't know Tupurupuru planned to kill them. They raced their tops down the slope, around, over and through the obstacles, but when they reached the huge pit not even they could make their tops reach the other side. The tops fell into the pit. The twins went to retrieve them and while they were in the pit, Tupurupuru leapt in and committed his murder.

'That's where the two magic kites come in,' Andrew continued. Mr Green was watching him, amused. His schoolmates, all except Simeon and Haromi, were giggling, but Andrew was determined to finish his story.

'When the twins did not return home their father, Kahutapere, knew they had been murdered. He made two kites and named them after his sons. He sent them up into the sky and called to them, "Show me the place of your murderer." The kites soared to a great height, hovered, and pointed at Rakaihikuroa's fortress. When Kahutapere went to see Rakaihikuroa, that old chief told him, "Let there be only one star shining in the sky." He then set upon Kahutapere, who escaped — but another two sons were killed. Kahutapere asked the assistance of his cousin, Mahaki. It was Mahaki's youngest son, Whakarau, who killed Tupurupuru in battle. This action changed the balance of power in the history of my ancestors.'

There was a long silence in the classroom. Mr Green coughed for attention.

'A lovely story, Andrew,' he said, 'but magic kites have no place in history.'

The class burst into loud laughter. Andrew's cheeks burned with embarrassment and anger.

'Shall we proceed with the lesson?' Mr Green asked.

'Don't lose heart,' Simeon whispered to him. 'One of these days you'll show him.'

'Are you ready, son?' Charlie Whatu called. He was still mucking around at the back of the house, looking for his scythe. Some beggar had taken it.

'Yes,' Andrew answered. He put the memory of Mr Green aside, getting on with life, getting on with the task to hand.

Charlie was the unofficial groundsman for Rongopai and, as he couldn't get back to sleep, he'd decided he might as well go and cut the grass — he'd been meaning to do it all week. 'Either that, son,' Dad said to Andrew, 'or else I'll just have to go and pester your mother.' The last thing Andrew wanted to do was sit outside and listen to his parents having sex, so he answered, 'I'll come with you.' He wasn't doing very well with his assignment for Miss Dalrymple anyway. Charlie went inside to see if Mana and Victor were awake and wanted to come and join them. He had only one hope — and that was no hope. Even if they had been awake, you think they would have come down to Rongopai to work? Better to pretend to be asleep.

'Found it,' Charlie said when he saw the scythe exactly where it was supposed to be. He picked it up, walked around to the front of the house and joined Andrew. 'Looks like it's only you and me,' he said. 'I tried to wake your brothers but Mana only rolled over and Victor farted in my face. How on earth do you stand sleeping in the same room?'

'Are you offering me my own bedroom, Dad?' Andrew answered.

'No use counting on Sonny either,' Charlie continued, turning a deaf ear to his son. 'His bed's not been slept in so he must still be over at Sam Walker's.'

'How long will we be at Rongopai?' Andrew asked. He was wishing he hadn't told Dad he would help. But if he was committed he wanted to get the job done, and the sooner the better.

'Let's see,' Charlie answered. 'The grass is so high you can hardly see the meeting house. It's two-thirty now. I reckon we should be finished by four. That is, if Albie Jones will lend us a second scythe for you to use. We'll drop by his place and ask him for it. Okay-ee, son, let's get to it.'

Charlie couldn't help putting a jaunty spring into his step and, when Andrew fell into step beside him, he gently mocked his dad by adding a two-step of his own. Charlie raised a finger at him, 'Don't get too smart,' and winked.

'So what are you daydreaming about now?' Andrew laughed.

'You were there, weren't you?' Charlie answered, offended. 'You saw me, didn't you, at last Saturday's rugby match, when I went on at the last minute and saved the day for Gisborne Old Boys?'

'I wish I hadn't asked,' Andrew groaned. His father was always hanging out at the rugby field hoping somebody would give him a game.

'I might be older than everyone else, son,' Charlie continued, 'but I'm still in my prime, still young enough to have some moves left. Okay, so I've got a few grey hairs but I've got my wind and my legs haven't let me down yet.'

To prove it, Charlie flexed his biceps and tried to pull in his pot gut. Ignoring Andrew's snort of suppressed laughter, he lost himself in last weekend's game.

'Some of my mates must have been really jealous of me,' Charlie boasted. 'They've only themselves to blame if they let their big eating and big boozing get the better of them.'

Yeah, so who had shown them up? Charlie Whatu, that's who. Who had come to the rescue when Gisborne Old Boys were down a player and the reserve hadn't turned up? The same Charlie Whatu himself, raring to go. 'Hey, Charlie,' his mates had yelled when he trotted onto the field. 'What do you think you're doing out there? Get off the field before you get hurt.' What a game it was! Even though he'd been put in as the fullback — 'You might get hurt, Charlie, so we'll put you in the back' — he'd been the one who got that try that clinched the game for Old Boys.

Charlie was acting it out for Andrew. 'Rufus Hickson passed the ball to the inner,' he said, 'who passed it on to the centre, who spun it out to the winger. The winger was getting all bunched up by the opposing Marist team. But did you see me, son? The way I blazed all the way from the back to help him? It must have been fifty yards at least. Do you think the winger would let the ball out? I yelled, Pass it out! Pass it out! but that kid didn't want to give the ball to an old man. The nerve of the little shit. Didn't he know I nearly made the provincial rep team when I was younger? I could have been a contender, son.'

Andrew was killing himself with laughter. Charlie chose to rise above it.

'In the end,' he said, 'that kid just had to let me have the ball. My goodness, it was a bad pass, but I managed to scoop it up, eh.' Charlie put the scythe down and replayed the move for Andrew. 'I saw those big Marist forwards and I thought I was a goner. They were waiting to tear me to pieces and make mincemeat out of me —'

Agnes was beside herself with worry on the sideline. 'You fellas leave my husband alone! Anybody who touches one hair of his head gets to answer to me,' she was yelling.

'Huh,' Charlie told Andrew. 'As if your mother should have worried.

It was chicken-feed to get past them. A sidestep here, a fend-off there, a little of the old magic Whatu footwork, and off I streaked — it must have been another fifty yards at least — to score the try right under the goal posts.'

Charlie struck a pose like a gladiator, but he was wearing a holey jersey and baggy pants, and that finished Andrew off. Snorting, he collapsed onto the road.

'What?' Charlie asked, opening his hands. 'What!'

'You were lucky, Dad,' Andrew answered. 'It was just a flash in the pan.'

'Flash in the pan my arse,' Charlie said. 'I can still show you a thing or two, son. You want to take me on? Let's have a race to Albie Jones' place. I'll fix you.'

'Forget it, Dad,' Andrew answered. 'You know I'll beat you, old man.'

'I'm an old man now am I?' Charlie bellowed. 'You've really asked for it now, son.' He scored a line on the ground with the heel of his boot, went behind it, spat on his hands, and took a crouching position. 'Put your feet where your mouth is,' he said and, because Andrew was still laughing, took hold of Andrew's hands and spat on them too.

'What did you do that for?' Andrew asked crossly. He wiped the spit off and lined up with his father. 'Right, you asked for it, so don't say I didn't warn you.'

'Ready,' Charlie counted. 'Steady.' Dad was looking so serious about all this and, because it still seemed such a farce, Andrew began to laugh again. As he was laughing, his father kicked the gravel and sprang. 'Go.'

'Hey, that's not fair,' Andrew said.

All right then, Dad. If you want a race, you're going to get it.

Andrew launched after his father. He thought he would overhaul him easily, but Charlie had put on a great burst of speed. Admiring the gall of the old man, Andrew kicked into higher gear. Along the road he sped, gaining on his father. The stones were spraying high behind Dad's heels and Andrew had to ratchet his speed up another notch.

Hell, Dad was quite a sprinter.

Ahead was a bend in the road. One hundred yards down the straight was Albie Jones' place. 'Gotcha,' Andrew laughed as he pulled up alongside his father on the bend.

They were running neck and neck, arms and legs pumping, running stride for stride. Charlie's neck muscles were popping and his face was straining with effort.

And Charlie looked across at Andrew — and in his face was fear.

Sometimes, your whole life can be illuminated by a moment. Sometimes a moment is all it takes for you to understand something important, something profound.

Andrew's world started to slow down. Slowly. Slower still. He saw that he and his father were running in slow motion, the gravel spraying like crystals from their feet, the landscape glowing like greenstone. Dad's body was leaping and straining in slow agony, his muscles rippling and pushing him forward. His face was a mask of pain. Again, that flash of fear.

The sun stopped. The world stopped moving. Andrew remembered his earlier conversation with his father. 'Look at my hands, son. All they know about is labouring work. Fencing and digging postholes, that's been my life.'

'We're only racing for fun, Dad,' Andrew thought, 'and yet your heart is set on winning. Why? Why is it so important to you? Why, Dad?'

And it came to Andrew that he owed an extraordinary debt to his father, this man who so disparaged what he was: a tiller of the soil, a guardian of the land. As he looked around at Waituhi, Andrew's sense of debt increased. A valley wasn't just a physical place made up of mountains, flat land and a river running through it. It was also a place where people had come to make a home, create a history and build a future. Generations of men, women and children had lived and died here. They had laughed and cried over this soil, contracted themselves to its welfare, and defended it to the death. They had kept the faith, had maintained the tribe and its history, and had done it against incredible odds. When there was nothing else to battle with except their physical strength, they had kept hold of their culture, fought for their valley and kept going when sometimes their only purchase on life itself had been by way of clinging fingertip and desperate toehold.

What had Dad said? 'Follow your ambitions, son. Let them take you out as far as you want to go, and even further. Go out and claim the world. Do what we could never do.' Andrew realised, however, that it was still a matter of pride for his father, for all his tribe, to count on their physical abilities to keep in place the structures of the world. Physical strength was what had kept the sky above, the earth below and the bright strand of light between.

It can all happen in a moment, such an epiphany, such an insight.

'My father, I acknowledge you and all who I come from.' Andrew and Charlie were running so slowly that Andrew was able to reach out and touch his father, caressing his skin. 'All your lives, you've all lived by your strength. Strength alone. I'll not take from you the belief you have in it.'

He fell back. He saw the gleam of surprise in his father's eyes and watched as his father, realising he had a chance to win the race, leapt in front.

And Andrew couldn't resist yelling at Charlie, 'Go, you old bastard.'

Oh, beat the drum slowly and play the fife lowly. This man running is the Lord of my life. These my people are my life's kings and queens, princes and princesses. They tamed the sun, pulled islands from the sea, and separated the earth from the sky so that I could stand upright and claim my inheritance. This my Lord, my father, made me from strong loins so that I would continue to carry the great stories of a people who were Vikings of the sunrise. These, my people, came to these savage islands far to the south and wrested a living from Mother Earth, the land. Over all these years they nurtured the seed that was planted in Raiatea and brought here, and have kept it safe. No matter who I become or where I go in the world, I will become a prince only because I am of such royal stock. Once, twice, thrice, I acknowledge you. Once, twice, thrice, I bow down and pay my homage to you.

'Hah,' Charlie snorted as Andrew joined him at Albie Jones' gate. 'What happened to you then, eh?' The sweat was pouring from Charlie's face and he was bending to get his wind back. 'Well?'

'A stone in my boot,' Andrew answered.

'Am I still an old man? I showed you a thing or two, didn't I! So aren't you going to apologise?' Charlie put Andrew into a playful headlock and wrestled him to the ground. 'The better man won, eh, son.'

Give a man an inch and he takes a mile.

'Yes, Dad. The better man won,' Andrew said.

'Nani?' Pene asked. 'Are you awake yet? We better start home now. Mum will be wondering where we are.'

Pene and Nani Paora had walked all the way along the ridge and now sat on the slope overlooking Rongopai. The old man flopped down on the grass and started to snore. A big blowfly was hovering just over Nani's mouth and, every time he breathed in, the blowfly had to beat his wings fast to make sure he didn't go down Nani's throat.

'Yes sirree,' Pene said to his sleeping Nani. 'Had I known you would get tired, I would have taken you on the second route for the Parade.' The second route was one that Pene took as an alternative whenever it rained or Nani was not feeling fit. For this route, they kept to the road. From Tawhiti Kaahu they went to Rongopai. On the way, if they were lucky, Mattie Jones was on the alert at the Matua's home and gave them some bread and a drink of cordial. Pene loved Mattie. She was too sad for such a pretty lady and he often hugged her, saying, 'I'll be your little boy, you can have me.' They would sit in the sunlight together and have their meal until the Matua came to growl at Mattie and tell her she had work to do.

From the Matua's place, Pene and Tamati Kota kept to the road all the way to Pakowhai settlement. A sad story attached to Pakowhai. The original settlement was Te Poho o Hiraina, named after a girl who died when she was sixteen. Her mother, Heni Te Auraki, couldn't stop weeping for Hiraina. Her sorrow was symbolised in the woven tears of the weavings in the original meeting house. Although fire and flood destroyed it in 1950, enough timber and iron was salvaged to build the new meeting house.

Pene saw two men racing along the road, around the bend and into the straight. He watched August and the other kids in the field opposite as they flew their kite. The kite was at the limit of the string's length, yet it tugged and pulled as if it wanted to go higher. Pene's heart wanted to go with the kite, to soar and swoop across the hills, and to look down upon this place where sheep and cattle grazed, on the village he loved, where Jerusalem had been built in Waituhi's green and pleasant hills.

Growing tired of waiting for Nani Paora to wake up, Pene chewed on a long straw. 'Some friend you are,' he said. The whole world was having fun but his Nani was still asleep. Who knew where the old man went in his dreams? Pene never liked missing out.

Then, oh no, the blowfly was sucked through Nani Paora's lips. Nani coughed, swallowed, licked his lips and, with a start, woke up. 'What flew into my mouth?' he asked. 'What's happening?' When he woke, Nani took a little while getting his bearings.

'At long last,' Pene sighed. 'It's time to go home.'

'Yes, we better go fast,' Nani Paora nodded. He pointed to some straggly sheep which were grazing closer and closer. 'Enemy soldiers, Grandson.'

Immediately, Pene's eyes lit up. Yay, it was time to go on with the Parade again. With excitement, he gave Nani Paora a rifle — a small fallen branch — and they waited until the sheep came in range. Up came Pene's arm and, 'Pow! Pow! Pow!' But some other soldiers were coming up from behind.

'Throw a grenade, Nani,' Pene yelled.

Quick as a flash, Nani Paora picked up a dried cowpat and, boom, bits and pieces of sheep rained through the air. But Nani wasn't fair. Swept up in the game he turned on Pene and said, 'Bang, you're dead.' Offended, Pene refused to lie down and chased Nani Paora through the bushes. 'I'll get you, you old cheat.'

What was this? Samson, the old bag-of-bones nag that Maka tiko bum owned, was waiting at the fenceline. Pene and Nani Paora were late for their rendezvous with him. He butted Pene impatiently, whinnied, and showed his teeth.

'All right, all right,' Pene complained. 'Don't blame me, it wasn't me who kept us late.' He put a hand in his pants and brought out a handful of sugar cubes. Nani Paora whinnied too — so he got a sugar cube as well. 'Count yourself lucky,' Pene said.

Then something bright settled around Samson and he reared as if a bee had stung him. Up and up he lifted, straight into the sun. Blinded, Pene had to look away. When he looked back, Samson was a magnificent white stallion. A man was riding him.

'Geronimo,' Pene whispered.

'No, not Geronimo,' Nani Paora said. 'Te Kooti. And he is riding his magic steed, Poukaiwhenua.'

*

'Quick,' Te Kooti said. 'We must escape, and there is no time to lose.' He was stoutly built, broad-shouldered and strong-limbed. His hair was black and glossy, and he was dressed in rebel clothing. He reached down and pulled Tamati Kota up behind him. When he reached down again for Pene, the young boy saw that the third finger was missing from Te Kooti's left hand.

All of a sudden, shell fire from two mortars exploded, and Pene realised they had returned to the siege of Ngatapa fortress, 1869. 'You came back,' Pene said, his eyes shining. 'You came back to rescue us.'

Te Kooti laughed. 'I have to save you, child, for are you not descended from she, Riripeti, who became my Left Hand of God?' He pulled on Poukaiwhenua's reins and the stallion wheeled and galloped out of the first defensive compartment, trying to make a break for freedom. A line of soldiers was waiting and let off a barrage of rifle fire.

'We're blocked,' Te Kooti said.

'How can we escape?' Pene asked. The adrenalin was rushing through his body.

'Fear not, child,' Te Kooti smiled. 'The Lord is with us and will show Poukaiwhenua the way.' He patted the stallion. 'Come, Poukaiwhenua, go as fast as the wind.'

And lo, the legends say that Te Kooti entered in unto the place of death, Ngatapa, and fought his way through the first compartment to the second compartment. In his right hand he held his sword — the Sword of Te Kooti, which some say is buried in a holy place near Makaraka — and he smote the many soldiers dead who came to try to stop him. Onward he pressed, into the third compartment, and his horse was also a deadly weapon fighting for its master, cleaving the air with its hooves so that many who tried to grab its bridle were trampled underneath.

'We're trapped,' Pene cried.

The soldiers were closing in. They were running fast, loading, discharging, reloading. Te Kooti was surrounded and pushed further and further to the cliff — the same place where many of his people had fallen to their death.

That was when Te Kooti called to the whirlwind path of Enoch. 'Come, whirlwinds, clothe us —'

He turned Poukaiwhenua to face the empty sky, the forest beneath.

147

It was a mackerel sky. From east to west stretched a broad band of cloud broken into long, thin, parallel masses, as if shoals of fish were teeming just below its surface. The sea was stormy with opalescent waves tinged with red, stretching to the end of forever.

Roaring and chanting, the whirlwinds came, make way, make way. They came out of the north, south, east and west, writhing across the sky like dazzling snakes searching for each other. They advanced, growing full-bellied, and found each other above Ngatapa. Immediately they coiled together into a single cone of turbulent winds. A storm broke out with a thunderclap, and laced the funnel with lightning. All the clouds of the universe came spiralling in, filling the funnel with phosphorescence. At the top was a field of bright stars in a clear black sky.

'Hold tight, child,' Te Kooti said.

Poukaiwhenua leapt from the cliff.

It was a leap into legend.

Caught up in the memory, Tamati Kota began to chant. His eyes were alive with fire and tears, fervour and prophetic vision. He was standing, Pene at his side, facing an old nag with bowed legs and a sag in the middle.

'*Na, tenei te haka* o *Te Kooti,*' he chanted. 'This is the song of Te Kooti, which is also the song that the prophet Joshua sang to the tribes of Israel concerning their inherited lands.'

The old man was holding a stick. With a dramatic gesture he lifted it and swept it across his body. As if commanded, Samson began to dance.

'*A ko Ihowa, ko o koutou Atua,*' Tamati Kota chanted. 'And the Lord your God, he shall expel them, your oppressors, from before you and drive them from out of your sight, and you shall possess this land, as the Lord your God has promised unto you.'

Tamati Kota joined in the dance. He stamped his feet and Samson imitated him. He lifted his arms and the stallion reared high. When he circled his stick, Samson turned in a complete revolution. The dust whirled from their feet like a cyclone. Stamp. Lift. Circle. Hiss. Slap. *Aue, hiii.*

'*A ka riro to ratou oneone i a koutou,*' Tamati Kota chanted. His eyeballs protruded. He clawed at his chest. He beat his hands against

148

his thighs. 'As long as we remain faithful the Lord will keep His word to us.'

Alert to the old man's movements, Samson snorted, shook his mane, tossing, bucking, neighing with anger. The hope of the people surged forward to overcome all their foes. Kneel. Leap. Stamp. Advance. Roar like the wind. *Aue, haaa.*

Watching, Pene jumped in beside Tamati Kota. He yelled at Samson, urging him to buck and kick even higher. 'Be ye therefore very courageous,' Tamati Kota continued, 'and keep and do all that is written in the book of the law of Moses.' Knees bent. Hip thrusting forward. Slap, slap, slap of hands against his chest. The tears spilling. Face gaunt with the weight of history. A young boy beside him, adding a chorus of battle cries and war whoops. *Aue hii, haa, hii.*

The dance reached its climax. 'Turn not aside from the fight, my people.' The dust was a whirlwind. The sun was immured in the storm that arose from stamping feet. 'Do not retreat either to the right or to the left.' The ground boomed. The earth moved. The universe split apart.

Dancing tall in the sunlight, Tamati Kota intoned the final challenge. 'Oh my people, go straight through the middle and fulfil your destiny.' He patterned the dust with quick movements. 'Make ready!' he cried. 'Charge!' He looked at Pene. 'Do not falter! Now fight —'

They were an old man and a young boy on the Parade. They were two tiny specks caught in the fierce heat of the bright overriding sun.

Pene began to throw sticks, rocks, stones, anything at the world.

'Yip, yip, yippee-aye-ay!'

Tamati Kota sank to his knees, weeping, exhausted. He picked up handfuls of dust, throwing them at everything, at nothing.

CHAPTER NINETEEN

Picture this:

A family group, waiting in a golden aureole of sun. Two are seated. The third stands behind them. Seated are the Matua, Miro Mananui, and her husband, Tama Mananui. Mattie Jones is the person standing behind them. They look as if they are posing to have a photograph taken, waiting for the photographer to say, 'Watch the dickey bird.'

Both Miro and Tama have dressed formally. Miro wears a dark blouse and ankle-length skirt. She sits with her legs together, her hands in her lap — she has black patent-leather shoes on her small, beautiful feet. Her grey hair is down around her shoulders. She wears greenstone earrings and a large *hei tiki* — a greenstone necklace. A touch of lipstick brings colour to her complexion. Mindful of the ceremonial nature of the forthcoming occasion, she has a feather cloak over all her garments. She chose the cloak specially because it is one of the most treasured heirlooms of Waituhi. Her mother, Mariah, gave it to her, this cloak which came from the times of Kai's two wives, Te Haaki and Whareana.

Tama is dressed in a black three-piece suit. He wears a high-necked white shirt and bowtie, and his sleeves are pinned with gold studs. In his left hand he holds a greenstone war implement, a fighting club that was used at the battle of Waerenga a Hika fortress. Mattie, standing behind him, barefoot, without make-up, wears a simple white lace dress with long sleeves. Her eyes are downcast, her hands clasped as if they should be holding a bouquet of flowers. She looks like a bride waiting for her groom.

A tall grandfather clock ticks loudly in the room. The Matua shifts impatiently and Tama pats her reassuringly. 'The boy will come,' he says. Tama has his doubts, however. He, the Matua and Mattie have been waiting like this, silent, unmoving and eternal, for over an hour. The Matua nods and surveys the room, acknowledging the people in the fading photographs and the spirits who are gathering. Bobbie and her mates are among them as they crowd into the room to witness this meeting. Here, the Matua must make her entreaty to Moses, he who is Prince of Egypt and lives in Pharaoh's Palace but who must be reminded that he is of the Israelites. They don't mind waiting. What's an extra few minutes when you have already been waiting over a hundred years?

A car draws up outside, crunching the gravel of the driveway. On the Matua's orders, Tama has left the front door open. In the sunlight, Tama sees a young man step out of the car and into a square of sunlight. The boy looks nervous. He straightens his jacket.

'He is here,' Tama says.

And Mattie walked to the doorway and lifted her face to the light.

'*Karanga mai, karanga mai, karanga mai*,' she called. 'Welcome, beloved son of Te Whanau a Kai, come to the call of love, come under love's protection.' Her appearance like this within such a formal setting, was the first shock for George Karepa. He had only known her as a party girl. He was not to know that after Miro and Tama had brought her to Waituhi, those three years ago, Miro had bonded Mattie to her services in exchange for a roof over her head — and Mattie had agreed. Even while pregnant, Mattie was taught to perform traditional duties; the *karanga*, for instance — the ritual call made by women to welcome visitors. She was also taught to function as ordained servant, acolyte for Miro at spiritual work, assisting the Matua and Tama as they took the Ringatu church services and prayers, escorting the elderly to their places, handing out the prayerbooks, making sure that Miro had her healing water and other sacred tools of trade, leading the prayers and, at the end of each service, collecting the prayerbooks. And was it Mattie's fault that she was also learning, by innocent observance, some of the Matua's more arcane and esoteric arts? Simply by watching, Mattie could not but absorb the methods by which Miro divined the welfare of the tribe: the arts of prophecy, dream, sign, making spells, reading the natural world, countering black magic, reinstating the order of things, and divination.

Sometimes Mattie was sent out to prepare potions and poultices for those who came to the Matua for healing: berry and bluegum juice for bruises, sprains and aching bones; tree sap for internal ailments and asthma; herbal tea for stomach problems; moss poultices for boils and other sores. The Matua was now instructing Mattie on the various massages to heal broken bones and to get the bones to knit. Mattie was also the kitchen worker, the cook who prepared the meals and, with Tama, kept the house going so that the Matua could perform her duties unfettered by such mundane matters.

Ah yes, the Matua had indeed bonded Mattie into her servitude, as Sarah had done to Hagar in the Bible. Miro considered such manual duties were little enough compensation for having taken Mattie into her house. Knowing that Mattie did her duties with reluctance and escaped whenever she had the opportunity to go to her parties only increased the friction between them. 'Will you not let me go?' Mattie would scream — for even after the baby was born, Miro still held her to her contract.

'Never,' the Matua answered. 'From this day onward you are in my service. Enjoy your moments of careless rest; they are your last. You are mine as surely as a master has his slave, a farmer his beast of burden, an organ grinder his monkey, and when I command you, you shall obey. You will get up in the morning when I say so and lie you down in the evening only when you have finished attending to me. To me will be your first duty. From me you will learn the meaning of some new words: obedience, silence and oblivion. I own you as strongly as I own —' she pointed to Tama '— him.'

Mattie beckoned George to approach, to come forward. As he did so she retreated into the house. He entered therein, saw a door to his left and the Matua and Tama sitting, waiting. Opposite them was the chair where he was to seat himself. He watched as Mattie resumed her place standing behind the Matua and Tama. Her eyes were still downcast. Not once had she looked at him.

With a cough, and a nervous glance at Miro, Tama stood to speak. He raised a hand. '*Kororia ki to Ingoa Tapu,*' Tama began. 'And so we praise His Holy Name.' His voice was quiet but authoritative, its soft cadences like feathers floating in the wind. '*Haere mai, nau mai, kua tae mai*,' he said. 'Welcome, welcome, come among us. Come back to your tribe, your people, your Matua, to all those who love you, to the lands of Te Whanau a Kai.'

As he spoke the ritual phrases, Tama paced back and forth. He invoked history to come to witness this encounter. He called upon the spirits to be true witnesses to the meeting. Although George could not see them, he felt them settling around him. They were in the cloaks on the walls, the photographs scattered throughout the room, the heirlooms of the tribe: prized greenstone weapons, whalebone pendants, and wood carvings. They came in shadow or in dazzling light. They filled the room. They listened as Tama read a passage from the Old Testament. This was the same reading, from Exodus, which the prophet Te Kooti had read at the Passover feast when he landed at Whareongaonga after escaping from the Chatham Islands:

'And ye shall take a bunch of hyssop and dip it in the blood that is in the basin and strike the lintel and the two side posts with the blood that is in the basin. And none of you shall go out at the door of his house until the morning. For the Lord will pass through to smite the Egyptians and when he seeth the blood on the lintel and on the two side posts, the Lord will pass over the door and will not suffer the destroyer to come in unto your houses to smite you.'

That's when the Matua stood up. No mucking around. Now that it was her turn she got straight down to business.

'Son,' Miro began. 'In 1869, after the fall of Waerenga a Hika fortress and the Te Kooti Wars, the Pakeha exacted his pound of flesh. I will talk briefly about the human cost. It is painful to acknowledge the dead, the limbless wounded and also the women who were forced to be the wives and concubines of the government soldiers. Fifty of the women from Ngatapa were put to service as comfort women, Son. I stand before you today and bear witness that I am descended from one of those concubine women, raped and brought to child. Ever since, I have heard the voice of my ancestress calling to me across the years asking for vengeance and also for my forgiveness for not having fought harder against her attacker. Never forget, Son, that women have always been the main victims of any war.

153

'Now I will turn to the land confiscations. Straight away Te Whanau a Kai, together with Te Aitanga a Mahaki and Rongowhakaata, were ordered to give up 5000 acres to the Crown. Our cousins of Te Aitanga a Mahaki and Rongowhakaata were bitter about this. They blamed us for what they considered was our fault, saying they had been tarred with the same brush and unfairly included in the cessions. The land we gave up was Patutahi–Kaimoe, vital to us because it was high quality, fertile, flat land with good access to the Waipaoa River. However, in the cession, the whole area ceded was expanded into a much more substantial confiscation of over 56,000 acres. All that land purloined unjustifiably by the Crown. Ever since we have tried to get it back.'

The Matua's words were strong and to the point, the saga related with clarity.

'Our first attempt, Son, was at a Royal commission presided over by Henry Tacey Clarke, a senior official of the Native Department, here in Gisborne in 1882. It was our ancestor, Wi Pere, who applied for the return of the land on our behalf. He placed us at the mercy of the court as being great sufferers through the cession of the Patutahi Block. Clarke recommended 500 acres be returned, but even this miserable pittance of compensation was not carried out. Instead, Te Whanau a Kai were given a worthless piece of land, nothing but pumice, where no food was able to grow, and a piece of steep hillside many miles away.'

And the shades in the room remembered, oh, how they remembered: Yes, yes, yes.

'Following the Clarke Commission,' Miro continued, 'Te Whanau a Kai made three major petitions in 1903, one put forward by Peka Kerekere and seventy-three others. There were more petitions in 1914, though the forgetful Crown has since denied we ever made any in respect of Patutahi — and particularly in our own right. In 1920, finally, the Government set up a Native Lands Commission, chaired by Robert Noble Jones, who at that time was both Under-Secretary of the Native Department and the Chief Judge of the Native Land Court. One of the diverse matters this Commission considered was the vexed problem of Patutahi. The Commission was welcomed in Gisborne by Te Kani Pere of Te Whanau a Kai and Lady Carroll of Rongowhakaata. At the hearings Rongowhakaata, Te Aitanga a Mahaki and Ngai Tamanuhiri were represented by Captain Wiremu Tutepuaki Pitt; Te Whanau a Kai was separately represented by a local solicitor, a Mr Dunlop. Chief Judge Jones did, in fact, recognise the injustice of Patutahi but couldn't find a way of sorting out the amount of land taken and the process by which it could be revested — and by then Rongowhakaata and Te Aitanga a Mahaki were making competing claims — and the whole Patutahi affair was sent back to the Native Land Court by means of evasive legislation, enacted as the Native Land Amendment and Native Land Claims Adjustment Act 1922. From July to December 1923, we were again separately represented in a hearing of the Native Land Court, and those who gave evidence on our behalf included Haare Matenga, Eria Raukura, Haerapo Kahuroa, Himiona Katipa, Taake Kerekere and others. But this case was calamitous because the court, in attempting to validate Te Whanau a Kai's claim, felt it necessary to define where the boundary line laid down in ancient times by Tui, our first ancestor, was for the tribe — and deemed that because Rongowhakaata and Te Aitanga a Mahaki were clearly involved, we did not have a separate case. Te Whanau a Kai immediately appealed against the 1923 judgment, and were again before the Native Appellate Court in 1925. The appeal was unsuccessful. There were two separate hearings on issues relating to Patutahi in 1929, more special legislation in 1930 and further negotiations with the Crown from 1935 to 1950. That, plus a stream of petitions.

'Then, in 1949, in an effort to solve the confusion of conflicting ownership, Te Whanau a Kai and Rongowhakaata met at Manutuke and worked out an arrangement between ourselves. It was resolved that the compensation for Patutahi would be £100,000 and that it would be split £60,000 for Rongowhakaata and £40,000 for Te Whanau a Kai. With this agreement, our representatives, Mafeking Pere for Te Whanau a Kai, and Reta Keiha for Rongowhakaata, met the National Minister of Maori Affairs, Corbett, at Wellington on 9 May 1950. Mr Corbett played a game of divide and rule. Compensation was made of £36,000, of which Te Whanau a Kai received £58, the rest going to Rongowhakaata.

'All this, and I have not accounted for the rest of the land taken under all the different acts like the Crown Purchasing Act, Native Land Act, the New Zealand Company dealings and other instruments of our dispossession.

'Thus we come to the present day, Son. We are still fighting the Government. Sadly we are also trying to prosecute our claim as a separate tribe in our own right against competing tribes. But Patutahi is not theirs. It is ours. Wherever we stand in our lands we have ownership. The claim remains our significant raupatu grievance. We have to get the land back.'

There, it was done. Sensing the approval around her, 'Well done, Matua, you have expressed our groans and our pains,' Miro took a particular pleasure in having done her job. Was that Bobbie, the old man Hopalong and the warrior with the bulging stomach nodding with approval? She had laid down the challenge, the purpose of the meeting, for George to take up. It was up to him now. She was confident of success.

George remained seated.

Watching him, Tama was impassive. George was a baby when the Matua went to collect him and, from the very beginning, Tama had never quite believed in him. George's parents had been killed in a car accident and when the Matua asked his immediate extended family if they would give George to her to raise as her adopted son, they agreed. After all, they reasoned, George would have all the benefits of Miro's hereditary status and power, and Arapeta persuaded them the adoption would also give George access to Miro's land. From that first day, when the Matua held the baby in her arms and wrapped him in the swaddling clothes she had hoped to dress her own child in, she indulged him.

'Why are you telling me this?' George began.

Tama saw Miro's momentary confusion at the question. 'I could have warned you, Matua,' Tama wanted to say to her, 'that all those years you brought him up would lead to this. Whenever he ran to you, you always gave him what he wanted. He took it, did not appreciate it and gave no thanks, considering that it was only his due. When, as a schoolboy, you sent him to Te Aute Maori Boys College, I could have told you he would become a man who would follow his own ambitions, appetites and avarice, but you thought he was just a prodigal son and would come back and take the place of honour at the head of your table. I would not have minded his taking my place. Although I have loved him in my own way, I have never expected him to be anything other than what he is.'

'Look around you, George,' Miro smiled, recovering. 'The people are still suffering. They are the same people who have loved you, honoured you and made you their prince.'

Listening, Mattie suddenly realised, 'Yes, that's it, that's the key to George Karepa.' When she first met him, George had told her of his successes as a schoolboy — dux, head prefect, captain of the First Fifteen — and that the Matua had planned for him to work for the Department of Maori Affairs. 'All that work,' George had laughed. 'Luckily, I got discovered for my sporting skills and, since then, I've been on a roll.' It was not that George was lazy. Oh no, the discipline that had kept him at the top as a rugby player proved the opposite. But when presented with an option George would always go for the more attractive or easier one. All his relationships had been conducted in the same way. Mattie felt so sorry for the Matua. She wanted to say to her, 'You mustn't blame him. Can't you see that he's exactly like you? You brought him up to expect that he would always have his way. As you have sown, now you reap.'

For a moment, George was silent. He looked at Tama and Mattie, wondering if, like many others had done during his life, they would come to the rescue. But they would not intervene. This was just between him and the Matua. He stood up, walked across and knelt before her. He looked deep into her eyes. His charm had always got him through difficult moments and would do so again.

'Matua, what do you want from me? All I have ever tried to do is to make you proud and I thought I had done that. I have fame and fortune and I've made it into the big time. Nobody here has ever achieved what I have achieved.'

'I am proud of you,' Miro answered. 'But what is fame, Son? What is fortune? They are like comets flaring brilliant trails, incandescent and beautiful of themselves, but they illuminate a Pakeha sky. Come back to your own heavens, Son. Achieve what must be done among your own constellations.'

And Miro was so certain that George would say 'Yes' to her, that she overplayed her cards, showing them too soon, laying them on the table as if she already possessed the winning hand.

'There is a very personal reason why you should do this. You are a direct descendant of the people who possessed Patutahi. I have done all

I can in my life to get the land back. I want to pass that job to you.' She reached into one of her sleeves and withdrew a document. 'Here, this will be your reward.'

'What is it?' George asked, unrolling the document.

'I referred earlier to my ancestress, one of the comfort women after the fall of Ngatapa. Her name was Aorangi and she was high-born and owned land at Patutahi. It was a double injustice to her that, as well as losing her land, she also became a concubine of the very soldiers who had taken the land. That land belongs to me, and whatever rights I have to the settlement that will occur, I am leaving to you. Everything.'

Mattie pressed Tama's shoulder. 'Did you know the Matua would do this?'

'No,' Tama answered. 'But it doesn't surprise me. Nothing the Matua does has ever surprised me.' Even so, he was saddened that she had not consulted him. He felt stranded, alienated, of little worth and no account. The Matua had always been a law unto herself.

George stood up. He took the document with him to his chair, sat, and read it. All the long nights of Miro whispering to him, 'When you grow older you will succeed me and work for the tribe,' were in the words on the paper. All her expectations that he would become a leader and deliver the people out of their darkness, that also was in the bold strokes of her signature. No matter that he had set his face in another direction, she had never ever understood that while prosecuting the Te Whanau a Kai claim was her life's work, it was not his. Becoming desperate, George wondered how he could get it through to Miro that, unlike many others who had left Waituhi, he was not coming back. He lived in a different universe now.

His head felt like it was splitting apart. He began to moan, rocking back and forth. All of a sudden he was howling. Howling like a crazed animal. Howling, howling, howling.

He dropped the document to the floor.

'I relinquish all my rights to the land,' George said.

The shadows in the room, the silent witnesses, began to weep at the words.

At first Miro thought she had heard him wrongly. 'What did you say?' Unbelieving. Uncomprehending.

'Everything that is my inheritance, I relinquish it,' George repeated. 'After all, I make plenty of money, I don't need your inheritance and —'

Before George could say another word, Miro was out of her chair, crossing the space between and slapping him hard — but it was Miro who had tears in her eyes.

'Is that what you think this is all about, George?' Her voice was full of loathing and disgust. 'I have raised you as my own, under this roof and among these people, and you have the gall to assume that all our efforts over all these years are about money?' She went to strike George again. Attack was the only way she knew of maintaining control, no matter the situation. It was as if attack was the only position she could take in the world, as if her fate and the fate of all who lived in her world depended on her.

'Don't do that, Matua,' George warned. 'So help me God, don't do that again.'

He stopped her with a firm grip, and she realised that her adopted boy had gone beyond any power she ever had over him. He was stronger than her now. The Pakeha world had seduced him totally and he would never be hers again.

'But I've worked and planned for this moment all these years,' Miro said. She was shocked, disbelieving.

Tama tried to intervene. 'You should have told the Matua earlier,' he said to George. 'You should never have led her to believe that you would take up the battle she has long fought for all of us.'

'Me?' George's laugh was hollow. 'This has never ever been about me. This has always ever been about her. What she wants. What she plans. What she dreams.' He turned to Miro. 'Well, what you want, Matua, is not what I want. Your plans are not my plans. I dream my own dreams. You're not even my real mother.'

George turned to leave. The unsaid had been said. No need for pretence any longer.

'Don't go, Son,' Miro pleaded. 'Don't relinquish your inheritance. Your land is your umbilical. Without it you are severed, ruptured, lost, gone forever. You become a man without a country or a history. Is that what you want?'

George kept walking. Out the door to his car.

'Are you really going to walk away?' Miro cried. 'Just like that? Your ancestors must be turning in their graves, George Karepa. Your ancestors — and your son.'

Mattie's face went white. 'You said you would never tell him, you manipulative old bitch,' she hissed.

George stopped in his tracks. He looked back at Miro and then at Mattie. His face was aghast. 'I had a son?' So that was why Mattie was living in Waituhi.

'Yes, you had a son,' Miro answered. 'Mattie gave birth to him here. He would have been my first grandson. I thought, one day he might be a trump card, might make the difference between your coming back and your not coming back. It doesn't matter now.'

'And he died? My baby son died?'

That's when some animus, some other presence that was in Mattie and of Mattie stepped up and out of her. All the barely repressed anger that Mattie had ever felt about George — for loving her, for leaving her, for destroying her life, for not coming back, for thinking he could waltz his way through life without paying his dues, for being successful, for marrying somebody else, for still being a handsome bastard, for getting away with it, for not knowing that he was supposed to be hers, oh, everything you could ever think of — came tumbling out of her. She began to shake apart and Tama saw the signs, but it was too late to stop her.

'Yes, George, he died,' Mattie said. 'Your son died. Do you want to know how?'

'Don't do this, girl,' Tama intervened.

Oh, but Mattie was really enjoying herself now. She'd never had the chance to say 'fuck you' to George and now she was going to take it.

'I killed him.'

For a moment there was silence. George's mouth went dry.

'You killed him, Mattie?'

His head was spinning, spinning, spinning. He couldn't take it in. He couldn't understand it. The incomprehensibility of it all. Mattie had killed her child? Their child? Why? It was insane. All of it.

George bowed his head and grieved. Throughout his life, if there was a door he didn't want to go through, he had always stepped back from it — and kept on walking. When he looked up again, all he said was:

'Goodbye, Matua. Goodbye, Tama. Mattie, I'm so sorry.'

He had to get away, get out, go. No asking questions. No looking back. If you looked back you would have to confront the past and you could be turned into a pillar of salt.

He stepped into his car, started the motor and drove away.

'Well,' Tama said, 'that's that.'

Miro tried to detain him but he pushed past her.

'Don't talk to me right now, Matua,' he said. 'I didn't deserve this. I feel betrayed. More than that, I am sorry for you. Today, heartache is your guest, Matua.'

Mattie began to laugh. 'Hey, Miro, guess what? For once we're on the same side.' After all these years of keeping the secret of their son from George she had expected to feel, oh, the sweetest revenge at telling him of the baby's death. Instead, the bitter taste of ashes filled her mouth.

The Matua regained her composure. 'Talk some sense for a change,' she answered. She was smouldering. Angry. Where had she gone wrong? Why had she let this happen?

'You and I are both losers,' Mattie said.

And Mattie was out of there, walking swiftly along the driveway, out onto the road and across it, to Sam Walker's place. On the skyline she saw two figures and an old white horse dancing in the sun. One of them was the boy, Pene. How Mattie would have loved to hold him tight and to love him. When her own baby was gone, Pene became her surrogate child. He said to her one day, 'I'll be your little boy now.' He was so candid about it that tears had stung her eyes. She watched out for him when he took the old man on the Parade, making sure that they both had a drink and bread before proceeding on their way. 'Goodbye, Mattie,' Pene would say, gravely, giving her a hug. 'Tomorrow the world will be in a different shack.'

A different place? Mattie gave a bitter laugh as she opened the door of Sam's shack.

'Hey, Mattie —' Jack Ropiho slurred.

'All you bastards still here?' Mattie asked. Same old people: Sam, Jack and Hine, Blacky, Sonny Whatu. They'd been joined by Kepa Jackson, bored out of his mind with Annie. Sitting around the old Mahana homestead was bad enough but Annie had actually wanted him to do some work, fixing a leak in the bathroom. It wasn't his house for fuck's sake. Let the Mahanas come and fix it.

Mattie walked through them and, on the way, pulled Sam after her to the doorway of his bedroom. He had never seen her quite like this, so basilisk, so frightening, and he wanted to say 'No' to her. But, 'I want to be alone with you,' she said, and slammed the door shut with her foot. Kepa gave a mocking wolf-whistle and Sonny made a few grunting noises, but Mattie didn't give a shit. Her eyes were wide, black, staring. She wanted to be punished. She wanted it to hurt.

'What's this about, Mattie?' Sam asked.

'I need a warm body,' Mattie said. 'Are you a warm body, Sam?'

'Not this time, girl,' Sam answered. 'Not like this.' He went to push past her but Mattie sprang at him. She put her arms around him and the coldness of her soul almost stopped his heart.

'Help me, Sam,' Mattie sobbed. 'Please. Help me.'

Something in Sam gave way. He let Mattie's chill, psychic, terrifying grief seep into him — and caught her as she fainted.

Back at Miro's house, the shades gathered around Miro where she sat in the waning light of the sitting-room. She could sense their lugubrious presence. Was that Bobbie, the old man Hopalong and the warrior with the bulging stomach, floating over to her?

'So, Matua, what now? Who is the successor you will anoint in the boy's place?'

'Oh lighten up and go and bother my brother,' Miro growled. 'There are others. It isn't the end of the world.'

Bobbie and her mates smiled indulgently at each other. They knew the Matua had remarkable recuperative powers. The Matua was a fighter.

'I will go to my Maker fighting,' Miro promised them. 'I will take Him on too if I have to.'

PART FOUR

Let My People Go

CHAPTER TWENTY

O sacred house, Rongopai, I greet you.

As in days of old, you still hold up the sky so that all your people can stand upright on the bright strand between. I greet you once, for you still stand triumphant. I greet you twice, for you have witnessed avarice and greed and yet emerged a symbol of resilience and resistance. I greet you a third time, for you have kept alive the millennial dreams of an unconquered tribe. Once, twice, thrice I acclaim you.

Listen, and I will sing you the song of Rongopai.

Following the pardoning of Te Kooti Arikirangi Te Turuki — in February 1883, fifteen years after his attack on the military garrison at Matawhero, in a general amnesty to all those who had 'committed crimes' during the Pakeha Wars — he settled at Te Tokangamutu, near the present town of Te Kuiti. He devoted his energies to developing the Ringatu faith, fusing Christianity and Maori traditions in a complementary relationship. Instead of building churches, he adopted the carved meeting house as the house of worship. The first, Te Whai a Te Motu, was begun in 1870 at Ruatahuna in the Urewera mountains, and its name enshrines Te Kooti's successful evasion of government forces. Te Tokanganui a Noho was begun two years later, in 1872. In 1882, Ruataupare was built by Te Kooti at Te Teko as an expression of gratitude to the people in that region for having supported him. Then, some time in 1886, four disciples from Gisborne journeyed to see the prophet and asked him to come back to Gisborne. He answered the elders, 'All right, go home and build the Gospel on charity and love.' The disciples interpreted their prophet's words literally by building four meeting houses, each one to be a station on Te Kooti's triumphal return: Te Whakahau, meaning 'to start something up', under the supervision of the Haronga family at Rangatira; Te Ngawari, meaning 'charity', supervised by the Peneha family at Mangatu; Te Aroha, meaning 'love', under the supervision of the Ruru family at Tapuihikitia; and Te Rongopai, meaning, 'the Gospel' supervised by the Pere family at Waituhi.

The site chosen for Rongopai was in the lee of a hill where the winds were coolest. It was also near a spring, so bountiful that it supplied the whole of Waituhi with water when there were long dry spells and the river was low. The spring water was reputed to have life-giving and medicinal qualities. Over 600 people from as far away as Tauranga and the villages of the East Coast came to join Te Whanau a Kai to erect Te Rongopai under the supervision of Wi Pere, Waituhi's most famous figure; he vested the responsibility to his son, Moanaroa Pere, and Ringatu elder, Pa Ruru.

From the very beginning Rongopai was built as a temple of the Lord, a cathedral for the Ringatu faith. The builders said prayers morning, noon and night and, in such a spirit of religious fervour, it is no wonder that erecting the meeting house took less than nine months. The deadline was strictly maintained because the plan was to have Rongopai ready for Te Kooti to be present at one of the two great annual Ringatu religious masses on 1 January 1888. Because of this, while some carvings exist, the interior features bravura folk-art painted frescoes that were revolutionary for their time.

The faithful camped out in tents on the hill above the place where Rongopai now stands. They must have been quite a spectacle. They lit bonfires every night and they sang all the day and night long. They travelled far and wide to gather the tree trunks for the framework of Rongopai. The long beam within was made from a log milled from a tall white pine, which was originally standing in the place called Purapurakapiti, some distance away in the Waikohu district. The log was launched into the Waipaoa River and, as it floated down the river, people guided it and sang love songs to it. At Pa Whakarau, a sacred site near Pakowhai settlement, the log ended its river odyssey and began its overland journey. Five hundred tribesmen carried it. The men were told that the work was sacred and, therefore, they should not sleep with their women. Within a quarter of a mile of their destination, while still on flat ground, the log suddenly became immovable. Try as they might, the men could not shift it. Pa Ruru realised the prohibition had been transgressed and asked the transgressors to leave the group. As soon as they did, the log became as light as a feather, and the journey to its destination was completed without any further problem. The meeting house was built, carved and painted on the ground and then lifted into place. The pillars were sunk straight into the earth. It was secured not with nails but by clever dovetailing of all the joints and spars so that they achieved a natural interlock. By October 1887 Te Rongopai was completed, with its kitchen, Te Pao, standing separately. Welcoming arrangements were underway for Te Kooti's arrival.

This is but one of the epic stories told about the building of the meeting house.

Come with me, now, through the gateway to Rongopai.

Do not be afraid. Come. Take my hand. I will tell you something of it, not all, for I don't know all there is to know about the house, but I do know something of its beautiful history and its sense of spirituality.

Rongopai is a large meeting house, and, of course, it does not look like it did when I was a young boy in the 1950s. The guardian of Rongopai is the Wi Pere Trust. The concrete courtyard and the exterior perimeter fencing, including the elaborate shelter for the local elders, are all recent, dating from 1986, as is the dining-hall which honours the great hereditary standing of Riria Mauaranui, the mother of Wi Pere. Regarding the shelter, the protocol for the Wi Pere family is to have the shelter on the left-hand side, not on the right. We owe the beauty of the new meeting-house complex to such as Mahanga Horsefall, Martin Baker, Rangi Edwards, Puku Smiler, Norma Horsefall Haronga, Jim Pere, Caesar Pere, Tom Smiler Snr and to the many young workers who continue with the work today.

One step, and one step further now. We are approaching the porch of Rongopai and it is time to take your shoes off before entering the meeting house. In the old days there was a humble fence with a four-foot-wide gate which you had to go through. Everything temporal, including money, watches and jewellery, were wrapped in a cloth or handkerchief and left at the gate. In those days nobody stole other people's things. It was shameful to steal from one another.

167

Take the time to look at the paintings on the porch. Moanaroa Pere, the architect of Rongopai, is portrayed with other ancestors. The words over the lintel of the front window, *E Nehe Taa*, 'They're the greatest', could be a tribute to the great work of the builders. The porch was lengthened in 1968 by an additional two-metre interior roof extension; the extensions and the supporting upright pillars were carved by John Taiapa.

Now, open the door and enter. The somewhat imperial bronze bust of Wi Pere was installed as part of the Wi Pere Centenary Celebrations in 1990, attended by some 3000 bloodline descendants. The bust was cast by Don ('Tiger') Smiler. Look past the bust and you will see the brightly painted garden that is Rongopai. Indeed, the absence of carvings is precisely why Rongopai is unique. It is a painted house, one of the few left in situ in the country. According to Tom Smiler Jnr, in the 1950s, Professor Trevor Lloyd, curator, Auckland War Memorial Museum, said, 'The paintings of the flora and other art forms in Rongopai compare favourably with the paintings in the Sistine Chapel in Italy. What a tremendous accolade and honour to the skill, courage and intestinal cleverness of all those men and women ancestors of yours. They had the unconquerable spirit of the undefeated.'

Professor Lloyd wanted to dismantle Rongopai in sections, transport it to Auckland, and reconstruct it there. The people of the village said, 'No'. They were right to keep the meeting place on its home soil, where it has become an inspiration to all who visit. However, they've also had to do a lot of work to restore it. Crucial advice has been given by the Gisborne Regional Committee of the New Zealand Historic Places Trust. The installation of protective cladding and a ventilation system has reinforced the structure and prevented it from aggravated dampness and fungicidal erosion. Artists like Cliff Whiting, Buck Nin, Para Matchitt and John Walsh have all assisted in advising on the restoration of the paintwork. Recently, Polly Whaitiri has led woven-panel conservation and Phillip Barry has been in charge of conserving the artwork. And what paintings! Although the exterior is drab, the interior still retains the magical and strange beauty and whimsical spirit with which it was painted those long years ago. They seem infused with an illumination that even the darkness of the house or the years cannot dim.

Look back and up. Above and to one side of the doorway you have just entered are two sets of eyes woven and separately painted within the reed panels. The eyes belong to Tarakiuta and Tarakitai, the twin boys murdered by Tupurupuru. They invoke legendary times involving magic kites. Follow the line of the ceiling. The rafters are painted in the typical designs of Maori native art: bold red, white and black curvilinear scrolls in the shapes of the unfolding fern, the double spiral, the hammerhead shark, the flower of the native berry and the red lips of the forest parrot. Now, bring your eyes down the walls. For as far as the eye can see there are alternating panels of wood and reed work. The reed work is superb: plaited dragon's teeth, the series of small triangles known as the little teeth, the double mouth, the armpit weave, the white crosses of the star seeds, and albatross tears, have all been woven with meticulous care by loving women. But now look through what you see, look at the Maori Garden of Eden which is Rongopai.

Behold the millennial dreams of the tribe.

The panels are tall trees, elaborately painted in greens, blues and reds. They are made of glowing wood and extend along both walls like a pathway into an illuminated forest. Here are the healing powers of the house, symbolised in the profusion of elaborate trees and vines, twining and climbing throughout the interior: reds and purples, brilliant flowers and pods pop out from large Victorian vases; oranges and yellows, sunbursting fruits defy botanical reality; the glorious purple of the Scotch thistle, the greens and creams of seeds float upward to the ceiling; the fabulous Tree of Knowledge of Good and Evil sprouts its twelve separate herbal flowers from a central trunk.

Fantastic birds fly through the forest. They are birds such as were dreamed of in Paradise, flying among bejewelled branches and darting like avian encrustations amid the painted foliage. They are not the only inhabitants of this enchanted forest. The fabulous monsters of the deep emerald oceans, the sea serpents and ocean creatures, the beaked bird-man, the lizard, the seahorse, the semi-human sea monster with the long tubular tongue capable of sucking in both fish and man, all slither within this glittering universe.

And the ancestors are everywhere. They stand, run, climb, fly. Kahungunu is painted on one pillar, handsome and wearing only a waist garment around his thighs to hide the sight of his fabled loins;

Kahungunu's daughter, Tauhei, and his grandson, Mahaki, also have places of honour. More ancestors are painted in the folk-art style, flourishing lances and clubs, but cleverly inflected with European references. A warrior stands with flax skirt and ornamental band around his head; in his hair he wears not the traditional royal huia feather but rather a purple Scotch thistle. A painted woman, Hine Hakirirangi, wears a pretty European dress with a hint of a Victorian bustle, and holds a red rose to her lips. Two men spar in a boxing match, stilted figures which seem to move, sway and bend toward each other; they are a sly reference to the ongoing conflict between the Crown and the tribe. A bushman holds an axe, a metaphoric reference to the clearing of bush for farmland and the future impact upon the people. Delicately daubed horses lift their hooves in a timeless race. Savage figures brandishing warrior weapons reach out from the darkness. Strange animals peer from behind the painted foliage. Wi Pere is also there, breaking with the usual tradition of incorporating images only of the dead. He is shown in the formal attire of black jacket, grey trousers, hat and spurs on his heels. His mother, Riria Mauaranui, from whom his inherited title descended, perches on his shoulder like a guardian owl. Wi Pere was in the Upper House at the time and the painted chair behind him indicates his position as a Maori Minister of the Crown.

Oh there is so much else to see. And remember: only the white paint has been retouched in the restoration work; the coloured paint is still the original paint of 1887. The four emblems from the deck of cards are painted on one end of a rafter beam and elsewhere in the house. The spade is upside down and is not an uncommon sight in a number of Ringatu houses. The cards represent the changing balances of political power. Of interest are also the nautical signs, the propellers, flags and tillers which reference Te Kooti's early personal history as a seaman.

Now seek you, the painting of Adam and Eve in the Garden. Of all the paintings this one is beyond comparison. To look at it is to weep. This Maori Adam and Eve are depicted clothed with cloaks and holding Maori weaponry in their hands. These are no passive representations of the first man and woman. This Adam and Eve come out fighting. In particular, they defy the old interpretation that Rongopai depicts the blending of Maori and Pakeha worlds, a new world of two races joining. The paintings were once seen as symbolising the twilight years of the

Maori, but these are interpretations which come from a colonised mind. Decolonise that same mind and you will see the paintings for what they really are: petroglyphs of resistance, iconographs of resilience, statements of Maori surviving within the colonial world. *Te Whanau a Kai pana pana maro*; we never retreat.

Indeed, there are other stories which need to be refuted. For instance, the hoary old tale that when some elders of the village came to view the work they were shocked with what they saw, closed the doors, and placed a ban on Rongopai. This story does not stand up. Surely the elders had plenty of time in the nine months of building the house to make their views known so that this somewhat radical step could be prevented? Not only that, but the oral histories of the Pere family record that the meeting house was an integral part of the lives of the people of Waituhi and other local areas who were generally part of the Ringatu faith. Any ban that was on Rongopai was resolved when it was lifted in 1952 by priests of the Ringatu.

Another ambiguous story relates to the Scotch thistle that once was there. Priests said that because of the thistle Te Kooti would never enter. Yet, this same purple thistle is emblematic of Waituhi; you see it all over the place. Nevertheless, in subsequent years, it came to be seen as heralding misfortune and was whitened out on the instruction of the seer, Hori Gage.

From the darkness of ignorance and colonised interpretation, Rongopai has emerged in all its magnificence. In the light of our times, we can now see it with all its political and aesthetic meanings intact. It gives life to the tribe; the tribe gives life to it. Away from it they will wither. Rongopai is in their blood and they are the blood of the land. Through the meeting house blood links blood, and blood links years, and blood links families now and over all the years past. It is good to have your ancestral place and your meeting house to belong to. If you have a meeting house you have a location. No matter where you live in the world, whether in Australia, the largest of all Maori diaspora, or the United States, you can fix your compass point from your meeting house knowing that no matter where you go you can always return to the centre.

Your meeting house will always transcend the tangled threads of history and the ebb and flow of human folly.

If you want to know what my heart looks like, look to Rongopai.

CHAPTER TWENTY-ONE

—— 1 ——

The kite turning, the kite turning. As it turned, the darkness lowered. A gust of wind flung the kite toward the hills, to the nearby community of Patutahi. There, shaking with grief, George Karepa stopped his car. The bravado he had exhibited at his meeting with the Matua fell away, leaving him an empty shell.

'What have I done? Oh, what have I done?' he asked himself.

The Matua had raised him, supported him, loved him and he had turned his back on her. George was so upset that he began to dry retch. The enormous price of his actions in also relinquishing his birthright was dawning on him. But he couldn't go back. Having burnt all his bridges, all he could do now was to keep on walking into his future. One step. And one step further now.

'And my son? I had a son? And Mattie killed him?'

The kite swooped back to earth. The world constricted. Below was Waituhi.

The valley was darkening with shadows but the old homestead where Riripeti Mahana once lived was still in sunlight. Annie Jackson was taking the opportunity to water her vegetable garden; she also had an eye out for Pene and Tamati Kota. It was getting late. Where were they? At last she saw Dinah Walker letting them out of her car.

'Have these two been playing hookey?' Dinah laughed. 'Do they belong to you?' She had seen them from her kitchen window hurrying home, knew they were late getting back from their Parade, and brought them the rest of the way. They looked beat.

'Thanks, Dinah,' Annie shouted. 'You just get in here, Pene. What do you mean keeping the old man out all afternoon? Look at him. He's absolutely stuffed.'

The houses looked small from this height and the people even smaller. Hana Walker was on the telephone to Janey Whatu; they were over their irritation with each other and chatting about whatever teenage girls talk about when there's actually nothing to talk about. Hine Ropiho was returning to the party after checking on Boy Boy; her grandmother Heni was not a fit babysitter. As Hine ducked into Sam's shack she heard Maka tiko bum shouting out her window, 'Sam, how long are you boozers going to keep up this ruckus?' Sam parted the curtains and Maka saw he had Mattie in bed with him, the wicked boy. 'Till the walls of Jericho come tumbling down, Auntie,' Sam laughed. Sonny Whatu wandered out yet again to water her flowers. He didn't even care Maka was watching. He unzipped his fly and, although she didn't want it, gave her a good close-up. 'Blacky's is bigger,' Maka yelled. She saw the alarm on Sonny's face; in his male world bigger always equated with better, and she was so glad she had ruined his day. She averted her eyes — well, one of them anyway — and saw Pita, Miriama, Waka and Ani, home from the hills, turning into their driveway.

Caught in the middle of the four winds, the kite became motionless. Suspended above Rongopai, it began to turn, look and seek.

2

Annie Jackson took a stick to Pene, whacking him hard across the legs.

'Look at your Nani,' she scolded him. 'He's really exhausted. What did you do with him out there on the Parade? You know better than to stay out at this hour.'

'Don't hit the boy,' Tamati Kota said. 'It wasn't his fault.'

Annie wasn't listening. She hustled them into the bathroom and ran the bath. She undressed Tamati Kota, helped him in and soaped him up. Pene waited his turn. 'Look at you both,' Annie glared at him while she slopped, slapped and scrubbed the old man down. 'Your clothes dirty,

173

your feet dirty, and what's this on your shirt, old man?' Uh oh, the blackberry stains. 'How am I going to get this out in the wash? Damn kid,' Annie said to Pene. 'Sometimes, I don't know what's the matter with you. Next time, I'll take the broom to you.'

Sometimes, when Annie was stressed out like this, both Pene and Tamati Kota knew it was better to stay quiet, keep out of trouble and not answer back. Mum sure was angry tonight. Not just at them, of course. They were unlucky enough to stray onto the shooting range when she had the rifle in her hand. No, she was stressing out over that drop-dead useless Kepa. When was he going to get some work and bring home some money? The only dollars coming into the house were his unemployment cheque, and the money that Social Welfare and Riripeti's will gave her fortnightly to care for Tamati Kota. The money from Riripeti's will was the lifesaver and, on its own, was enough to keep them going. But what did Kepa do? Spend it as if he had won the lottery.

Annie helped the old man out of the bath, put a towel around him and rubbed him down. 'Your dinner's on the table, Paora,' she said. 'Let's go and eat. As for you, Pene, you wash yourself all over. Don't come to the table until everything, and I mean everything, is clean, folded and tucked away. Is that clear?'

'All right, Mum,' Pene answered. 'Sorry, Mum.' He was snivelling because he was sorry for himself. He hopped into Nani Paora's water, hoping the old man hadn't urinated in it. The water was cold and he didn't want to stay in too long. He soaped and flannelled and by the time he finished, he was shivering. He put on his pyjamas and went to the kitchen.

'Are you all right, Grandchild?' Tamati Kota asked. 'Poor Grand-child, you always get the blame.' The old man stroked Pene's head and made soft reassuring noises.

'It's his own fault,' Annie said, her anger still boiling over. Part of Tamati Kota's cheque was supposed to go to keeping up the homestead, and Kepa had done nothing on any repairs. Where was he now? Boozing over at Sam's. Let's face it, Annie had married the wrong man. 'Pene, you ready for your dinner now?' Pene wasn't hungry. 'My goodness,' Annie growled. 'I made it for you and you better eat it, boy.' Pene seated himself at the table and Mum dished the food out. 'If it's cold, tough. Dinner won't be waiting for you next time.'

While Pene was eating his dinner, Annie took Tamati Kota down the hallway to his bedroom. She put his dressing-gown on and sat him in a chair so that he could watch television. For some strange reason, perhaps because she had seen old people treated like this at an old people's home she once visited, she assumed that this was what you were supposed to do with an old person at night: bathe him, give him his dinner, let him watch television for an hour and then put him to bed. 'Let's see what's on tonight,' she said. 'Look at this! Your favourite programme, *Lost in Space*.' She gave him a kiss on the forehead. The volume wasn't on loud enough so she turned it up enough to pierce his eardrums and closed the door.

'Good, one out of the way.' Annie returned to the kitchen. Pene had finished his dinner. 'All done, Mum,' he called. It hadn't been much fun having dinner alone. 'Do your dishes then,' Annie answered. Pene took his dishes to the sink. He ran water into the basin. He washed and dried the dishes, wiped the table down and set the chairs neatly around it. When Annie saw how carefully he had tidied up, she felt awful for hitting him. He was such a good boy really. But she had to be firm.

'You were very naughty today. Go to bed now.'

Pene flung his arms around her. 'I'm sorry, Mum.'

Annie took out a cigarette and lit it. She began to shake. She, Kepa and Pene were already close enough to the breadline. They had been lucky that somebody — who was it? — had suggested to her, 'Hey, why don't you make the application to be your great-grandfather's caregiver?' Of course Kepa, out of work, had jumped at it as a way of putting them on easy street. Because of it they had a roof over their heads. Tamati Kota was their meal ticket. What would happen when the old man went?

Pene ran down the hallway. He took his usual detour into Nani Paora's room. Nani was waiting for him. 'Hello, my little mate,' he said. 'We're both in the doghouse, eh?' He kissed Pene on the forehead. 'You better go before you get another whack.'

But Annie had already forgotten about Pene and the old man. Sitting in the kitchen, she got moodier and moodier. In the end she stubbed out her cigarette. 'Dammit,' she swore as she decided to join Kepa at Sam Walker's, 'I need a party too.' She went to the bathroom, looked critically at her image, ran a comb through her hair and put lipstick on. Pene and Tamati Kota would be all right. She and Kepa had left them alone plenty of times. The boys wouldn't even know she was gone. She slipped silently out of the house and over to Sam's. 'The more the merrier,' Blacky greeted her.

Tamati Kota sat in the blue light of a dark bedroom watching bizarre images of a world he could not comprehend: a boy, a robot, a scientist, a family lost on an asteroid floating in the universe. The images were all accompanied by recorded studio laughter as if what the people on the television screen were doing was humorous. It was a surreal world making no sense and without any sacredness to it. At first, Tamati Kota watched in silence. He swayed back and forth. His mouth cracked open.

In his room, Tamati Kota began to chant.

————— 3 —————

It was getting dark. 'Time to bring in the kite,' August said.

He tugged the kite quickly earthward. From the outer perimeter of the village he pulled it, over Rongopai and back down to where he was standing with his brothers and sisters, June, July, Anzac, Crete, Daisy and Hope. Just in time. Big Mama appeared at the doorway calling for them. 'You kids come inside before the ghosts get you,' she yelled. 'Quick.'

The sight of their mother gave the children pause. Within the lighted square of the doorway she looked so vulnerable. August looked at his siblings and put out his hand to them. One by one they put their hands on top of his. They had made a pact about their mother to look after her forever. On the night August had fought their father, the other children had stood by, screaming. When Dad came out of prison, and if it happened again, they had vowed that August wasn't fighting alone.

Nodding, and war whooping, the children darted through the paddock, over the fence and up to the steps of their house where Teria counted them in.

'Good. All accounted for. Time to wash behind your ears, have dinner and go to bed.'

At Rongopai, Andrew Whatu was surprised at the sudden fall of darkness.

176

He looked at his watch. His father was rhythmically bending to the work of scything. After a long apprenticeship on the land, he worked with a freedom and fluidity of movement beautiful to see. He worked at his own pace, each action measured to that pace. Time did not control him. He didn't seem aware of time at all. It didn't really matter how long a task might take. Only that it was done.

'Hey, Dad,' Andrew called. 'You said we'd be finished by four and it's almost six.'

Charlie took his hat off and wiped at his brow. Hard work this, and his back felt sore, but there was a deep sense of satisfaction in working the land, a pleasurable feeling of achievement. He and Andrew had accomplished a lot this day. 'Right-oh,' he said. 'Why don't you go and wash up? I'll finish off what I'm doing. I hope your mother has a good dinner ready for us when we get home.'

With a nod, Andrew walked around Rongopai to the tap at the back. He loved his meeting house and had never been afraid of it. Why should he be? People told mystical stories about the house — of miraculous happenings, bushes on fire but not on fire, men and women speaking in the tongues of angels, visitations by the Holy Ghost, spirits congregating among the faithful and praying with them, comets appearing over the hills. They were manifestations of godliness and, unless evil resided in you, nobody needed to be afraid of them.

But people *were* afraid. Certainly the Pakeha had been afraid. The Pakeha stopped Te Kooti from returning to see the beautiful cathedral the faithful built for him. In the *Poverty Bay Herald* edition of 24 October 1887, the *Herald* spoke for the majority of the Pakeha citizens in objecting to what was happening at Waituhi:

'There is not the slightest use in appealing to the natives who are taking a hand in honouring Te Kooti. They are utterly beyond any influence of civilisation save that of the strong arm of the law. There is little doubt that the place selected for the gathering has been chosen for the purpose of showing contempt for and in defiance of the opinion of the English settlers.'

A vigilance committee was set up and local settlers contributed to a Poverty Bay Defence Fund. A force comprising sixty-seven members of the fully armed Permanent Artillery, sixty-five East Coast Hussars with carbine weapons, ten members of the Armed Corps with revolvers and batons and thirty-five Ngati Porou soldiers intercepted Te Kooti at Waiotahi fortress, issued a warrant for disturbing the peace and illegal assembly, and turned him back. He died seven years later on 17 April 1893 in exile at Wainui, adjacent to Ohiwa Harbour, never having seen Rongopai at all. It was left to others, like Riripeti whom some called Artemis, to carry on the prophet's work in Waituhi.

Andrew rinsed his face and hands. The bargeboards of Rongopai loomed above him like a huge arrow pointing at the sky. Directly behind Rongopai was the sacred altar where the Ringatu held prayers and healed the sick. Sometimes copper coins bearing the effigies of the British crown were burnt or buried in the ground. Looking across at the altar, Andrew stood up and called out, as if there were people there, listening.

'They never wanted peace,' Andrew said. 'Although Te Kooti entreated them, "*Kia hora te maungarongo,*" let peace be widespread, it suited their purposes to continue their war with us.'

He sprinkled water over his head for protection. Tomorrow would be a good day to start with, to begin battle from.

———— 4 ————

Karangatia ra! Karangatia ra! Powhiritia ra!
Nga iwi o te motu! Haere mai!

Charlie and Andrew Whatu weren't the only ones working in the twilight. So was Rongo Mahana, bending to the harvesting. The truth was that Rongo had completely forgotten the time. He was enjoying himself. As he worked he sang a popular Maori song:

'Let the call go out for all to assemble here —'

The words arrowed sharply through his mind and he began to think of the great Maori sports and cultural tournaments that used to happen throughout Maoridom. Whose idea was it? That's right, it was Apirana Ngata in the 1920s who got the people started. Te Apirana knew that because Maori loved their sports, they should have competitions of their own in hockey, rugby, tennis and golf and, while they were at it, hey, they could also combine sports with Maori cultural dance competitions. Sport and culture would keep intratribal relationships going in a changing world and enable tribal connections to be maintained between Ngati Porou, Waikato, Kahungunu, Te Arawa and Te Whanau a Kai. A renaissance might occur of Maori culture and Maori art. All that which had been lost after the wars with the Pakeha could be regained, perhaps, perhaps.

Guess which village was one of the first to front up to the challenge? Waituhi, that's who, with hockey teams dating from 1928 and offering up trophies like the Hine Te Ariki cup, the Hana Konewa shield and the Riripeti Mahana Challenge Trophy — in the shape of a huge attacking spider — for competition. By the 1940s, over fifty teams from all over Maori country were competing.

'Come, welcome,' Rongo sang, 'join together in unity —'

Rongo couldn't help putting some high-stepping style into his harvesting. Teams came from Whangarei to the Bluff. By bus, by train, by car they came, gathering together, playing and laughing together. They slept together on straw in large marquees too, haw haw, because the tournaments were an opportunity for the young people to fall in love and, if they got lucky, to make out. Of course, making out in those days was different to making out in these days and you had to get married before you could — you know — do *it*. During the daytime the sport was furious. During the night time the cultural competitions were just as furious, the boys trying to show off their fabulous bodies in the war dance and the girls swinging their hips and showing off their child-bearing properties. You think those boys got married just to have *sex*? No, they also got married so that they could raise their own First Fifteen or First Eleven.

Yes sirree, such good memories of good times. Even when it rained there were good times because the rain gave everybody an excuse to cuddle up a little closer, baby, and to escape the raindrops falling through holes in the canvas onto their heads. Somebody was bound to refer to Taraipine Tutaki who sang the Te Whanau a Kai rain song — but somehow got confused about her directions and caused a flood way down in the Hawke's Bay, good grief. 'Not her again,' they would laugh. They washed together, they got dressed in front of each other, and there was no embarrassment. The older (married) couples made love while the others pretended to sleep. Some of the cheeky ones, though, would yell, 'Hey, is that an earthquake I can feel?' or, 'Would somebody tell that volcano to hurry up and erupt?' or, when, after an hour, it was finally over, 'Gee, that was quick.'

'Come, welcome —' Rongo whistled.

He remembered that he had met his wife, Huia, at one of the tournaments. She was a Ngati Porou girl from Ruatoria, and the captain of her hockey team. Rongo had his eye on her all that week and just loved her forthright — some would call it bossy — captaining and the way she led her team. From her position as halfback she yelled her loving comments across the field.

'You call yourself a hockey player, Henrietta? Get after that ball and be quick about it. And you, Wiki Hiroki, what are you standing around for? The goal posts are the only ones supposed to stand still! Hey, Arihia, this isn't a beauty contest so never mind about your hair and just chase that ball eh! Oh, my giddy aunt, Karen, if you can't stop that girl, what the heck are you doing on the field! She hit you? Well hit her back then. Are you a mouse or something? Quick now, here's our chance. Hit the ball into the circle, Henrietta. Hurry up, Wiki, chase after that ball. Never mind about those legs being in the way. Hit the ball. Hit it! Hit it, stupid! Well, what do you know. We actually got a goal. About time, eh. But no time to rest. Back to the start again, girls. And let me see you play some real hockey for a change.'

'That's the girl for me,' Rongo had decided. He made his play for her straight after a game that her team had actually lost. He thought if he told her how sorry he was that they didn't win, that would give him a few brownie points. No such luck. Huia was giving a debriefing to her team:

'Well, we were good today, but not good enough. Henrietta, you better start losing some weight. Wiki, it's about time you went for some training runs. As for you, Arihia, the next time I see you patting at your hair instead of swinging at the ball, I'm going to get my scissors and cut your hair all off. I've seen kids play better hockey than you girls do.' That's when Rongo stepped up to the plate with his idiotic grin and flushed face. Huia took one look at him and had his number. 'Just what I don't need,' she muttered. 'Another fan.' How was he to know there had been a few other boys after Huia? Or that she had taken to heart the advice her mother had given her about boys from Te Whanau a Kai: 'They have a hundred lovers and they are not faithful.'

But Rongo and Huia had managed to work through their differences and, before he knew it, Rongo was all trussed up like a turkey and married. He would not have wanted anything else in the world. When you had a Ngati Porou woman in your life, you were fortunate indeed.

Rongo stood up for a breather. Charlie Whatu saw him as he and Andrew walked home. 'Hey, Rongo, if you do everything today, you won't leave anything for tomorrow,' Charlie laughed good-naturedly.

'My God,' Rongo said. 'Is that the time?' Hurriedly he put his spade and sacks in the back of the truck. 'Huia will be really cross if I get home too late.'

But the memories of the Maori sports tournaments hadn't finished with him. He felt a kick to his guts for, over the last few years, the hockey tournaments had gone into recess. Oh, face the facts, hockey had been declining for some time and, after all, wasn't that just the way life was? Sometimes you were on the way up on the wheel of fortune and other times you were on the way down.

Even so, nobody had expected Maori hockey to drop completely off the board. Each year, fewer and fewer teams participated at the district level and a Waituhi team had struggled on only because the Matua had bullied everybody to keep it on the field. Like her commitment to her church and to her land, sport, too, was part of her strategy in maintaining her tribe. She had organised the annual meetings, throwing in a church service just so that she could justify her efforts on religious grounds, and Tama drove the bus whenever their teams competed with other tribes. Lately she had begun to bully Rongo to get the tournaments started again.

Rongo got into his truck and set off down the track towards the road. He was just about to turn left back into Gisborne when, in his mind's eye, he saw Miro wagging a finger at him. 'Never put off till tomorrow what you can do today.' He turned right in the direction of his brother Pita's place to talk about taking responsibility for the sports tournaments.

'Ah well, if I'm going to be late I may as well be really late so that Huia can give me a really good growling.'

The hills were quiet now, the shadows falling. The land sighed for Rongo's return for he was the blood of the land. Throughout the valley lights were coming on, the houses twinkling like fireflies in the night.

We call you! We call you here! Assemble here,
All the people, welcome! Welcome!

———— 5 ————

'Are you ready, Miriama?' Pita asked. He was getting anxious about the visit to Annie and Kepa Jackson's place. He was so nervous that he had decided to put on a white shirt and good trousers and a jacket. Going to see Tamati Kota required such formality.

A knock sounded at the door. 'Not another Maori to ask for a big favour,' Miriama groaned. She was secretly glad. She wasn't looking forward to visiting Annie and Kepa at all and a visitor might mean that Pita would get to talking, and that might lead to cancelling going out.

'Hello, brother,' Pita said when he saw Rongo at the doorway. Then, 'Oh no,' he groaned, 'the harvesting.' Rongo had brought him a couple of sacks of spuds. 'I'm sorry, brother, I got a call this morning from Wayne at Mairangi Station. Me and Miriama went out to help him and we've only just got back. I guess Teria didn't turn up either? No.'

'Well, there's always tomorrow,' Rongo answered. He could see Pita was really pissed off with himself.

'I'll make a cup of tea,' Miriama said.

'No,' Rongo answered. 'I can see you're going somewhere, but this won't take long. Pita, the Matua came to see me last week. She told me she wants to start up the Maori sports tournaments again.'

What Miro had really said was, 'Me and Tama have got too much on our plates with our church business, so I want to delegate this responsibility to somebody else. That somebody is you, Rongo Mahana.' She had cocked a beady eye at him, indicating this was an offer that was not to be refused. 'After all, you are a descendant of Riripeti Mahana and she was the one who donated her shield.'

'So what did you say to her?' Pita asked. How strange it was that things came in twos. Here he was, ready to go and rectify the situation of the Mahana family's own making, and here was Rongo, coming to see him on a similar matter.

'I said yes,' Rongo said. 'Our family must take a leadership position again, brother. I know that must sound rich coming from me, now that I live in Gisborne, but since the days of Riripeti we've gone backward.

We've got nobody to blame except ourselves, but we've got to start thinking about the family again.'

And everything in Pita's body said, *Yes*. This was it. This was what his visit to Tamati Kota was all about. A symbolic reclaiming of all that the Mahana family had stood for. Reclaiming the inherited title of the Mahanas. Although Rongo was talking about this in the context of sport, it was still the same objective.

'As far as the tournaments are concerned,' Rongo continued, 'I need you to help me. Financially, I can raise the money needed to ensure the tournaments don't keep running at a loss. I want you to talk to the people out here to start working together again like they did in the old days. We need an organising and planning committee; Hepa Walker would be good at chairing that. We also need a committee to look after catering. I was thinking that our sis, Teria, could do that — she could go around getting people to promise to donate what they can — pork, poultry, fish, cabbages, you know the sort of thing. I'm thinking that we should hold the first tournament next Easter.'

'That soon?' Pita asked, his eyes glowing. 'I'm right behind you, brother. I want this to happen as much as you do. In fact it's been bothering me all day, this question of taking back the leadership role our family had once in Waituhi. Although Riripeti is no longer with us, we have to take over where she left off. We have to bring everyone together again, all the people who have been scattered to the four winds.'

Then, oh so casually, Pita added something else. 'Oh, brother, did I tell you? Miriama and I are going over to look in on Tamati Kota.'

'Tamati Kota?' Rongo answered. His voice was hushed with reverence. 'I haven't seen that old man for years.

'I'll come with you,' he said.

CHAPTER TWENTY-TWO

————— 1 —————

An old man chanting in the dark, looking into the dark, invoking the dark. As he chanted, passionate, eloquent, the wind changed direction. Before, it had been blowing from the warmth of the north. Now it came from the cold of the south. The owl nesting with its young was surprised, ruffling its feathers and huddling its chicks closer for warmth. Soon it would have to go on its mission. The chant grew stronger, cleaving a pathway, come rain, come wind, come elements, come storm, come to Waituhi, come.

'*Pinepine te kura,*' Tamati Kota sang, his eyes wide with lightning. 'Here then are the tidings of peace made welcome. Let us go together to Turanga, so that there I may lay down before you the machinery, the arms, the murderous weapons of the Pakeha. Arise! Let us ascend by the whirlwind path of Enoch.'

His voice slashed the air to shreds. 'Even in being shaped by the mouth, the law is twisted, yet it touches all. Standing above even the Queen's power, even over the covenant made by our ancestor, David. Search for the bridge, O people, the shedding of light, revealing how men can live in grace in the world.

'O people, seek that good word. It is you, Pakeha, alone who hate,' the old man sang, his words wild with the wind. 'From the porch, I look across the sea and see the mist rising. My people, I tell you that your relation yearns to return to you, to provide you sustenance, but your banquet was of the bullets you fired at me. Dig the wax from your ears and listen; although it was I who warned you not to strike me, I alone am banished. This is a false truce.'

He pointed a finger and spittle sprayed from his lips. 'You never were satisfied with victory at Waerenga a Hika. My people you imprisoned. Myself you exiled to the Chathams, yet I returned to you across the sea, landing at Whareongaonga. Then was to be heard the cry of the Government.

'Your power was brought against me by mistake,' he accused, his voice rising, breaking, roaring, 'and now the bitter taste cannot be drowned in strong drink. Your animosity feeds on shame and jealousy. O my people, leave such evil things behind.'

Tamati Kota stopped chanting. Just like that. And waited.

——— 2 ———

The moon went out.

From out of nowhere, the storm burst across the sky. It came out of Te Kore, the dark void at the very beginning of Time, and split the heavens apart. The landscape quaked. The universe was torn apart by sudden winds.

'Where the hell did that come from?' Rongo asked. He, Pita and Miriama had just parked their vehicles in the driveway of the homestead. The landscape was so dark he could hardly see his way. But lights were on in the homestead and guided them. They reached the verandah just in time. The rain came squalling down.

Pene heard a rapping at the door. 'Annie? Kepa? Is anyone at home?'

The rapping became more insistent. Pene looked out the window. Darkness and rain. Three people at the front door. Where was Mum? He pondered whether he should go to see what the visitors wanted, but Mum had always told him that if she or Dad weren't home, he was not to answer the door at night. Instead, Pene pushed back the blankets and ran to Nani Paora's room.

'Some people are outside,' Pene said. Nani Paora was sitting in his chair. The television set bathed the room in bizarre flickering blue light. Nani Paora looked at Pene and saw the boy was afraid. He opened his arms and Pene climbed into his lap. His fingers fluttered across Pene's face. He traced the boy's profile and caressed his cheeks. He waited.

And the Three Wise Men found him and came in unto him.

'This must be the old man's room,' Pita said. He turned the doorknob. He saw the old man and boy sitting together watching television. With tears in his eyes, he went forward unto Tamati Kota, fell on his knees and kissed the old man's left hand. He turned to look at his brother, Rongo. 'See?' he asked. 'See what the bastards have done to our old one? They have left him here, alone with the boy, in a bedroom without light.'

Rongo approached Tamati Kota, this man who had been Riripeti's priest, who had anointed her to her calling. This same man, the oldest living member of Te Whanau a Kai had helped Artemis, she who wore pearls in her hair, to build the Ship of God during the flu epidemic of 1918. Through his ministrations, many of the people had been saved from the plague. Tamati Kota, for it truly was he, had survived the Second World War and, with Riripeti, had tried to keep the people together during those great and turbulent post-war years when the faithful streamed to the cities, leaving only the survivors behind. At Artemis's funeral, he had wanted to die with her.

Bending beside his brother, Rongo pressed noses with the old man.

'Friend,' he began, 'beloved priest. Is this really you?' The old man's face was gaunt. Lined. Ancient.

'Yes,' Tamati Kota answered. 'I recognise you, son, you who are descended from she whom I served.' He hit his breast with a fist. 'A wilful and stubborn heart still pumps the blood rich red through my veins.'

Miriama intervened, trying to placate the two brothers. 'Maybe Kepa and Annie are out the back,' she said. 'My sister would never leave Tamati Kota alone for long.'

The old man was eager to know something. He looked at Pita, at Rongo, and behind them to see if they had brought somebody else with them. 'Is he who is the king yet to come, is he among you?'

'The old man's rambling,' Rongo said. He saw the disappointed look on the old man's face. 'Do you know where your parents are, boy?' he asked Pene.

'They must have gone to Sam Walker's place,' Pene answered. 'And Nani's not alone. I look after him. I'm good at looking after him.'

'The bastards,' Pita said. 'Boozing all day and night. Who knows what might happen while they're away? The house could burn down. The old man could have a heart attack. Would they care? Oh no, they'd be too drunk to care.' His eyes set with determination. He had made up his mind what to do even before he came tonight. 'Help me with him, brother, I'm taking him home with me.'

'Dear,' Miriama interrupted, 'I don't think that is a good idea. Why don't we come back in the morning.' She was gentling him, soothing him, thinking of the court order which had awarded the care of Tamati Kota to Annie. 'Yes, let's come back in the morning.'

Tamati Kota started coughing, a low wheezing cough, arching out from deep inside his body. 'Are you all right, Nani?' Pene asked, alarmed. He held Nani Paora close to him but the spasm would not pass. Desperately, Pene put his hands across the old man's mouth to stop the noise coming out. Pita took it away.

'Come, old one,' Pita said. 'You should be among people who respect you and love you.'

He picked the old man up in his arms.

--------- 3 ---------

Rimurimu, tere tere, e rere ki te moana e
Tere ana ki te ripo i waho e

'I have a band of men and all they do is play for me. They come from miles around to hear them play a melody. Beneath the stars my ten guitars will play a song for you. And if you're with the one you love, this is what you do.'

The rain was coming down in torrents. The moon came out and in the wan moonlight, the rain looked like thousands of silver javelins being thrown from heaven.

Mattie was alone in Sam Walker's bedroom. When she'd recovered from her faint, Sam had given her the comfort she wanted. Skin on skin. Two people trying to find some solace from the world. Animal gratification. It meant nothing, and after they'd made love — what a joke that something made of lust and sweat should be considered love —

they'd lain in each other's arms. Some bugger had barged in, it might have been Sonny Whatu, to tell Sam that the beer was running out and they needed to go and get some more supplies. Sonny knew a hotel where you could bribe the owner if you had sufficient cash. Sam went off with him and they made it back just before the storm. Mattie decided to get up, wash herself, pull a brush through her hair, and go out and join him.

'Oh oh hula, hula, hula to my ten guitars. And very soon you'll know just where you are. Through the eyes of love you'll see a thousand stars. When you hula, hula, hula to my ten guitars.'

'Look at the rain,' Blacky said. 'It's pissing down.'

Sam's shack was really rocking. It didn't take long for people around here to smell the beer and, before you knew it, the whole of Waituhi was there to party. One sniff and they came to drink, laugh, talk the night away, and to sing. The last one to come on board had been Annie Jackson, and now she was dancing up a storm with Sonny Whatu. Nothing much else to do on a Sunday anyway, and partying was at least some compensation, some reward, for working your butt off from Monday to Friday. If you got too boozed to make work tomorrow, not to worry. Plenty of other jobs. If not, something would turn up.

Mattie couldn't even make it to the door of Sam's bedroom. All of a sudden she collapsed, sobbing her heart out. She was cold, empty, and nothing — not fucking or partying — could stop her from mourning her life, George, her dead baby, oh her dead baby. 'You want to know how your baby boy died, George Karepa? I killed him. His own mother killed him.'

And Mattie began to sing a sad lament for her dead boy, a song about the sea and a dead child floating away across the waves.

Rimurimu, tere tere, e rere ki te moana e. *Seaweed drifting, drifting, drifting. Carrying my child away from me. Drifting, floating, floating, drifting, toward the whirlpool on the sea.*

Lightning flared, luminous, foreboding.

Who knows why a woman has a child to a man who has left her? If you really want to know, ask this woman, Mattie Jones, because only a woman who has carried such a child for nine months can tell you. Love must have a lot to do with it because, look at her. She's still in love with George Karepa. Nothing can burn him out of her soul. He is there until she goes to her grave.

When she discovered she was pregnant, Mattie could have terminated the pregnancy, but she didn't. In Wellington, her friends Whetu and Marama pleaded with her to see an abortionist they knew, but she closed her ears to them. Why? Surely, love for George Karepa, because she wanted to bear his son. During those months she carried the child in her, she loved it, surely. When Miro Mananui and Tama turned up at her doorstep to ask her to return with them to Waituhi, it was only right that she should take up their offer of a place to give birth to her boy. That was love, surely, because Waituhi was George Karepa's ancestral birthplace and, like George, his son would be a son of this earth. No mother could honour a man more than to bear a son for the tribe.

Do you want to hear a story? One day this woman, Mattie, rocking herself in the cradle of her own arms, went to the afternoon movies in Gisborne. She was in her eighth month, not uncomfortable, still carrying the baby high. The filmgoers in the audience were a mix of children with grownups. When the movie began Mattie realised she'd come to the wrong film. This one was for children. It was about a mother elephant who had a boy child with big flappy ears that enabled him to fly. But they were separated and the mother elephant was chained up, and the poor boy elephant was all alone and lonely for his mother. He came to see her while she was locked up and she put her trunk through the bars and sang him a lullaby: 'Baby mine, don't you cry.' Coming out into the light, Mattie's eyes streamed with tears and, for the rest of her pregnancy, that was the song she would sing to her boy whenever he kicked and squirmed and moved inside her: 'Don't you cry, baby mine.'

It was all for love, surely.

Then why is it that this woman, spangled with a thousand tears, hugging herself, trying to stop herself from breaking apart, is mourning so terribly, so deeply?

I'll tell you why. Mattie Jones didn't have her baby out of love. She had her baby out of hatred.

189

Kei te tio, te huka, i runga o nga hiwi. *Look out yonder, all is calm there. But my heart rains with stormy tears. Seaweed drifting, drifting, drifting. My child floating away on the sea.*

The rain, like stormy tears, falling.

When Mattie Jones had her boy, love had nothing to do with it. From the very beginning she planned him to be an instrument of blackmail. For nine months she carried him out of anger. What kind of mother would do that? What kind of mother would whisper to her foetus all the angry and smouldering thoughts she had about his father? What kind of mother would dream of how she would punish George with this child and then send the dreams to the child so that it would know its role in her madness? What kind of mother would dream of flaunting her boy child in his father's face, offer him up to his father, and then snatch him back, 'Fuck you, George Karepa'? And what kind of mother would say to her unborn child, 'When you grow up, I want you to hate your father as much as I hate him.' From the very beginning, she wanted to have the baby to punish George for what he did to her. She had the child out of hatred.

And when the child was born, what else should anybody have expected but a child blackened, bruised and misshapen by all the evil his mother had poured into him?

The doctors suspected there might be complications when the pregnancy developed alarming signs. They took X-rays. The negatives showed that the baby was malformed, with a large encephalic head and abnormally stunted arms and legs. They didn't want to tell Mattie. It was better not to let the mother know. She already had enough on her mind. But they did tell the Matua to expect the worst.

'Oh, Mattie, what have you done?' the Matua asked. She touched Mattie's stomach and gave an involuntary cry because she felt the baby writhing with pain. At the same time she heard its tiny soul screaming for help.

The birth was supposed to be Mattie's moment of triumph. When she came to labour and was taken into the delivery room she was ecstatic. She had worked hard for this, and the pain was going to be worth it. Perspiring, hysterical with joy, she gave a huge powerful push and he came spilling out of her. The doctor scooped him up, cleared a passage for the baby and prayed, 'Please don't breathe, little boy, please don't breathe.' But he did, and when the nurses delayed bringing her baby to her, Mattie wanted to ask, 'Does he have big elephant ears so that he can fly?'

The Matua was in the delivery room. When she saw the child, she began a grief-filled prayer. He looked as if he had been born in a crucible of fire, all red, squealing, with a red O for a mouth.

Mattie couldn't understand why her baby wasn't handsome like his father.

'May God have mercy on your soul, Mattie,' Miro said.

Against all odds, the baby lived. He cried a lot. His head was large, like Humpty Dumpty, and the weight must have been awful. All his internal organs were around the wrong way and gave him terrible pain. There were holes in his stomach lining, abnormalities everywhere.

He lived for two months. Mattie was allowed to take him home. When he died, the doctors were glad for the little tike. However, the post-mortem revealed suspicious bruising around his nostrils, as if somebody had pinched them together so that he would not breathe. There was talk of Mattie being charged with murder and, indeed, the police wanted her to stand before the court. But the doctors said that the baby would have died anyway, and her lawyers said they would plead postnatal depression. The Matua told the judge at the deposition hearing that Mattie had been through enough already, and the judge dismissed any police action. He passed Mattie over into Miro's custodianship.

All this time, Mattie sat wild-eyed, staring into nothing. Just before the judge agreed not to take the case to court, she stood up and called to the vacant air:

'Oh baby mine, forgive me —'

The tears spilled like stones vomited from her eyes.

Oh, hula, hula, hula to my ten guitars. Seaweed drifting, drifting, drifting, carrying my child away from me. Very soon you'll know just where you are. Look out yonder, all is calm there. Through the eyes of love you'll see a thousand stars. My child floating away on the sea. When you hula, hula, hula to my ten guitars.

Lightning flashed its spectral light.

Hine Ropiho saw Mattie slumped against the door and rushed to her, cradling her. Hine, who had her own boy child, Boy Boy, knew exactly what Mattie was grieving about. For three years Mattie had been like this. Her life was her vale of tears, her penance, her suffering.

'It's going to be all right, Mattie,' she said. 'You'll be all right.' But it wasn't going to be all right. Mattie had sinned. She had committed infanticide. She had hell in her and would go straight to hell.

'I used to rock my baby to sleep,' Mattie sobbed. 'I would sing to him, Baby mine, don't you cry. The night he died, I was drunk. I went to bed but I was feeling cold, so I got the baby out of his cot and brought him to bed with me. I liked to have him lying beside me. He smelt so lovely. I didn't care what he looked like. He was my child. When I woke the next morning, he was dead.'

Sam Walker came into the room. 'What's wrong, Mattie?' he asked.

Mattie looked at him with haunted eyes. 'They say I killed my baby, Sam,' she said. 'But if I did, the Lord our God knows I didn't mean it. He who knows all our hearts knows that although I didn't want him, I grew to love him. The police tried to make me confess that I had murdered my boy. Then they buried him in the deep, deep earth. If I did kill him, it was an accident. I didn't mean to do it. Oh my son, wherever you are, believe your mother and forgive me.'

Seaweed drifting, drifting, drifting
My child floats away on the sea

——— 4 ———

A thunderclap cracked overhead.

Annie Jackson was having a great time. There was nothing better than to hula away a Sunday night. She plonked herself down next to Kepa where he was smoking. She took a few puffs herself and felt even better than best, sweeter than sweet.

That is, until the door opened and, in the squalling rain, Annie saw Pene. 'Mum? Dad? They're trying to take Nani Paora with them.'

Together, Annie and Kepa followed quickly in the footsteps of their son. They passed, shimmering, underneath the window where Mattie was still mourning in Hine's arms.

The door exploded open just as Pita was carrying Tamati Kota from the homestead. Annie Jackson stormed into the house. Her face was wet with the rain, her eyes grim. She strode into the sitting-room where Rongo and Miriama were packing Tamati Kota's clothes into a suitcase.

Pita put Tamati Kota down and turned to Pene. 'Take the old man back to his room, son. Stay there.' Pene nodded and took Nani Paora's hand. 'Come, Nani Paora,' he said. No sooner had the door shut behind them than Annie took control. She started to push Pita, Rongo and Miriama out the door, manhandling Miriama in a way which caused her to cry out in pain.

'Get out of my house,' Annie said. 'Get out before I throw you out. You Mahanas have no business here. And that includes you too, Miriama. You may be my sister but you're one of them now.'

Pita took Annie's left arm, twisted, and it was her turn to cry out. 'Don't you ever call it your house,' he said dangerously, 'because you and your arsehole husband are not fit to walk across its sacred threshold.'

Annie backed away, but she was still on the offensive. 'Your family may have owned it once,' she said, 'but you don't own it now. Don't think you can come in here strong-arming anybody and throwing your weight around. You and your family are dead meat as far as I'm concerned. Get out before I call the cops.'

'Yeah, and who are you calling an arsehole?' Kepa asked. His eyes were bulging and he was bunching his fists to throw one at Pita. Rongo restrained him and, instead, Kepa let one loose on him. Rongo blocked, deflected and moved to one side. 'I wouldn't do that again, Kepa, if I was you.'

'Annie, we just came around to see if Tamati Kota was all right,' Miriama said. 'We found him and the boy alone.'

'Was he complaining?' Annie asked. 'Had he pissed or shit himself? Did he have any bruises on his body? Did he ask you to take him away? No, he didn't, did he?'

'He's still coming with me,' Pita said.

'You try to take him out of this house and you'll be dead before you touch the door,' Annie answered. 'The last people I would ever let him

193

go with are the very gutless people who kicked him shitless when he was already down. If your conscience is bothering you after all this time, that's your problem. Now get out. Get out.'

The sounds of the argument escalated. In Nani Paora's room, Pene put his hands over his ears and closed his eyes. How long he was like this he didn't know. But when he opened them, Nani Paora was at the door looking to his right and listening to Rongo, Pita, Miriama fighting with Annie and Kepa. Nani Paora saw that Pene was alert, raised a finger to his lips, and gestured:

'Be very quiet,' Tamati Kota said. 'Soldiers.'

CHAPTER TWENTY-THREE

—— 1 ——

Miro Mananui was in the sitting-room looking at her genealogy books. She heard a crack, thump and boom as one of the trees at the back of the house was uprooted by the wind and fell against the wall. Next minute there was a scattered hail of noises as broken branches skittered across the roof — and the lights went out.

'What was that?' Miro said. She had been playing the radio while she worked and, now that the electricity had failed, she could hear the wind shrieking outside. She'd also been working with the curtains closed. When she drew them to take a look she was stunned by the intensity of the lightning and squalling rain.

Tama appeared at the doorway dressed in an oilskin and carrying a torch. 'Are you all right, Matua?' They were the first words he had spoken to her since George Karepa's visit that afternoon. She counted them: five words, the big spender. Yes, she was regretful about not telling Tama her intentions about leaving George the land at Patutahi, but it was her business, not Tama's, and she was not going to apologise for it.

'I'm fine,' Miro answered. 'You're not going out in this, are you? All those flying branches, you could get killed out there.'

'As if you would care,' Tama said. 'I have to look at the damage and see if I can get the generator going. The rest of Waituhi still have lights, so it might just be us that's out. The matches and a lamp are somewhere in the kitchen. If you want to keep on working, no use doing it in the dark.' He opened the door and closed it — but something rushed in with the wind, sidling by, before the door clicked shut.

Grumbling to herself, Miro went to the kitchen. Was she supposed to remember where everything was? Luckily the moon was out, full, and gave her some light. Where did Mattie put the emergency supplies? After banging and crashing around ineffectually she found them in the pantry: matches, kerosene for the lamp, and the lamp itself — exactly where she had told Mattie to put them. She lit the lamp and went to the bedroom to look out the window. What was Tama doing? Oh my giddy aunt, he was up a ladder playing with electric wires. Angrily, she rapped on the window to gain his attention. 'Don't do that, you fool,' she yelled, as if he could hear her. He saw her making vigorous movements with her head and gave her the thumbs up to indicate he knew what he was doing — which he didn't. He was still cross with her and feeling exhilarated out here in the wind, the rain and the hurtling branches. Better to be out here than to wait for the Matua to get over her mood and apologise to him as she eventually would.

Miro went back down the hallway. When Tama was like this, she just had to wait for him to come around. She noticed a pale glow coming from under the door of the sitting room. 'Huh?' she asked. 'But we haven't got any lights.' She opened the door.

A spirit child had come into the house. He had flown down between the cold moon and earth, slipped past Tama when he went out, and was floating in the sitting-room. When the spirit child saw Miro, he pointed a finger at her and, giggling, began to run upside down, chasing his shadow across the ceiling.

Miro couldn't help it. The sight of the young spirit child enjoying himself at his upside down games made her bubble with laughter. She should have known better than to be taken unawares because it was that kind of fearful night when the graves are all gaping wide, and every one has let forth its sprite. She should have felt the chill of the stormy wanton winds which had brought him to her. But she was completely taken in by his beauty. He was gorgeous, a boy child so beautiful and chubby, with such a perfect face and limbs that she was made radiant by looking at his perfection.

She called to him, 'Come down, child, and rest in my arms.' With joy, the child left his ghostly moonlight revels and tumbled, looped and swooped down, saying, 'Hello, Matua.' He had sparkling eyes, a perfect nose, a rosebud mouth and white, white teeth. His hair was crowned with a chaplet of sweet summer buds. He was about three years old. He rested in Miro's arms and twined some strands of her hair in his fingers and *pulled*. 'Ouch, don't do that,' Miro laughed. She was overwhelmed with love. She rocked him in her arms.

Lightning flashed and, in that horrid moment, scarred the child with the pallor of death. But the lightning was soon gone, the child restored, and he began to chuckle, his voice like a bubbling brook. 'You don't recognise me, do you?' he asked. 'No,' Miro answered, puzzled. Even then she should have known that appearances were deceiving. 'Should I know you?' The spirit child chuckled again. Dead leaves floated in a stream. A chill current carried dead frogs and lizards within it.

The spirit child looked at Miro with its sparkling eyes and smiled. 'This is what I would have grown up to look like if you had not murdered me.'

Only then did Miro see the pinch marks at his nostrils.

'Oh no, darling,' Miro said, 'please tell me it's not true.'

The happiness she had felt on first seeing the spirit child turned to grief. This couldn't be the same horribly malformed boy child which Mattie had given birth to. Not this perfect child. That other child had an encephalic head and limbs like paddles without fingers or toes. She couldn't bear to think that other child might have grown up to be such a perfect being. No, she had killed some other child.

'No,' she sobbed, 'it can't be you, darling. You were already so damaged outside and inside. Whenever I touched you I could feel your pain. It came with the laying on of my hands on your head and your limbs. I heard your little soul asking me to help you. I could never understand how you could withstand the agony, darling. Oh, so much pain from all your organs twisted and out of place. I tried with all the powers I possessed to fix you, I tried to command your organs, Go, go to your right places, go, but they would not obey me. Not even I, your Matua, could do it for you. No, you're not that child. No.'

That other child, Mattie's child, had screamed in pain all day and all night. That other child had cried unceasingly, so filled with the sadness of living that even after it had used up all its tears, it still cried. That other child found it so painful to suckle that whenever it put its red mouth to Mattie's breast, it screamed because the milk looped through its herniated stomach and flowed where it wasn't supposed to go. Oh, it hurt so, the milk that was its mother's milk.

'But it is me,' the spirit child pouted. 'Even though I asked your help, didn't you know my mummy loved me?'

Oh, that was the matter that Miro couldn't understand at all. It defied all understanding that after all the hate Mattie poured into the child, she loved him. She wouldn't let him out of her sight. She took the gruesome boy with her everywhere, showing him off as if there was nothing unusual about him. 'You're always fussing over that child,' Miro yelled to her, 'instead of praying to the Lord to take him off your hands, to take him off our hands. He screams and frets all the time and drains me of my blood and my senses.'

In the end, Miro decided it. Every night she hoped the baby would never see the sight of the next day — but it always did, screaming and fretting. Every week she hoped it would stop drawing breath — but it always did, gasping, choking, vomiting and screaming. Every night. Every day. Every week. Every second.

Even she, the Matua, as strong as she was, couldn't take it any longer. And the child kept crying, crying, crying.

It was so easy really. One evening, Sam asked Mattie to go to a party, and Miro encouraged her to go. Mattie came home happy and tipsy and took the baby to bed. Later in the night, when the stars were shining bright, Miro went in to Mattie and took that other baby from his mother's arms. She kissed him on the forehead. Simply pinched the nostrils of the child closed. Tightly. Tighter still.

That other child didn't even move. Didn't fight. He never struggled, uttered not a sound. He opened his eyes and looked at her. So trusting. Did the child know that she was doing it for the best? 'Child, your life would be awful; I have to do this.' All that Miro felt was a slight tensing of his left hand as he took his last breath. His eyes were still open at the point of death, staring at her, as he went so softly to his lasting sleep. She waited until he was not breathing any longer. Closed his eyes. Kissed their lids. She put him back in Mattie's arms.

'But I never expected that Mattie would be accused of murder,' Miro told the spirit child. 'I held my tongue, trusting to God that He would make things right, and He did.'

The spirit child watched as the tears flowed down Miro's face. He laughed and laughed, mocking, gleeful, as if he had just played a wonderful trick. Through her tears, Miro saw that the gorgeous face was a mask. When she looked again she saw that behind the mask was that other child. It had been him all along.

'Fooled ya,' the spirit child said.

He was a forgery. He was ill met by moonlight, a goblin child, a counterfeit, a changeling. He leapt out of her arms and, as Tama came in and switched on the lights, slipped out and away.

As soon as he saw the Matua, Tama rushed to succour her. Even as he held her, felt her shuddering and giving up to him the residue of her encounter with the spirit child, he knew what had happened. He had known it for years. When Mattie took all the guilt onto herself he had tried to convince her that she was not to blame.

He calmed Miro's bitter tears. It was not easy to live with the guilt and responsibility of deciding who should live and who should die but, after all, she was the Matua. That was her job. Even so, there was a task she still had to perform. She knew it and should have done it three years ago. 'I'll keep that one for a rainy day,' she kept saying in jest, her eyes haunted.

Well, that day had just turned up.

'It's about time, Matua, you told Mattie,' Tama said.

There was a sharp staccato rapping on the door. Tama seated Miro and went to see who it was. Rongo Mahana was standing there in the storm. The headlights of his pick-up truck illuminated the driving rain.

'I'm here to see the Matua,' Rongo said. 'We've got a problem. Tamati Kota and Pene have disappeared.'

'They're out in this weather?' Tama asked.

'Yes,' Rongo answered. 'Can I use your phone? I want to tell Huia I won't be home for a while.'

He heard the Matua's voice, tired, disembodied. She had forgotten that this was supposed to happen. Ever since the owl had made its early morning call and given her the foresight, she had been waiting; but there had been so many other things on her mind. Of course she hadn't known in what way the events would occur, nobody could predict that. But when the owl screeched out a name, she knew that Tamati Kota and Pene were involved. At that same moment she had seen them wandering in a beautiful garden. The garden had looked strange, brightly coloured, familiar, but Miro had not been able to place it. Now she knew where the garden was.

'They're heading for Rongopai,' she said.

———— 2 ————

Let us ascend by the whirlwind path of Enoch. Even in being shaped by the mouth, the law is twisted, yet it touches all. Search for the bridge, O people, the shedding of light, revealing how men can live in grace in the world.

Tamati Kota was in a low crouch, running swiftly from the homestead. 'Come, Grandchild, quick, Grandchild. We must go far away.' In one second they were drenched to the skin and, already, Pene had a hard time seeing where Nani Paora was. Suddenly he wasn't there at all. He had slipped through a curtain of rain and disappeared.

'Nani?' Pene called. He liked this game; they had never played at night before. But Nani had moved too fast for him and he was having trouble keeping up. He saw some footprints in the mud and, following them, came to a stile over a fence. On the other side was a paddock filled with tall, slapping maize. Pene climbed the stile and jumped. At the last moment a hand reached out, Pene grabbed it, and Tamati Kota pulled him through the curtain and down onto the ground. He put his hand over Pene's mouth. Looked back at the homestead. Raised, panicking voices came through the air like dying birds. Already their absence had been discovered.

'Let's go,' Tamati Kota said.

The lightning forked as Pita and Miriama ran to their car. Rongo had already gone ahead to alert the Matua about Tamati Kota and the boy. Pita jumped in and gunned the motor.

'If they've kept to the road,' he said to Miriama, 'we'll have them in a second.'

'I hope so,' Miriama answered. 'That old man had pneumonia last winter. We've got to get him out of this weather as soon as we can.'

Kepa Jackson stopped the car. 'Which way will they have gone?' The lightning showed that Tamati Kota and Pene could have gone to the right toward the main road through Waituhi — or to the left, which led to the river.

'Oh no,' Annie Jackson blanched. 'The water comes down the hills so fast and next minute the river rises and —'

In her mind's eye she saw the old man and Pene running along the bank. There was a sudden swell, an expansion of wild water swirling higher like watery hands clutching at them, sweeping them off their feet and pulling them down into the cold, cold depths.

'I blame you for this, Pita Mahana,' Annie said. 'If anything happens to the old man or my son, I'm blaming you, you bastard.'

Hepa Walker was watching television when the telephone rang. He nudged Hana to answer. She scowled at him. Was she his social secretary? 'Hello? Oh, hello Tama.' She gave her father a dirty look: See, I knew it was for you. 'You want Dad? Hang on.'

'Good evening, Hepa,' Tama said. 'Tamati Kota and young Pene have disappeared.'

'Disappeared?' Hepa asked. 'Have they run away or what? When were they last seen? Did anybody see them leave?' He sounded like a military man, and already he was looking through the window, scoping the situation. From his house he looked straight across the valley to the old homestead. He saw two sets of headlights as Pita and Miriama went one way and Kepa and Annie went the other. The rain, my God, the rain.

'The Matua thinks they're headed for Rongopai,' Tama said. 'You know how she is with these things. Would you take your car and go to the crossroads? If they come your way, pick them up and bring them to the meeting house. If they don't turn up within five minutes, look in the maize paddocks on the left-hand side of the road. Could you do that?'

'Yes,' Hepa answered. He walked quickly into the bedroom. Dinah was reading in bed. 'We've got an emergency,' Hepa told her. 'Tamati Kota and Pene are missing.'

'I'm coming with you,' Dinah said.

'Stop,' Miriama shouted. While Pita was watching the road ahead, she had been pointing the torch through the opened window, shining it along the paddock on her side of the car. There were big ditches running parallel to the road and, you never knew, Tamati Kota and Pene might hide there. She saw a movement.

Pita braked, jumped out of the car, leapt across the drain, and peered into the paddock. The electric whine of the windscreen wipers flicked aside the rain. In the cone of Miriama's flashlight, tall maize waved back and forth like defensive spears.

'I'm sure I saw something,' Miriama said.

It is you, Pakeha, alone who hate. From the porch, I look across the sea and see the mist rising. Your banquet was of the bullets at Paparatu. I warned you not to strike me. You never were satisfied with your victory at Waerenga a Hika.

'Come, Nani, quick,' Pene said. Although Nani Paora had been the leader, now he was the follower. They had just about been discovered by Pita and Miriama but, phew, the car passed by, heading for the main road through Waituhi.

'Alas, my little mate,' Tamati Kota smiled when he caught up. 'I've lost my puff. I'm not as fit as I used to be.' He was wheezing hard, his breath rattling.

'I'll help you, Nani,' Pene said. He put his hands to Nani Paora's chest and pressed hard, assisting him to breathe. 'In, out, in, out.' The old man felt very small and very bony. His hands and face were like ice. But Pene kept on, warming him with his own young warmth. 'There,' Pene laughed.

Pene was so excited. 'So where are we heading for?' he asked. He saw a strange light in Nani Paora's eyes and, when Nani spoke to him, his voice was reverent and filled with awe. With joy he kissed Pene.

'To Rongopai, of course,' Tamati Kota said, 'to await the return of the king.'

But Pene saw that the soldiers had set up a barrier. A car, Hepa Walker's car, was at the crossroads. 'We're going to have to make a detour,' Pene whispered. He grabbed Nani's hand and pulled him through the maize. They wriggled through the fence, slid into the ditch, and waited again. A dark cloud slid over the moon.

'Now,' Pene said. Under cover of darkness they crossed the road and went through the blackberry patch to the ridge beyond.

Andrew Whatu saw torches moving along the road. Every now and then, they converged before separating again: Rongo Mahana and Hepa Walker conferring. Puzzled, Andrew walked to his parents' bedroom and knocked. 'Dad?' Oh no, they weren't having sex in there, were they? Married people were so disgusting.

The door opened. 'No,' Dad said, 'me and your mother didn't order room service.' Behind him, Agnes giggled.

'Something's happening outside,' Andrew said. Quickly, Charlie walked to the front porch, opened the door and looked out. Agnes came to see too. My goodness, this wind, this rain.

'Hello?' Charlie yelled. 'Who's there?' A voice yelled out, 'It's us.' Charlie responded, 'Us who! Has there been a car accident?' He went off to see what was happening. Meantime, Mana and Victor had finally woken up, yawning and scratching their balls, and Janey had come to look too. As for Agnes, she couldn't help thinking of her cousin Mohi, so young, so handsome, killed on a road just like this, on a night just like this. She prayed that nobody had been hurt.

Charlie returned to the house. His face was grim. 'Okay, it's not a car accident — but somewhere out there in all this muck are Tamati Kota and Pene. Let's get dressed and go out and find them. Mum, you get that big lamp of mine. Janey, if you like, you can go over and team up with Hana. Hepa tells me he left her alone in the house and she might be getting scared. He's gone off to drum up some other volunteers. We have to find the old man and the boy soon. If we do, we take them to Rongopai. If we don't, let's all meet there anyway in half an hour. The Matua is insistent that they are heading there. Rongo's already had a quick look. So far, nobody.'

Down by the river, Annie Jackson was going out of her mind. The water level had already risen, spilling over the embankment. The earth underfoot was slippery. It would be very easy to fall and disappear forever into the swirling water.

'Pene? Tamati? Pene?'

Hepa Walker strode quickly through the rain. When he got to his son Sam's place, he picked up a batten and started banging it against the tin shed. Hepa's intervention had the desired effect. Out they poured, ears ringing: Sam, Mattie, Hine and Jack Ropiho, Sonny Whatu, Blacky and God knows who else. Even Maka tiko bum came out of her house to find out who was banging on a gong.

The rain blurred Sam's vision so that he didn't see the bastard who had interrupted the party until the last minute. When he did, fucked if he knew what to say. 'Uh, hi Dad,' he began, 'you've got an interesting way of knocking. Something up?'

Hepa should have been pissed with his failure of a son. Seeing him there, getting drenched, his anger deserted him. 'Your party just got cancelled, son. I'd appreciate it if you and your mates would help us. We're looking for Tamati Kota and Pene.'

At the sound of their names, Maka tiko bum wailed as if they were dead already. 'Alas, they have gone to God,' she cried.

Mattie's head came up with a snap. Tamati Kota and Pene, gone? Immediately she was looking beyond the shack, her eyes searching the dark skyline. She loved that little boy. 'Tomorrow will be a different place, Auntie Mattie.' She willed the curtain of rain to part so that she could *see*. In a lightning strike, a tree flamed like a sword and burned a hole in the rain big enough to look through. On the other side, something flashed whitely in the dark. What was that? An old white horse, disappearing over the ridge. An old man on the horse, a young boy leading it. Oh merciful God.

'They'll be heading for Rongopai,' she said. Something else alerted her senses. A blur of wings, a flash of cryptic colours, something flying fast through the valley.

Immediately, she was on the run.

My people you imprisoned. Myself you exiled to the Chathams, yet I returned to you across the sea, landing at Whareongaonga. Then was to be heard the cry of the Government.

'Hup! Hup!' Pene was having such fun. Phew, who would have thought that Samson, that old bag of bones, would be waiting just beyond the blackberry patch to take them the rest of the way? In the nick of time, too, because Nani Paora was pretending to be exhausted again.

'I can't go any further,' Nani had said, lying down in the mud. 'You go on, Pene, and welcome the king who is coming.' But what was this? Samson had snorted in the dark, scaring Pene out of his wits until he realised who it was.

'We'll be safe now, Nani,' Pene said as he pushed Nani Paora onto Samson's back. He took off his belt and used it as a bridle, pulling the horse up the mud-slippery slope. 'Hup!' he ordered. 'Hup!'

Suddenly, halfway up the slope, lightning crackled. 'Nani!' Pene cried. The air was filled with ozone and a tree just above them flamed like a sword.

Tamati Kota saw the boy's fear. He pulled Pene up behind him. 'Hold tight, child.' In front was a cliff. In the darkness below was Rongopai.

'Come, Poukaiwhenua,' Tamati Kota commanded, 'ride as fast as the wind.' The horse reared, its hooves stamping the ground. It began to gallop toward the raging, storm-filled sky. A bridge, like a bow of burning gold, opened up before them. In front, all the whirlwinds had gathered into a single funnel, dazzling, kaleidoscopic, whirling, whirling, whirling, pulling everything in. The cone was a spiral cloud lit with phosphorescence and laced by lightning. Enoch's path, vertiginous, circled up the funnel to the field of bright stars in a clear black sky.

Poukaiwhenua jumped over the cliff.

Your power was brought against me by mistake. Now the bitter taste cannot be drowned by strong drink. Your animosity feeds on shame and jealousy. O, Pakeha, why can you not leave your evil behind?

Two hours later.

The eye of the storm had located itself above Rongopai, swirling, swirling, swirling.

From her home, Miro saw that the people had all begun to gather at Rongopai. The meeting house was ablaze with light. Cars and trucks were parked on the perimeter. The villagers were huddled in groups, whispering, mournful. Beyond the village, the storm still squalled. The river was running very high, swollen with silt; trees as big as canoes roared into the darkness. One by one, groups of searchers were heading empty-handed to Rongopai. Across the hills, trees had been brought down.

Annie Jackson was bereft, insane with grief. 'Have you found them?' She could not be calmed down.

Miro's face was grim. She had called Rongo, Hepa, Pita, Charlie and Tama to the house. They were cross with her and she was cross with them. She purposely kept them waiting while she pretended to do some work on her genealogy books. To one side, Mattie waited.

Miro slammed the books shut and took off her reading glasses. 'I told you once,' Miro said, 'I told you twice, and I will tell you again, they were heading for Rongopai. You should have stopped them from getting there and going in. Now it's too late because they are already inside.'

'You are mistaken, Matua,' Rongo answered. 'We've searched throughout. They didn't make it. They're still out there in the dark somewhere.'

Miro looked at them all with irritation. 'When was the last time you looked?' She herself had ordered Pita to look again.

'They're not there,' Pita said. 'How many times do we have to tell you?'

'Oh, why do I have to do everything myself?' Miro said. 'Get the car, Tama, and bring it around to the front. I don't want to get my feet wet walking in the mud.' She put on a warm coat, gloves and black scarf. Just as she was about to get into the car, she turned to Mattie. She knew Mattie had a close relationship with the boy, Pene. You only had to look at them together, sitting, breaking bread in the sun, to know they had made a special covenant.

'I know you love the boy but, whatever happens down there, don't interfere,' she said.

CHAPTER TWENTY-FOUR

The eye of the storm, swirling above Rongopai.

Miro waited for Tama to open the door of the car for her but August, Teria Mahana's eldest, beat him to it. 'Looking to take over my job, are you?' Tama asked. He liked August and often gave him and his brothers and sisters pocket money to clean the car. If they learnt to respect the car they might treat it better than Maka tiko bum's old horse.

'You kids should be in bed,' Miro scolded as she stepped out and straight into a cowpat; she hoped that wasn't going to be a sign for what was to come. She saw Teria taking scones over to the kitchen. 'Teria? These children should be all at home in bed.' Plenty of time for them to come back tomorrow for the mourning.

'They're good mates of Pene's,' Teria answered. 'They want to be here when he and Tamati Kota are brought back safe and sound.'

Miro made a gesture of understanding. She saw Sam Walker standing with his mates, Blacky, Sonny Whatu, and Hine and Jack Ropiho. Sam Walker was always a flirtatious boy with his sparkling eyes and ready wit. He stopped Miro with a wink, asked Sonny for his neck scarf, and wiped the green shit from her shoes. Sonny spluttered with indignation, but Sam waved aside his objections. 'Can't have the Matua walking around with cow crap on her feet,' he said.

'Thank you,' Miro smiled. 'Sober, I see. You better watch out. With all the good works you are doing, you might end up coming to church on Sundays.' Blacky and Sonny guffawed. 'Thank you all,' Miro continued, 'for your work tonight. I know you looked hard for the old man and Pene.' Then, turning to Hine and Jack Ropiho, she offered a gentle rebuke. 'Don't leave Boy Boy all day with his grandmother. And you, Jack Ropiho, get a job.'

One step and one step further now. Toward the painted porch of Rongopai, Miro proceeded. Mattie was on her left. Tama was on her right. Following her came Rongo, Pita, Hepa and Charlie Whatu. Miro saw Andrew Whatu standing with his hopeless brothers and nodded to him. She stopped to kiss Janey Whatu on the forehead. Before she forgot, she motioned to Hepa Walker:

'Hepa, that boy of yours, Sam,' she said. 'Time to forgive him and let him get on with his life.'

Ahead, sitting in the porch comforting Annie Jackson, were Miriama, Dinah Walker and her daughter, Hana, and, of course, Maka tiko bum. Why was it that it was always women who waited, always waited, for their husbands or sons to be brought home?

As soon as Maka saw Miro, swivelling her left eye to keep Miro in her sights, she began to wail and moan. 'Have you found the boy yet? Have you found Tamati Kota?' Maka always carried on as if the world was coming to an end.

'No, not yet,' Miro answered. Maka set off a fusillade of little cries, Yip yip yip, as if they were already dead.

Miro knelt to Annie Jackson and lifted her face to hers. She pressed noses. 'You must get some rest,' she said. 'Tomorrow comes.' Standing beside her, Mattie sensed the unspoken text in the Matua's words.

'You know something, Matua. Something has already happened, or will happen, and you know what it is.'

'I'm going inside,' Miro said.

'But we've already looked,' Pita answered.

Miro ignored him. Mattie stepped behind her, ready to follow. 'No,' Miro stopped her. She turned to Tama. 'Don't let anybody follow me,' she said.

Hush, Nani. Can you hear, Nani? Somebody else is coming. Be still, be quiet. Don't make a noise. Don't move. Don't talk. If we are quiet, whoever it is won't hear us. They'll never hear us. No matter what happens, we'll always be together, eh Nani. Always. Oh, what a good game this is.

The meeting house was filled with a strange glow. The light seeped in from the sky outside. Through every crack, fissure, gap and opening it filtered, sparkling on the dust within. It illuminated the interior with magic and beauty, transforming it into a garden. It could have been the Garden of Eden glistening at twilight. It could also have been the garden of the Queen of Sheba, where hoopoes sang. Or a garden in fabled Babylon, one of many hanging in the palace of Nebuchadnezzar. Or the garden of the New Testament at the place called Gethsemane, where a bright broken Christ was laid to his death and resurrection. Overhead was an illuminated heaven studded with stars. Around were tall decorated trunks of giant, ancient trees taking root in the dark earth. Between the trees, fantastic birds flew among exotic, brilliant fruits, vines and flowers. The atmosphere was rich with promise and hope.

Miro peered into every corner. Pita was correct. Nobody was there. Only a chair in the middle of the meeting house and the painted ancestors of Te Whanau a Kai looking on. With a sigh she walked to the chair and sat down. She was in the stomach of the meeting house. The ridgepole was the backbone. The rafters were the ribs. The exterior gable was the head. The bargeboards were the arms and legs.

Still no sign of the old man and the young boy.

Minutes passed. 'Maybe I'm mistaken,' Miro thought. 'Maybe they're still out there after all.' She was relieved. She had divined that the Parade was bringing Tamati Kota closer to Rongopai and, keeping watch, had been ready to prevent him crossing the threshold with the boy. If they had come this far they would have been lost to her, gone already into the Garden — and, this time, Tamati Kota might not have wanted to come out.

Then Miro heard someone giggle. Swiftly she tried to trace the sound. Had it come from the rafters with their unfolding ferns, double spirals, hammerhead sharks and red lips of the forest parrot? Or had it come from the panels stitched with the stars, the thousand seeds of heaven? Perhaps it had come from behind Hine Hakirirangi, she who wore a Victorian dress and held a red rose to her lips? No, it had come from the darkest recess where strange animals lurked.

Someone giggled again. A boy's giggle. Following it was the soft laughter of an old man. The voices were coming from behind Miro. They came from above the doorway she had just come through.

Slowly, the Matua turned in her chair. She looked up to the wall where two sets of eyes were woven and separately painted. The eyes belonged to Tarakiuta and Tarakitai, twin boys.

They had been joined by another two sets of eyes. One set of eyes *blinked*.

'Come down from there, old one,' Miro commanded, 'and bring the boy with you.'

Oh, Nani, she's seen us. Trust her to spoil our fun. All the people who have been running in and out haven't seen us. You must have moved, Nani. It wasn't me who moved. You must have coughed. But she hasn't caught us yet. Let's play hide and seek. No matter what happens, we'll always be together, eh Nani. Always.

The eyes blinked out.

Miro heard feet running along the ridgepole. Immediately she was out of her chair and in pursuit of the sound. She caught a glimpse of Pene behind the flower of the native berry.

'I can see you,' Miro said. But the boy thought it was just a game and, giggling, pulled his grandfather down from the ridgepole into the shadows of the rafters. He tried to sneak off to the left but, 'Again I see you,' Miro shouted. She almost had Tamati Kota and Pene but they dived down the woven panels to hide behind a Victorian vase ablaze with reds and purples, brilliant flowers and pods.

Panicking, Miro tried to catch them as they ran past her, along the walls, weaving in and out of the illuminated forest.

'Come, Nani,' Pene called. 'Quickly, Nani.' There he was, peering from behind the Tree of Life. There, climbing through the legs of Wi Pere's chair. He was running round and round the meeting house, rustling overhead in the painted branches, climbing down the vines.

Miro's heart began to thud with anxiety. The boy had already gone far beyond her reach. Her only hope was to call for Tamati Kota.

'Old one,' she commanded. 'Enough. Bring the boy out before it is too late. Bring him to me.' Her voice was peremptory. Authoritative. 'You must bring the boy back. He does not belong in the Garden. Neither do you. I order you. Come out. Now. Do it.'

And suddenly, the whole house was filled with sobbing. All the sorrows of the world were in those sounds of grief. All the pain of lost hopes, lost lands, lost expectations, lost voices, lost promises, lost peoples, lost histories. The Matua saw that the sobbing was coming from the painting of Adam and Eve in the Garden of Eden. Adam and Eve were looking on as Tamati Kota cried and Pene, confused, tried to console him. The old man and boy were trying to get in but, already, the golden angel was on guard gently turning them away. He wore glowing armour and in his hands he wielded a shining sword.

'But we await the king,' Tamati Kota wept.

The golden angel made way for the Matua. She reached in, gathered Tamati Kota and the young boy in her arms and brought them out. There was no way back into the Garden. All had been banished and forever wandered in the Wilderness. A new way had to be found, a bright, shining pathway to a different kind of Deliverance.

Miro kissed the old man's vein-wrinkled hands.

'He is not coming,' she said.

And the Matua brought them out from the Garden.

Watching, Mattie wondered why the Matua was still grieving. Annie Jackson gave a cry of joy and hugged her son to her as if she would never let go.

'Get Tamati Kota a drink of water, cover him with a blanket, and take him home,' the Matua ordered. But still she grieved.

Then the Matua looked skyward.

Mattie caught a glimpse of something flying down to perch opposite the meeting house. The owl had arrived from its place by the Pouarua Stream. Waiting. Ready to fly. Ready to call out a name. With a sudden insight, Mattie looked at Miro and understood. The name that the owl would cry would not be the old man's. It would be the name of the boy. She loved that boy.

Nobody except Miro saw Mattie as she strode toward the owl. Nobody was even looking her way when she confronted it, staring into its wide, dark, eyes. The owl was ready to take flight. Mattie put up her hands in warning.

'A life for a life, owl,' she bargained. 'You took my baby's life.' She pointed to Pene. 'Give me his.'

The owl bristled. Grew large, ominous, enraged. It bobbed its head to left and right, trying to find a passage past Mattie. Its cryptic colours flashed with anger.

'Give him to me, you bastard,' Mattie said.

Carry Me Home

CHAPTER TWENTY-FIVE

——— 1 ———

The stars were trickling in the dark. Tamati Kota lay in bed, looking at the moon, his face agleam with light. He could see light under his doorway and hear raised voices along the hallway; Annie and Kepa were arguing again. He closed his eyes and grieved. When he opened them, Riripeti, the Matriarch, her pearls shimmering in her hair, was sitting beside him.

'So, my faithful servant.'

'I will not fail you,' Tamati Kota answered. 'I will continue to await the return of the king.'

'He is already among you,' Riripeti said.

The squall which, two hours earlier, had swept Waituhi, descended on Auckland just as the late night flight for Sydney, Australia, lifted from Auckland International Airport.

'Whoa,' George Karepa laughed. The plane rocked, rolled and bounced through the night sky. He and Hayley were seated in first class and, although he was laughing, he was nervous. The storm brought sad, sorrowing voices with it: 'Let us in, let us in, oh, let us in.'

'Don't worry, ladies and gentlemen,' the purser reassured his passengers. 'The turbulence is unexpected, but the captain says we should be in calm air soon.'

'Are you all right, George?' Hayley asked. He was clutching the seat. Sweat beaded his forehead. Hayley threaded her fingers in his: George might be big and strong on the rugby field but he was just a baby really — and, now that they were married and going back to Australia, he was all hers. She'd been uncomfortable among his Maori relatives and she was glad that he had sorted that out.

There was an increase in the plane's elevation and, with a sudden whining roar, the flight lurched through the clouds and away from the storm. George closed his eyes with relief. The moon came out, shining a pathway across the clouds. Far on the other side was Waituhi, like another country really.

'Champagne?' The purser offered two glasses to George and Hayley. The champagne bubbled with promise.

'To us,' Hayley whispered. 'To the future.' George was still brooding about what had occurred with his Matua in Waituhi. 'Things will work out, darling,' Hayley said. 'You'll see. People will come round to your way of thinking. It's never too late.' What did George's people expect, for goodness sake? They had no right to try to hold him back.

'Maybe you're right,' George nodded. But even as he drank, he felt a terrible emptiness, a desolation, a void. Ah yes, what profits a man if he loses his country and his history? *Your ancestors must be turning in their graves, George Karepa.*

'No, I made the right choice,' he said to himself with conviction. 'Not just for me but for everyone.' Tears threatened as he thought of his dead son and Mattie, but there was nothing he could do about them, now or ever. 'This way the kill is quick, the cut is clear and the wound is clean.'

The moon went behind a cloud and the pathway disappeared.

The moon was a chaste goddess bringing benediction to the land. Miriama Mahana walked quickly through the moonlight, heading for Miro's house. Slipping an overcoat over her nightdress, she had left the side of her husband, Pita. He was unrepentant about taking Tamati Kota and, even though he had been thwarted tonight, he was planning to see the family lawyers in the morning. 'The old man belongs to us,' he said. 'He is the vessel by which our family hopes can be delivered back to us.'

In Miro's house, the Matua was ready to go to bed. Tama was already there, warming her side of the bed. It was one of the small pleasures he liked to give her. When she arrived he would roll over to his side of the bed as if, after all, this was what a husband was supposed to do for his wife. And maybe she might say sorry while she was about it.

Before going to bed, however, Miro wanted to have a few words with Mattie. She walked to Mattie's door, knocked, and entered. Mattie was brushing her hair at the dresser. 'Yes?' Mattie asked. The word was a challenge — and both Mattie and Miro knew it.

'I saw what you did out there,' Miro said. 'Don't think I don't know what's going on. When the owl came for the boy, I saw you bargain with it and deflect it from its purpose. You shouldn't have done that.'

'Well, you weren't going to do it,' Mattie answered. 'You would have let the boy die, wouldn't you?'

Miro gave Mattie a hard look. 'Stay out of things you know nothing about. I warned you not to interfere and you disobeyed me. When you change the way things are supposed to be, there is always a reckoning. The price still has to be paid, missy. All you've done is shift it to some other person.'

Miro heard a knock at the front door. Was the reckoning already happening? She left Mattie and went to answer. Miriama was standing there. 'I know it's late, Matua, but I need to see you.'

In the bedroom, Tama became grumpy. That was the trouble with the Matua's life. People calling at all hours of the night and day as if she had nothing better to do than to attend to their troubles and needs.

Miro led Miriama into the sitting-room and went to put on the light. 'No,' Miriama said. 'Please, I would prefer to speak to you in darkness. I have a lump in my breast.' She opened her coat and unbuttoned her nightdress. The Matua slipped her hands in and gave a sad sigh as she felt the cancer. 'Have you been to see the Pakeha doctor?' she asked.

'Yes,' Miriama answered. 'Doctor Hewitt.'

'Did he tell you what ails you?' When Miriama nodded, 'Then why come to me?' Miro asked 'I'm not a miracle worker.'

'I'm sorry, Matua,' Miriama wept. 'Can you do anything at all?'

Miro closed Miriama's nightdress and buttoned her coat. 'The cancer has already taken root and grows like a tree,' she told Miriama. 'Its flowers and fruit are already blossoming and, where they fall, they take root again.'

'How can I tell Pita?' Miriama sobbed. 'How will he get on without me?'

'Send him to me tomorrow and I will tell him for you.' Miro kissed Miriama on the forehead. 'I will give you some remedies for the pain when it comes.'

Still weeping, Miriama kissed Miro's hands. Miro watched her disappearing into the night. People always came to see her after first trusting to the diagnosis of the Pakeha doctor. If he couldn't treat them, they came to her for a miracle cure. Well, her powers didn't work that way.

'Now to bed,' Miro said. But as she was going along the hallway she saw that Mattie was still up. *Matua, it's about time you told Mattie.* She also remembered what the spirit child had said to her. *Didn't you know my mummy loved me?* Miro took a deep breath and walked back to Mattie's doorway.

'There's something I have to tell you,' she said.

'You get ready for bed, dear,' Dinah Walker said to Hepa. 'Hana and I will finish up.' After finding Tamati Kota and Pene, Dinah had invited everybody around to the house for a warm cup of tea and biscuits. To her pleasant surprise, quite a few had taken her invitation up, among them Pita and Miriama, Charlie and Agnes Whatu, Rongo and his sister Teria, Maka — and even the Matua and Tama had briefly graced the evening. The last people to leave were Rongo and Teria; Rongo was dropping her home before heading back to Gisborne.

'Okay,' Hepa answered. He was tired and already thinking ahead to tomorrow's council meeting. Rongo had mentioned the restriction on building on less than ten acres, and he had decided to raise the issue with the other councillors. Something definitely had to be done about that.

'Good,' Dinah said to herself when Hepa left the kitchen and went to the bathroom. She had been waiting to have a talk with Hana without Hepa around. She saw Hana coming into the kitchen carrying more cups and saucers. As Hana went to go back into the sitting-room, Dinah put out an arm, stopped her, and gave her a hug.

'What was that for, Mum?' Hana asked, surprised.

'I was just thinking about how helpful you were tonight,' Dinah answered. 'I know it's sometimes a bore to pass around tea and biscuits, but I really appreciated it.' Oh well, she was on a roll now, so she may as well press on regardless. 'Also, Hana, I want you to understand why your father has so many expectations of you. I know you think he treats you like a baby but, after all, you're his only daughter. Be patient with him.'

'I don't know what you're talking about,' Hana lied.

'Yes you do,' Dinah answered firmly. 'You and I have to figure out how to get your father to understand who you are and what you want.'

Hana looked at Dinah, stunned. 'But how did you know, Mum?'

'Meantime,' Dinah continued, 'I want you to promise that whatever you do that your father might not like, don't let him find out. It's easier that way. What he doesn't see won't hurt him. He's a proud man, your father. Too proud. He also thinks he knows what's best but he doesn't. For that, come to me. Now go to bed. School in the morning.'

Dinah kissed Hana on the cheek. She couldn't help a furtive tear because the thought of Hana growing up and, no doubt, leaving home soon enough, only amplified her sense of isolation. For that evening, even as she was being the good hostess, making sure that people were happy and chatting, an epiphany came to her: 'I love my husband and my children, and they belong here — but I don't.' It occurred between the buns she was giving to Maka and the second cup of tea she was pouring for Tama and, when it burst around her, she took it in her stride. But Miro must have known — that old woman knew everything — because when she was leaving she said, 'I always enjoy coming to your home, Dinah. You are a credit to Hepa.'

'No use feeling sorry for myself,' Dinah said, as she began to wash the dishes.

'That was a lovely gesture, dear,' Hepa said to her when he came back from the bathroom. 'Having everybody here to our home. I know they appreciated it.'

Dinah turned to him with sparkling eyes. 'You think so? That makes me feel very pleased, darling. I won't be long.' As she finished up, she was reminded of her mother. She switched off the light but her memories of her mother stayed with her, and she addressed a fearful question into the dark:

When the time comes to lay me down to my final sleep, to my deep deep rest in the dark dark ground, Mother, if the Maoris don't want me and if there's no room in Hepa's graveyard, can I come home to you?

*

All of a sudden Tama heard a loud scream, a slap and somebody hitting the floor. He leapt out of bed and ran to Mattie's room. Mattie was standing over the Matua, hitting her across the face and body. 'You bitch,' Mattie screamed. 'You fucking bitch.' The Matua wasn't even defending herself. She saw Tama and put up a hand.

'No, don't interfere, husband,' she said. 'This is my retribution. This is the price I have to pay, and I will gladly pay it.'

The Matua's face was ashen. She should have realised how much Mattie had been hurting. Now she understood. Even so, the ferocity of Mattie's attack staggered her.

'Murderer,' Mattie yelled, her face a rictus of rage and fury. 'Assassin. Child killer. Who are you to decide who must live and who must die? Who?' Blood was coming from the Matua's mouth. She was clutching her side where Mattie was kicking her. Kicking. Kicking. Kicking.

Only then did Tama step between them. He picked Mattie up and threw her across the room. Mattie leapt up and was at him, snarling, lashing out.

'Mattie,' he said. 'Mattie, the baby was already dying. He was in pain. He was calling the Matua to help him. She did it for love. Do you hear me? For love, Mattie.'

Mattie gave a huge, deep moan. She wasn't about to forgive the Matua, but she trusted Tama and knew he never lied to her. Shivering, she took both his hands and kissed them, wiping them with her hair. They were both outsiders and they had only each other.

And suddenly all the agony, all the guilt, all the terror Mattie had felt about being a mother came pouring out of her.

'But why didn't she tell me?' Mattie wept, her face streaming with tears. 'What kind of woman lets a mother think she murdered her own child?' She looked at the Matua, entreating her. 'Why leave me all that time, Matua, in limbo where lost souls go? Why?'

She collapsed into Tama's arms.

——— 2 ———

It is after midnight. High above the village the clouds break apart and the moon floods the earth with its pale light. So wan. So calm.

Along the road which passes through the village, Miriama hurries swiftly home. As she passes each house the lights wink out. Slowly. One after the other.

'You kids in bed yet?' Teria Mahana asks. 'August? July? Turn your light off. Now.'

'Okay, Mum. We love you, Mum.' They are talking about the kite and how high it had flown. 'Next time, let's aim it all the way to the top of the sky.'

Listening, Teria begins to shiver. 'I've got to turn my life around. I've got to give my kids the best shot at life. What happens to me is of no account. What happens to the kids, though, that's what matters.'

Tama carries the Matua to the bathroom. Her face is bruised and her lip is torn. She holds one arm against the side where Mattie has kicked her. Tama pours water over her face and begins to clean her.

'This is all your fault,' Miro says. 'Now I'm going to be uglier than ever, which means,' she tries to hit him, 'you'll be more beautiful. If I hadn't taken your advice, this wouldn't have happened. How am I going to explain this to everybody?'

'You did the right thing,' Tama answers. 'And when did other people's opinions ever matter to you?' He looks at her and remembers: *I can give you a life, Tama Mananui, that has a purpose to it. At the end of it you would know you had truly lived.*

The *Matua* has fulfilled her promise. Tama kisses her.

'What was that for?' she asks. 'Are you going all sentimental on me? Well, don't.'

Maka tiko bum is gleeful. Boy oh boy she has been waiting all day for this. She sees Sam Walker's lights go off, puts cottonwool in her ears, opens her sitting-room window, and then switches the volume on her stereo way up.

Annie and Kepa Jackson look in at Pene. At last he is asleep. Something happened at the meeting house tonight — they don't know what it was — but Mattie was involved somehow. She bundled Pene in a blanket and said, 'Take him away and love him, oh, you better love him like never before because we have all been fortunate tonight.' He loves his

Nani Paora so much. Sometimes they have heard him scratching at Nani Paora's door like a little puppy trying to attract the old man's attention. If Nani Paora doesn't answer, there are a few sniffles and the sound of a blanket dragging as Pene goes back to his own bedroom. They know that tomorrow morning they will find him lying at the old man's door, waiting for him to wake up. And when the day comes when the old man doesn't wake up?

'How will he get on without his old mate?' Annie asks. 'The old man's not going to last forever.' She looks at Kepa. 'How are we going to get on, Kepa? How?'

Rongo Mahana drives back to the city. 'Call all the tribes, come to Waituhi,' he sings. Tomorrow is rich with promise.

Mother mine, don't you cry.

In her bedroom, Mattie Jones is still crying. But this time the reason is different. Just before Tama had carried the Matua from the room, Miro had turned to her:

'I have a message for you,' the Matua said. 'Your baby son loved you. He knows that you loved him.'

Oh, she so needed to hear that. She so needed to know that.

Andrew Whatu climbs onto his bunk. 'Magic kites have no place in history.'

Oh yeah? Tomorrow will be a good day to begin with, to start battle from. Take the universe if you want, Mr Green, but leave our valley to us.

Miriama reaches her home. She opens the gate and steps into her house, away from the night. Only three lights are shining now. Look into one window, and Annie and Kepa Jackson are watching over their son Pene. At the second is Mattie Jones, her face calm, looking across a calm sea; yes, tomorrow *will* be in a different place. At the third, Tama is putting the Matua to bed, covering her with the quilt. He picks up his Bible for the last reading of the day:

'Oh Heavenly Father, Divine Deliverer, place Thy Holy Spirit within us this night. Glory to Thy Holy Name. *Kororia ki to Ingoa Tapu.* Amen.'

Only two lights remain. Then one light. Then it too winks out and the village is left in darkness.

But I have not yet appointed my successor.

Fear not, Matua, and be at peace. Look to the margins where she is coming, still covered in red earth, raw, bleeding, uncomprehending but healing, from east of Eden, out of the Land of Nod.

The village sleeps, still dreaming its millennial dreams. *Te Whanau a Kai pana pana maro.* We never retreat.

Rongopai, the painted meeting house, still holds up the sky.

ACKNOWLEDGEMENTS

I acknowledge the following sources and works consulted and quoted from: J.B. Mackay's *Old Poverty Bay*, and the following contributors and authors of submissions made to the Waitangi Tribunal Hearing on the Te Whanau a Kai claim, Waituhi: David Hawea, Tom Smiler Jnr, Joe Pere, Josephine Smiler, Bub Ngapo Wehi, Dr Bryan Gilling, Garry Wayne Clapperton and the counsel (KPMG Legal) for Te Whanau a Kai. The Patutahi issue is a very substantial one in terms of documentation, with the main Native Department file accounting for two entire volumes of the Waitangi Tribunal's Raupatu Document Bank, over 1000 pages of documents in all. In addition there is a substantial mass of evidence generated by the various commissions of inquiry, court hearings, appeals and so on which took place during the twentieth century, many of which were recorded in the Gisborne Minute Books of the Native Land Court or in parliamentary papers. It was undoubtedly the single biggest and most convoluted twentieth-century inquiry into any Gisborne land issue. I thank all my uncles, aunties and *whanaunga*, my cousin Kiki Kerekere Smiler and the many others who have been so vigilant in prosecuting the Te Whanau a Kai claim in the past and present. The *haka* that Nani Paora does with the horse, Samson, is based on the Book of Joshua, chapter 23, verses 5 and 6. I thank Jane, Jessica and Olivia for their love. From the bottom of my heart I also thank Jenny Gibbs for her unfailing support and *aroha*.

Finally, although I have located *Band of Angels* in Waituhi, a real place with a very real history, and have based some of the characters on people I have known and loved — particularly my father and mother, Te Haa o Ruhia Ihimaera Smiler Jnr and Julia Keelan, my grandparents Pera Punahamoa Ihimaera Smiler and Teria Pere, my Nani Mini Tupara and mentor Te Aomuhurangi Te Mamaaka Jones — the novel is primarily a work of fiction and should be read as such.

Since the times in which *Band of Angels* is set, Te Whanau a Kai have continued from strength to strength, with a younger generation having qualities of leadership that the older generation would have been proud of. I pay tribute to the great people that I have sprung from and to the valley that has been the constant inspiration of my life.

Author of the bestselling *The Whale Rider*

WITI IHIMAERA

THE UNCLE'S STORY

WITI IHIMAERA

THE WHALE RIDER